Shadows on a
Cape Cod Wedding

Books by Lea Wait

In the Maggie Summer "Shadows" Antique Print Mystery Series
Shadows at the Fair
Shadows on the Coast of Maine
Shadows on the Ivy
Shadows at the Spring Show
Shadows of a Down East Summer
Shadows on a Cape Cod Wedding

Novels for children and young adults
Stopping to Home
Seaward Born
Wintering Well
Finest Kind

Praise for *Shadows of a Down East Summer*
by Lea Wait

"Engaging... Wait, herself an antiques dealer who lives on the Maine coast, does a good job depicting small-town Maine."
—*Publishers Weekly*

"VERDICT: This gentle regional mystery involving the art community in Maine will appeal to readers of Jane Cleland and Sharon Fiffer."
—JoAnn Vicarel, *Library Journal*

"... a homey yet suspenseful setting. Fans of the series will enjoy meeting up with Maggie again.... As in the previous books, each chapter begins with information about antique prints and the artists who hand-colored them, making the series not only enjoyable, but educational."
—Betty Webb, *Mystery Scene*

"The mystery plot is convincing and well thought out, made all the more interesting by the engaging Maggie Summer as amateur sleuth and the descriptions of the local art scene in Maine. That this whodunit includes a credible cast of suspects helps as well. The historical backstory provides a fascinating and colorful context, and there's enough of an edge to keep this cozy from being, well, too cozy."
—*Hidden Staircase Mystery Books*

"Wait includes the colorful characters expected for this small-town setting and a sufficient dose of suspense. She also adds plenty of educational details on the antiques trade and many mouthwatering examples of Down East cuisine. Recommended."
—Sarah Johnson, *Historical Novels Review*

"Filling her mystery with background on Winslow Homer, antique prints, and antiques shows, Wait seamlessly interweaves the past (through the diary entries) and the present."
—*Booklist*

Shadows on a Cape Cod Wedding

An Antique Print Mystery

LEA WAIT

2013· Perseverance Press / John Daniel & Company
Palo Alto / McKinleyville, California

This is a work of fiction. Characters, places, and events are the product of the author's imagination or are used fictitiously. Any resemblance to real people, companies, institutions, organizations, or incidents is entirely coincidental.

The interior design and the cover design of this book are intended for and limited to the publisher's first print edition of the book and related marketing display purposes. All other use of those designs without the publisher's permission is prohibited.

Copyright © 2013 by Lea Wait
All rights reserved
Printed in the United States of America

A Perseverance Press Book
Published by John Daniel & Company
A division of Daniel & Daniel, Publishers, Inc.
Post Office Box 2790
McKinleyville, California 95519
www.danielpublishing.com/perseverance

Distributed by SCB Distributors (800) 729-6423

Book design by Eric Larson, Studio E Books, Santa Barbara, www.studio-e-books.com

Cover image: *Red Dory*, © Christopher Seufert Photography, www.CapeCodPhoto.net

10 9 8 7 6 5 4 3 2 1

LIBRARY OF CONGRESS CATALOGING-IN-PUBLICATION DATA
Wait, Lea.
Shadows on a Cape Cod wedding : an antique print mystery / Lea Wait.
    p. cm.
ISBN 978-1-56474-531-6 (pbk. : alk. paper)
1. Summer, Maggie (Fictitious character)—Fiction. 2. Antique dealers—Fiction. 3. Prints—Collectors and collecting—Fiction. 4. Murder—Investigation—Massachusetts—Fiction. 5. Cape Cod (Mass.)—Fiction. I. Title.
PS3623.A42S5346 2012
813'.6—dc23
                    2012030707

Dedicated to my aunt Jane Bennett Smart (1926–2011),
one of several people who, together, were my
models for Gussie White

and

to my husband, Bob,
who believed in my dreams decades before anyone else did,
and who hasn't given up on me yet.
It's impossible to fully return such faith and love with words,
so I hope ample supplies of chocolate and Scotch
will also be acceptable.

*Shadows on a
Cape Cod Wedding*

Chapter 1

The Wreck of the "Atlantic"—Cast Up By the Sea. Wood Engraving by Winslow Homer (1836–1910) from *Harper's Weekly*, April 26, 1873. Body of drowned woman, lying in surf on rocky shore, being discovered by fisherman. A ship is sinking in the distance. On April 1, 1873, the transatlantic liner RMS *Atlantic*, whose route was Liverpool to New York City, ran into rocks off the coast of Nova Scotia and sank. Although residents of nearby fishing villages tried to rescue passengers, 535 people were drowned, including all the women and children on board. The *Atlantic* was owned and operated by the White Star Line, which later owned the *Titanic*. Winslow Homer, one of America's most important artists, was still working as an illustrator for *Harper's Weekly* in 1873, and this full-page illustration was his tribute to those who'd perished. 9.125 x 13.75 inches. Price: $250.

THE BODY WAS BLOATED and discolored, and mercifully half-covered by the rockweed tangled around the sand-encrusted legs and torso. It sprawled on the sand just within the dark high-tide line, a few feet from where breakers of ebbing waters were slowly returning to Cape Cod Bay. Gulls and crabs hadn't feasted. Much.

"Welcome to Massachusetts," Maggie Summer thought, and immediately gave herself a mental slap. Whoever this poor man was, he deserved respect. Someone, somewhere, had loved him. Maybe he had a wife and children waiting for him to return home.

She pulled her challis scarf closer against the chill October sea breezes, glanced at the dunes above the boardwalk, and looked up and down the beach. Empty. Bleak.

Her drive from New Jersey had taken less time than she'd estimated. Ten minutes ago she'd thought a quiet beach walk in salt air would relax her while she waited for Gussie to return home. Winslow's town beach was only a short block from the house Gussie and Jim were having refurbished, where they'd planned to meet. She'd parked in their driveway and headed for the dunes.

But right now being the only person on the beach, or at least the only living one, wasn't relieving her stress levels.

Maggie pulled out her cell phone and dialed 911.

Police on Cape Cod would be prepared for occasional drownings. But she hated that, on top of everything else that had gone wrong, this unfortunate soul had been washed ashore so close to Gussie's new home days before the wedding.

Only one thing could be worse, Maggie thought, as she waited for the emergency operator to answer. That would be if Gussie or Jim, her husband-to-be, had known him.

"Dan Jeffrey. His daughter called a couple of days ago and said he hadn't come home," Winslow Police Chief Ike Irons pronounced as he looked down at the body. "I didn't worry much. He's a grown man, known to hoist a few. I figgered he and his cousin Cordelia'd had a spat, and he'd gone for a long walk. Or was visiting someone in Boston for a day or two." He shook his head. "Poor fellow. Guess I should've paid more attention."

The chief had shown up at about the same time as the ambulance. "Looks drowned to me, but the law says someone official's got to tell me that," he said to the driver, as though the situation needed explaining. "He goes to the state medical examiner's office in Sandwich." The EMTs half lifted, half rolled the unfortunate Dan Jeffrey into a body bag, lifted the bag onto a stretcher, and wheeled him up the dune and into the back of the waiting ambulance.

Then Irons returned to Maggie. "You're the one found him, so I guess I'd better get basic information." He pulled out the black notebook that's a part of every crime fighter's equipment. "Name?"

She already had her driver's license out. "Margaret—Maggie—Summer, from New Jersey. I'm here visiting Augusta White, for her wedding a week from Saturday."

"So you're a friend of Gussie's, eh?" said Chief Irons, glancing at the license, and then looking her over, from her long wind-blown hair to her L.L. Bean jacket and jeans. He made a point of checking out her naked ring finger, so she did the same to his. The fourth finger of his left hand was clearly taken.

The significant ring Will had given Maggie, the Victorian ring whose small Ruby-Emerald-Garnet-Amethyst-Ruby-and-Diamond spelled out the word "regard," wasn't on her left hand, but she flashed it anyway. That ring had been given in serious friendship, but had come to mean more than friendship to both Will and Maggie. She never took it off.

Chief Irons glanced up toward the road above the dunes. "I didn't think they'd moved in yet. Their fancy house's still under construction, far as I know."

"Gussie's going to meet me there."

He refocused on the purpose of their conversation. "How'd you happen to find Mr. Jeffrey?"

"I came down to the beach to walk. To stretch my legs after my drive from Jersey."

"Did you touch the body?"

Maggie recoiled slightly, without meaning to. "No. It was obvious he was dead."

"Right."

"I called 911. And went up to the road to wait for someone to come." She hadn't exactly wanted to hang around with the body, and clearly the tide was going out. The body wasn't going anywhere.

Chief Irons snapped his notebook shut. "Okay. That's about it. If I think of anything else to ask, will you be staying with Gussie, or at one of the B and Bs in town?"

"I'll be with Gussie until the wedding. At her old house."

"I'll be seeing you around, then," he said, giving Maggie another head-to-toe look. "Nothing much happens in this town I don't know about. Jim Dryden, Gussie's intended, and I, we've worked together on some cases. He's a lawyer, you know."

"I know," Maggie said. Gussie'd been her best friend for years, and yes, she did know Gussie's fiancé. The maid of honor tended to be informed about such things.

They walked together back up toward the road. Somehow Maggie didn't feel in the mood to continue her beach walk.

As they reached the pavement Gussie's familiar beige van pulled into her wide driveway and parked next to Maggie's red one.

"You can give your friend the news about her neighbor," said Chief Irons, as he headed for the black Buick with WINSLOW POLICE CHIEF printed on the side. "I've got paperwork to take care of. Welcome to the Cape, Ms. Maggie Summer. Enjoy your stay."

Chapter 2

In October. Lithograph of painting by Sarah S. Stilwell (Sarah S. Stilwell Weber, who sometimes signed her work "SSS"). Girl in white dress of period (1905) holding a bunch of purple grapes and eating them while standing in front of a vine heavy with ripe grapes. Her eyes are wide, as though she's been caught in the act. Stilwell (1878–1939) was one of Howard Pyle's students, and a close friend of his sister, Katherine, for whom she illustrated many poems and stories for children. She also illustrated stories and advertisements for many leading magazines of the early twentieth century. 5.75 x 8.50 inches. Price: $60.

"MAGGIE! YOU'RE HERE!" Gussie called out. She waved from the window of her van and then maneuvered her electric scooter from the driver's side to the wheelchair lift, and pressed the buttons so the lift would deliver her to the ground. "Sorry I wasn't here when you arrived. My dentist's appointment ran late."

Maggie hugged her as soon as she was safely on the driveway. "It's been—what—three months? It seems forever!"

"It *is* forever," Gussie agreed. "In July when you were here Jim and I hadn't even decided to get married. And then this house came up for sale, and we loved it, and we thought it only needed a few modifications to be completely accessible. Of course, we were crazy!"

"I know, I know. You've gone completely mad, and I'm thrilled for you!" Maggie said, gesturing at the house and land. "What a location! I haven't seen the inside of the house, of course, but I did walk around a little. So close to the beach! And it's not far from the boardwalk, so that makes easy for you to get there, too."

"Exactly. Unless it's really low tide and the sand is wet, beaches aren't great for wheelchairs or scooters. The town built the boardwalk after a hurricane twenty years ago destroyed most of the original one. It makes the beach much easier to navigate for folks like me."

"And the house is gorgeous! Very different from your old place!"

"Not exactly an apartment above a store, is it?" Gussie smiled. "Or Jim's Victorian, either. We've gone contemporary. Come on! I can hardly wait to show you the inside. Jim's going to join us any minute, too." She led the way up the ramp over a yard of broken shells and sea stones. "The outside of the house, both the original house, and the addition we've added, is finished, but the inside isn't quite done, as you'll see. That's one of the reasons we're going a bit crazy." She opened the door, which Maggie noted had a handle and lock at just the right height for someone in a wheelchair.

"It's wonderful, Gussie!" Maggie said immediately. "But…you're planning to live here right after the wedding, right?"

"That's my Maggie! A woman who grasps the obvious," laughed Gussie. "Yes; we think it's going to be perfect. And the plan is for me to move here right before the wedding and Jim to join me as soon as we're legal. But as you can see, it's not quite ready yet." She steered her scooter around the pile of cartons filling most of the entrance to the large living room. On one side was the kitchen; on the other was a large open stone fireplace. Straight ahead a wall of glass windows looked out over Cape Cod Bay. "We opened up three rooms to get this space," she explained, "and we totally redid the kitchen. It's the only part of the house that's completely finished. See?" She zoomed over to demonstrate.

Maggie followed her.

"I worked with the architect on everything," she said, with pride. "It's designed not just for someone in a chair, but for me, personally! Every cabinet and shelf the right height. The insides of some of the cabinets have lazy-Susan shelves so I can turn them to get plates or pans in the back. I can reach every burner on the stove, and the oven, too. It's perfect. Jim doesn't mind bending over a little if he has to do some cooking, and we had a second microwave installed at his level. For the first time in years I have a kitchen where I can cook safely and comfortably."

"It's wonderful, Gussie." Maggie walked through the wide aisle, peeking into the drawers and checking the shelves in the cabinets. "I love it!"

"Now all we have to do is get the rest of the house finished. And all of our furniture and books and clothes moved in!"

"What still needs to be done?"

"Our master bedroom was finished yesterday, thank goodness. The guest bedroom only needs molding and paint. It's close. Jim's office needs more. We're going to have cabinets built there, and bookcases built in all the rooms, but that won't happen for another month. The problem is that my old place needs to be emptied in the next couple of days."

"No office for you?"

"My office is down at my new store."

Maggie nodded. "Which I can hardly wait to see! And of course, the newlyweds' bedroom had to be finished first."

"Naturally!" They grinned at each other. "A glass of wine? The kitchen's operational now."

"I'd love a glass," Maggie said. She watched as Gussie, clearly proud to show off her kitchen, got out three wineglasses ("one for Jim, when he gets here") and a bottle of Chardonnay from the refrigerator, and poured them each a glass.

"Luckily, we do have a few chairs here," said Gussie, handing Maggie her glass, and pointing at a chair near the fireplace. "We've been gradually moving in furniture from my apartment and Jim's house, as we agree on pieces we want to keep. I, of course, come equipped with my own seating."

"Cheers!" said Maggie, raising her glass. "And best wishes, on your house, and your upcoming nuptials."

"Thank you for coming. You haven't heard all the reasons I need you yet," said Gussie, raising her glass, too. "So take some sips. I don't want you turning around and changing your mind about being here."

"There's something I should tell you, too," Maggie started to say, when Jim walked in.

Tall and confident, his white hair windblown, he reached down and focused first on his bride-to-be. "Survived another day?" he said quietly.

"I'm happy as a clam," Gussie replied. "Now that Maggie's here I'll have someone on my side. You can cope with the painters and carpenters and with any telephone calls from your mother."

Jim grinned. "No problem. And I can deal with my mother. I've been doing it all my life, I keep telling you. Hi, Maggie. Welcome to our frenetic world. I see you ladies have already opened a bottle of wine, so I'm going to join you." He poured himself a generous glass. "I'm glad you're here. This getting married has turned out to be a bit more complicated than we'd thought. We're beginning to think eloping would have been the best idea."

"We've been considering it, actually," Gussie threw in, a bit grimly.

"Unfortunately, it's a bit late for that. If we eloped now my mother would probably murder one or both of us."

They smiled at each other.

Maggie put down her wineglass. "I hate to interrupt, but before we talk about the wedding I need to tell you what happened this afternoon when I was walking on the beach."

"What? Did you find a whale? Or the man of your dreams? If it's that, we'd better call Will and tell him not to drive down from Maine after all," Gussie teased.

"No calls to Maine necessary," said Maggie. "But I did find a man. A dead man."

Chapter 3

Godey's Fashions for April, 1873. Hand-colored steel engraving from *Godey's Lady's Book*. Trifold, as usual for large *Godey's* fashion plates, so it would fold inside the monthly magazine. Depicts five women and one young girl, all wearing bustled dresses. One, a bride, in white satin dress and transparent veil, so readers could see the dress. Another, in purple mourning attire, with a black cape. The others are wearing elaborate dresses of beige, bright blue, and pale blue. The girl, who's playing with a rabbit pull-toy, wears a similar dress, with a capelet top and shorter ruffled skirt. *Godey's* was published between 1830 and 1898. It included black and white and colored fashion plates, recipes, embroidery patterns, beauty hints, and fiction, essays, and poetry by luminaries like Hawthorne, Emerson, Poe, Longfellow, and Stowe. Sarah Josepha Hale, its editor from 1836 until 1877, advocated for women's education and child welfare. 11.25 x 9.25 inches. Price: $65.

"WHAT?" JIM PUT HIS wineglass down, and Maggie could almost see him wanting to reach for a legal pad and pencil. He *was* a lawyer.

"Where? What happened?" asked Gussie.

"I found a man's body on the beach, not far from here." Maggie pointed out the window toward the beach. "I called 911. Your local police chief, Ike Irons? He said he knew you, Jim."

Jim and Gussie exchanged looks. "Everyone in Winslow knows Ike Irons. Go on."

"He came, and so did the ambulance. They confirmed what was obvious. The man was dead. Irons had them take the body to the medical examiner's office."

"I thought I saw a police car leaving when I drove up! I was so excited to see you I didn't think anything of it. What did the man look like? Did Ike say who he might be?" Gussie asked.

"He did, actually. The man's name was Dan Jeffrey."

Gussie's hand went to her mouth. "Oh, no. Poor Cordelia."

"You knew him, then?" Irons had said the man was a neighbor, but "neighbor" could mean proximity, not necessarily friendship.

"We didn't know him well," Jim put in. "He'd only lived in Winslow a couple of years. But his cousin Cordelia's been here for—what would you say, Gussie? Ten or fifteen years? She was here when I moved to town, and that was more than ten years ago now."

Gussie nodded slowly. "I'd say closer to twenty years. I remember a young family lived in that house about the time my nephew Ben was born. I think they had a baby about his age. He's twenty-one now. And dying to see you, by the way, Maggie. You're his favorite unofficial aunt."

"None of that's important now, Gussie," Jim reminded her gently. "What's important is that Cordelia's going to be alone again, with no one to share her loss."

"What about his daughter?" Maggie asked.

"What daughter?" Gussie looked at her.

"Maybe I misunderstood," said Maggie. "I thought the police chief said Dan Jeffrey's daughter had called to report him missing a couple of days ago."

"There's no daughter I know of," said Jim, shaking his head. "Only his cousin, Cordelia West. Maybe Ike was confused."

Gussie turned to Maggie. "Cordelia's a dear woman, but very shy. She's deaf. She doesn't read lips, she only signs. And very few people here in Winslow sign. So she's alone."

Maggie frowned. "I wonder why she chose to live here, then. So many people do sign today. And there are lots of ways those who are hearing impaired can communicate."

Gussie shrugged. "I've wondered that myself. But she keeps to herself. Or she did until about two years ago, when her cousin Dan appeared and moved in with her. He signs, and he took her out with him places. She seemed to enjoy being with people more. And now he's gone."

"He wasn't like Cordelia, that was for sure," said Jim. "He had a bit of a drinking problem, and from what I heard, could be a nasty drunk."

"It's a small town," Gussie added, "and he was new in town. So he was the one blamed when problems came up."

"I wouldn't be surprised if Ike Irons had a file on him, that's for sure," Jim agreed. "But except for that fight he and Bob Silva got into over at the Lazy Lobster a while back, I don't know of any real trouble he got into."

"Well, he won't be able to blame Dan for anything that happens in the future," said Gussie. "I only met the man a few times and didn't see a lot in him, but I feel sorry for Cordelia. Tomorrow I'll stop in and let her know I'm thinking of her."

"I'd be happy to go with you," Maggie volunteered. "I can sign a little. We have ASL interpreters in classrooms at Somerset County for students who need them, of course, but I took courses so I could start to communicate a little with my students who were hearing impaired."

"That would be wonderful," said Gussie. "We'll do it."

"I hope you ladies won't mind my leaving you alone tonight, but I have a lot of paperwork to catch up with," said Jim.

"Bless you, Jim," said Gussie. "You'll be missed, but somehow I think we'll cope. Maggie and I have so much to talk about."

"I had a feeling that might be the case," he said. "In fact, I arranged with the Winslow Inn to have a double order of your favorite steamed mussels and two stuffed lobsters delivered to your place," he paused and looked at his watch, "about ninety minutes from now."

"No wonder you're marrying this man!" Maggie said. "He's perfect. Except for ensuring that we have wine chilling in the refrigerator there. You forgot that, Jim!"

"Actually, I didn't," he grinned back. "I just forgot to mention it."

"Thank you, dear," said Gussie. "I hope you don't have to work too late."

"Not to worry. I'd rather work now than the first week after I'm married. I want to have a clean desk then. So I have an agenda, too. Shall we all be off?" He stood up, and Maggie followed.

"Wait! Before we leave here, I want to give Maggie a preview of the wedding," Gussie said, a bit slyly. "I thought I'd show her the dress your mother chose for her. And had shipped all the way from Atlanta."

"You haven't told her?" Jim looked at his bride-to-be incredulously. "I can't believe you haven't told her."

"I wanted it to be a surprise," Gussie said, with a stern look at him.

"You have a dress for me?" Maggie asked. "When we talked about dresses a month ago you said the wedding wasn't going to be formal, and I should bring my favorite cocktail dress. I brought a couple with me; I thought you could choose whichever one you thought would work best with whatever you'd decided to wear."

Gussie shook her head. "Remember, I said I needed you to come to the Cape early?"

"Of course. I had to pull in a lot of favors to get people to cover all my classes for ten days," said Maggie. "I assumed you needed help getting the house ready before the wedding." She gestured at the unpacked boxes.

"I do. Believe me. At my old home, and here, and at both the old and the new Aunt Agatha's Attics," said Gussie. "I still can't believe that in this housing market my dear sister Ellen managed to sell the building with both my house and store, so I need to move both before the wedding." Gussie paused for a moment and shook her head, as though still trying to convince herself it was true. Then she looked back at Maggie. "But, no, those little details are only the beginning." She headed her scooter toward the closed door to the future guest room. "Follow me."

Maggie glanced at Jim, who had suddenly become fascinated by the view out the window, and followed Gussie.

"*That,*" said Gussie, throwing the door to the guest room open dramatically and pointing, "is the dress Jim's mother sent for you to wear to the wedding."

For a moment Maggie said nothing. She stared in horror at the pink-green-and-yellow-flowered, off-the-shoulder, Scarlett O'Hara–style dress, complete with flounces, stays, and a hoop skirt, that was hanging from the wrought iron chandelier in the middle of the empty guest room. The dress occupied a space that might have been filled by a table seating eight.

"You're my best friend in all the world, Gussie," she finally said, breaking the silence. "You know I'd do anything for you. But you cannot expect me to wear *that*."

Gussie's knuckles on the hand control of her electric scooter were almost white. "I told you it was an emergency. *That* is only the beginning."

Maggie took a deep breath. "I brought you and Jim a case of special champagne as a wedding present. I'd thought maybe tonight, after dinner, you and I could break out a similar bottle, so I also brought a couple of extras. When we get to your old house I'm going to put them in the refrigerator. While we're eating dinner I want you to tell me what's really going on with this wedding. And then, after a few more drinks, I want you to tell me everything you won't have told me over dinner."

Gussie grinned. "Have I told you how really, really happy I am that you're here?"

"Just keep saying that, my friend. Because I have a feeling that before the next ten days are over you're going to owe me. Big time!"

Chapter 4

Picturesque New England Industries: Lobstering Off Scituate. **(From Sketches by Joseph Becker.)** Full page from *Frank Leslie's Illustrated Newspaper,* May 21, 1887, including a paragraph on the lobster industry, and sketches of setting the traps ("lobster boats are a species of small lugger, with one large sail and one small one"), measuring the lobster ("none less than 10½ inches long may be kept"), pegging the claws, and arriving at a boiling and canning factory. Black and white. The way life used to be. 10.5 x 16 inches. Price: $65.

"DON'T PANIC ABOUT the dress I showed you," Gussie said after she and Maggie were settled at her old home and the wine was flowing. "It's being shipped back to Atlanta tomorrow. I told Lily, Jim's mother: this is my wedding, and Jim's. I only kept the dresses this long because I wanted to show you the sort of challenge we've been facing."

"Along with the painters and carpenters and moving your home and store, and basically, changing your entire life," Maggie added.

"That's all!" said Gussie. "Now, let's relax and enjoy the mussels. They should be eaten while they're still warm."

"No problem here," Maggie agreed. "There's no place to get decent food on the road, and the 'everything' bagel I bought at the Bridgewater Diner this morning was gone a long time ago."

The wine-and-herb-steamed mussels disappeared much too fast, and they dug into their baked lobsters stuffed with crabmeat with gusto.

"Mmmm. Nothing like this in Jersey. Just promise you won't tell Will I ate a lobster caught outside Maine waters," Maggie said, leaning back and taking a sip of her wine. "He won't even consider Massachusetts lobsters."

"Maine lobsters are pretty darn good," Gussie acknowledged, savoring a particularly sweet piece of the tail, "but I believe in comparison eating. Especially when you can get lobsters locally."

"And this restaurant really knows how to prepare seafood," Maggie agreed. "Fresh, and not overcooked. Too many chefs have a heavy hand with shellfish."

"Which is why we're having our reception at the Winslow Inn," said Gussie. "No baked lobsters, I'm afraid, but we think they'll do a great job. We're taking over a room for about seventy-five, which should be the number of guests."

"You don't know yet?"

"People are notorious about not returning those RSVP cards. Everyone who warned us was right. We've only heard from about half those we invited."

"That's incredibly inconsiderate," said Maggie.

"Indeed," agreed Gussie. "Another day and we'll have to start telephoning people. We've just had too many other things to do."

"Well, I'm here to help now. And Jim gets major points for having a scrumptious feast prepared that the two of us could eat in peace this first night."

Maggie looked around the living room of what had been Gussie's home for as long as they'd been friends: the second floor above Aunt Augusta's Attic, the shop where Gussie sold her antique dolls, toys, and children's books. Several years ago the progression of Gussie's Post-Polio Syndrome had convinced her to add a chairlift from the downstairs to her apartment. She still used her old wheelchair, and sometimes a walker, to go a few steps when she was at home, but doctors had told her to stress her muscles as little as possible, and at forty-nine, she knew it was time to listen. Two years ago she'd moved to an electric scooter for when she was at the shop or "out in the world," as she put it.

"It looks as though you've packed most of your things," Maggie commented. "Your bookcases are empty, and except for the furniture we're using, this room is empty."

Gussie nodded. "Except for the biggest pieces of furniture, and those in my bedroom, we've been moving things to the other house. But the closets are still full. I need your help packing seasonal things, and treasures like the Limoges dinner set my Great-aunt Jane left me that I've never used, but never could bear to sell. A lot is stored higher than I can reach."

"I hear my marching orders," Maggie said, nodding between bites. "No problem. Just tell me what you want packed, and what you don't want to take."

"At this point, pack everything. I'll make decisions at the other end," said Gussie. "I'll finish the packing in the shop so I'll know exactly what's in each carton. I have to get the new store up and running as soon as possible."

"I'm impressed that you have a new location for the store already."

"I'll show you tomorrow. The economy was on my side, and I actually had a few choices. Several businesses in Winslow failed recently."

"Ouch."

"I know. But it meant I got a good price on a shop that's closer to the center of town, so traffic should be good. It's bigger than the one I had, too, with a back-room office that will be a big help."

"And it's accessible?"

"Carpenters are working on that. Plumbers have already put the fixtures in a handicapped-accessible bathroom. The new shelving and counters are about done, and the whole space is being painted. I'm hoping you can help me unpack and set up while you're here. I'm aiming at opening the new and improved Aunt Augusta's Attic the week after the wedding."

"In time for the Christmas season."

"In time for Thanksgiving, if all works out. My busiest time of the year is October through December. I've lost most of October this year, but I'm hoping the new space will help me catch up. That's one reason Jim and I aren't taking a honeymoon right now. We want to get our house in order, my shop opened, and then, maybe in January or February, when everything's slowed to a frozen snail's pace on the Cape, we'll take a cruise to somewhere warm."

"I can't get over how much you've done, so fast," said Maggie. "When I was here in July for the Provincetown show you and Jim were just a—dare I say, comfortable?—couple! And now...everything's changed." The shadows of where paintings and prints had once hung were now ghost-like shapes on the muted wallpaper, empty cartons were stacked next to full ones, and the room where she and Gussie had sat and shared dreams and confidences so many times already looked vacant. Maggie felt a little queasy. Maybe it was the mussels. Or maybe it was Gussie's life, changing so quickly.

"It's good, Maggie. It's good not to get so set in your ways that you can't allow your world to be shaken up a little," said Gussie. "Jim had to push me, I'll admit. But he was right. The new house is going to be wonderful, and the new shop is better than I dreamed. I needed that push."

"You're making a lot of decisions, fast."

"Maybe. But it all makes sense. Jim was the right guy, and it was time to move on. And I finally admitted it to myself," agreed Gussie. "He doesn't seem to mind that I come equipped with wheels and can't do everything I'd love to do. It bothers me a lot more than it seems to bother him. It took me a long time to believe that, but now I do."

"I'm so happy for you!" said Maggie. "I am." She stood up. "In fact, I think it's time to open the first bottle of that champagne I brought for us. Then we can talk about whatever wedding issues are pending. Besides that hideous dress you showed me, which I'm very glad to hear will be heading south tomorrow." She went toward the kitchen, hoping for a minute to take a deep breath. She was happy for Gussie. She was. Gussie was her best friend, and now she had everything she wanted. It all sounded so easy. Why wasn't life as easy for her?

"Maybe all this talk about weddings will give you and Will some ideas," Gussie called out to her.

Maggie yanked the cork out of the champagne bottle and bubbly wine ran down the sides.

"Will and I are fine," said Maggie, returning with the bottle and two glasses. "He's moved himself and his business from Buffalo to

Maine so he can keep an eye on his Aunt Nettie, who's in her nineties. He has his hands full, and I have my teaching."

"There are schools in Maine. You're not wedded to New Jersey, Maggie, any more than I was wedded to this building."

Maggie handed Gussie a glass and then raised her own. "To us. And to decisions. The ones we've made, and the ones we're making now. May they enrich our lives!"

They touched glasses, and each took a generous sip.

Gussie looked at Maggie quizzically. "All right, old friend. We're here tonight because of my wedding. But I've known you long enough to know we just drank to something else, too. What's happening? What decision?"

"You mustn't tell Will. It's between you and me for now."

Gussie put her glass down. "Oh, Maggie! You've met someone else? Tell me. I promise. I won't say anything."

"No! Nothing like that. Or," Maggie hesitated, "not exactly like that. I've finally decided to go ahead and adopt a child. Or children. As a single parent. I filled out my application last week. My home study should be finished by Christmas."

"Oh, Maggie!" Gussie put down her glass and looked at Maggie. "What should I say?"

"Say you're happy for me! You know I've wanted to be a mother for years. I've finally gotten up the courage to do something about it. I've applied to Our World, Our Children, the agency that benefitted from the antiques show we did last May. I've told them I'd like to adopt a girl between the ages of five and nine, but two sisters would be fine, too."

Gussie hesitated. "Are you sure, Maggie? That's a big step. Especially when you know Will doesn't want to be a father."

"I'm sure," said Maggie, holding tightly to her glass and taking another, deeper sip of champagne. "I'm getting older. I need to make this decision now. Will moved to Maine to take care of his aunt. That's important to him, and I love Aunt Nettie, too. But being a mother is important to me. I don't want to wake up and realize I've given up something I really wanted to do because someone else didn't want to do it. This decision is mine. Will's decisions, whatever they are, are his."

"I have to ask. Is there any chance he'll change his mind about parenthood?"

"I hope so. He's told me he likes children. Oh, hell, Gussie, he used to be a high school teacher! But his wife had an ectopic pregnancy and bled to death, and he got it in his mind that he didn't want children. He stopped teaching after she died, and decided he didn't wanted the responsibility of being a father. He's been clear on that point. Believe me. But I keep hoping."

"When will you tell him what you've done?"

"I don't know. I don't even know if my home study will be approved."

"You've been involved with that agency for almost a year. They know you. The chances are very good you'll be approved, aren't they?"

"Yes," Maggie said quietly. "I think I'll be approved."

"Then you have to tell him, Maggie. He's a big part of your life. You have to tell him now. You can't wait until you have a referral for a child. You have to give him another chance to think about what you're doing."

"I will, Gussie. I promise. But not right now. This week is all about your wedding!"

That's when Gussie's phone rang.

Chapter 5

The Georgia Delegation in Congress. Winslow Homer wood engraving published on cover of *Harper's Weekly (The Journal of Civilization)* Saturday, January 5, 1861. A montage of the faces of the Georgia delegation, by Winslow Homer, based on photographs taken by famous Civil War photographer Mathew Brady at his studio in Washington, D.C. The Georgia delegation pictured had already seceded from the Union when this newspaper was printed. 11 x 16 inches. Edges slightly uneven; otherwise, excellent condition. Price: $225.

GUSSIE PUT DOWN her champagne, picked up her cell phone, and looked at the caller ID. "It's Ike Irons." She looked at Maggie. "Guess I'd better pick it up. Yes, Ike? Yes, she's here. Just a minute." She put her hand over the phone. "It's for you."

Maggie raised her eyebrows, but took the phone. "Hello? This is Maggie Summer. Yes, this afternoon, on the beach." There was a pause. "I see. No. I told you; I didn't touch the body. I'd be happy to come down to the station." She looked over at Gussie. "Gussie will tell me where it is." Gussie nodded. "I see. No. I'll be in town until after the wedding. Thank you." Maggie handed the phone back.

"What was that all about? I mean, I know it was about Dan Jeffrey's body, that was clear from this end of the conversation. Did Ike forget to have you sign some paper or other?" Gussie picked up her glass again.

"No; it was more than that," Maggie said slowly. "He just heard from the medical examiner. Dan Jeffrey didn't drown. He was shot."

"No," said Gussie. "That means…"

"He was murdered. Shot in the head, before he went into the water. So now they need a more detailed statement than they did when

I'd just found the body of a man who'd drowned. It seems I found a murder victim."

"Now we *have* to go to see Cordelia in the morning," said Gussie. "I guess after you make your statement. The poor woman."

"You said she didn't have many friends here?"

"Not that I know of. I see her at the post office, and the library. I've seen her more often in the past few months because she lives down the beach from our new house, but off another road. I smile and nod, and she does the same. Once last August she brought over a tray of muffins while Jim and I were talking with the contractor."

"What about the man who was killed?"

"Jim knew him a little. He'd lived with Cordelia a couple of years, I think. He may have been her cousin, but he wasn't at all like her. He was much rougher around the edges. You remember Jim said he drank; he'd seen him at the Lazy Lobster a few times."

"The Lazy Lobster?"

"It's a sports bar popular with local fishermen. Where you can hoist a draft and fill up on thick chowder or a burger while you're watching the Pats or Sox and not worry anyone's going to complain you smell of fish. Not the kind of place where a lot of people order champagne." Gussie lifted her glass in Maggie's direction.

"I'm sorry this Dan Jeffrey was murdered, Gussie, but I won't be able to help the police. I didn't see anything that will help their investigation. I'm here to help you and Jim with your move and your wedding. I've got my marching orders: pack closets, and when directed, help unpack at the new and brilliantly improved Aunt Augusta's Attic."

Gussie raised her arm and saluted. "Exactly!" She reached out her glass. "Is there a little more of that champagne? Between the move and the wedding, and now a murder, I think I could use another glass."

"Filling up, Captain!" Maggie topped off both of their glasses. "And now I need to hear about that wedding. Somehow we've managed to put it off long enough. The happiest day in a woman's life and all that, you know."

"That's what people say, don't they?" Gussie smiled, a little lopsidedly. "Well, like I told you when I called in August to tell you the news. We planned a small wedding. After all, I'm not exactly a blushing bride. It'll be my second wedding, and although Jim's managed to escape the joys of matrimony so far, he's a typical man. The simpler the better for him. We invited our friends from Winslow, of course, and you and Will, and a few of my antiques friends. Jim's family is in Georgia and South Carolina, and he's an only child, so we didn't think any of them would come except his mother, and maybe a stray cousin. I have Ellen and Ben and a couple of relatives near Boston who might decide to drive down and see who I finally decided to marry. Add everyone together and we thought, maximum, maybe fifty people. Since we were sure we'd have the house fixed up by then," here Gussie rolled her eyes, "we planned a catered reception there, sort of a combination wedding and housewarming. Then, when it was clear the house wouldn't be in party shape, we moved the reception to the Winslow Inn. And that would be it. You and Ellen would be my attendants, and Jim's invited Ben, and Andy Sullivan, his best friend and law partner, to stand up with him. So that covers the wedding party."

"All sounds great so far," said Maggie. "Just large enough. Manageable. Festive. Perfect! And how sweet of Jim to ask Ben."

"Wasn't it?" said Gussie. "Ben's thrilled, of course. Now that he's twenty-one he's been invited to a few weddings of people he grew up with, but it's been a little hard for him. He's never had a girlfriend, and he talks about girls all the time. Other than that he seems happy to live at home with Ellen and work for me at the shop and at shows. Ellen and I've talked about whether it might be better for him if he spread his wings and lived in a halfway house, with other young people who have the same challenges he does. Maybe he'd meet a young woman who has Down's, like he does, or find other friends."

"Are there any group homes near here?"

"Only a few on the Cape, and those have long waiting lists."

Maggie shook her head. "I can see the issues. Well, that's Ben. And you've told me what you and Jim wanted your wedding to be like. So I assume something happened to change your plans. Talk!"

Gussie sighed. "It's Jim's mother. She'd met me once, about two years ago, so she knew about the PPS. Jim was worried she'd feel he shouldn't marry someone with a disability, so he didn't even tell her about the wedding right away. He waited until we had our plans made. He made reservations for her at the nicest B and B in town, the same place you'll be staying after I move into the new house. Then he told her."

"She was upset?"

"Turned out my PPS wasn't an issue. She was delighted! Finally her baby boy—Jim's fifty-two, Maggie—is getting married, and she's thrilled. Jim was so relieved he didn't see the flags flying when she started asking about my family."

"Your family? You and Ellen?"

"That's it. Ellen and Ben and I are about it. When Jim told her my parents had died years ago she went into overdrive. She set out to help us. She sees herself as the mother of the bride."

"*What?*"

"Turns out she's spent the last fifty years dreaming of her baby boy's wedding day, and she's dying to make sure it turns out just right. The way *she's* always dreamed it would be. She wanted to come here in September, as soon as she heard. Jim's held her off because of our moving. But she's been calling Jim or me four or five times a day, always with new, helpful, ideas. And doing things, like sending the dresses, as 'surprises'! If I hear the word 'surprise!' one more time…!"

Maggie tried not to laugh. She held up the bottle of champagne and poured what was left into Gussie's glass. "Keep talking. I assume you and Jim explained to her, like the grown-ups you most assuredly are, that this was your wedding, and it was arranged the way you both wanted it."

"That would be about the time she started crying." Gussie grimaced. "For the first time. That woman is a master manipulator. How Jim emerged as a sane adult is beyond me."

"Let me guess. You and Jim decided to compromise. Let her contribute a little to the wedding."

"Exactly. It seemed the kindest thing to do. And after all, we were so tied up with the construction on the house, and the store, and moving, and Jim can't exactly put his law practice on hold, even for a wedding. We decided to turn over some of the details to her, since most of the wedding was planned anyway. What harm could she do? We'd tell her what we'd decided, and let her make some of the minor decisions."

"And?"

"It's gone downhill from there." Gussie drained her champagne glass. "You saw the dress she rented for you. She thought it was awful that I'd told you and Ellen you could wear whatever you'd like, and that I'd decided to wear a pale yellow dress. Horrors! All on her very own, believe me, she found a place in Georgia that would deliver overnight and ordered two dresses like the one you saw, for you and Ellen, and a flower girl dress, since every wedding must have a flower girl. She's still calling around to relatives Jim didn't even know he had trying to find one who'll fly in and play that role. Her alternative suggestion, I swear, is for me to go to the local elementary school and find 'a cute little miss with curls' to fit the costume."

"She really wanted Ellen and me to wear *Gone With the Wind* sorts of dresses in a New England Congregational Church in the twenty-first century?" Maggie asked, still fixated on the vision she'd seen earlier.

Gussie nodded. "Believe it. You should have seen Ellen's expression. She took one look at her dress and asked if we were changing the date of our wedding to Halloween. And by the way, Lily even made you both dressmaker's appointments with a woman in Provincetown. Bless the Internet."

"But at least she left you alone? You already had a dress you'd chosen."

Gussie chortled until the tears rolled down her face. "No, Maggie. Not a chance. She ordered a dress for me, too. Open the door of the closet in back of you."

Maggie got up, a bit unsteadily, and threw open the door, more dramatically than she'd planned.

Inside was hanging something that appeared to be an enormous white balloon, above which was a small tight bodice. Maggie looked again. The balloon was supported by the largest hoop she'd ever seen.

She turned back to Gussie. "What is it?"

"Lily's choice for my wedding dress," Gussie explained. "It has a hoop, which Lily somehow felt I could wear by putting the hoop over my scooter. She also sent a veil, which Jim's great-grandmother wore, so I could carry on a family tradition."

Gussie and Maggie looked at each other, and looked at the dress.

"We have to burn it," said Maggie. "Not the veil. That would be mean. But the dress? Definitely."

Gussie started to giggle. And then they both burst into hysterical laughter.

Chapter 6

Cinnamomum Cassia Blume. Chromolithograph from Kohler's four-volume *Medizenal Pflanzen*, Germany, 1887, showing a sprig of the plant and details of the flower. These four volumes picturing plants used for medical purposes (Cassia was said to relieve flatulence, vomiting, nausea, and diarrhea, and decrease the secretion of milk in nursing mothers) were considered an authority when they were published. During the nineteenth century Cassia, also called "Bastard Cinnamon" or "Chinese Cinnamon," was also used as a substitute for *Cinnamomum zeylanicum* from Ceylon, which it closely resembles. The stronger flavor of the inside of its bark (where the "cinnamon" is) was preferred by chocolate makers in Germany and Russia. Cassia's buds, similar to small cloves, were often used in potpourri. 9 x 11.5 inches. Toned edges. $55.

AFTER A LATE NIGHT of talk and wine and more talk and champagne, not to speak of an almost seven-hour drive, finding a body, and hearing about both a wedding and a murder, Maggie hadn't slept well. Her head hurt, her back ached, and her mind kept jumping from Gussie's wedding to how and when she was going to tell Will she'd decided to adopt.

She'd hoped Gussie would be more supportive. Even her best friend sounded as though she was on Will's side. Or at least on the side of telling him. Soon.

She hit the pillow and turned over, trying to block the sunlight coming through the cracks in the blinds in Gussie's guest bedroom. The only piece of furniture left in the room was the bed, and it was directly in the path of those cheerful rays.

Maggie groaned and closed her eyes. It really was morning. Already.

She heard voices, and the tapping of Gussie's walker in the hall. "Maggie? Maggie, wake up! Jim's here. He thinks he should go with you to the police station."

"I'm awake." Maggie raised her head. "Just a minute." She rummaged through the suitcase she'd left on the floor next to the bed and found clean underwear, jeans, and a red turtleneck, and managed to get a comb through her long, wavy hair. Five minutes later she was as presentable as she was going to get.

"Here," said Gussie, handing her a Diet Pepsi. "I got in a supply, knowing you were coming."

"Thank you. Nectar of the gods," said Maggie, inhaling the liquid that she required the way others in the universe require coffee or tea. After a few gulps she managed to ask, "Do you have any aspirin?"

"I think there's still a bottle in the bathroom medicine cabinet," said Gussie.

Jim stood, bemused, sipping the cup of coffee he'd brought for himself. Gussie had a similar cup that held tea. He'd been warned Maggie would drink neither, but hadn't seen her in action before.

She was back in a moment. "Okay. That's all the personal restoration I can manage at the moment."

"I assume you ladies had a late night?" said Jim, clearly trying to keep a straight face.

"The dinner you had delivered was delicious," said Gussie. "And you were right. We had a lot to talk about."

"So I can see," he said, looking from one of them to the other. "Gussie told me Ike called about Dan Jeffrey. I thought I'd drive you to the police station this morning."

"I don't need you to do that," said Maggie.

"I think you should have a lawyer with you."

"A lawyer? Because I happened to be the one to find a body on the beach?"

"It won't do any harm. In a murder investigation it never hurts to have a lawyer around."

"This isn't the first time I've been involved with a murder, Jim. I've never had any reason to have a lawyer."

Gussie maneuvered her walker so she stood slightly in front of

Jim. "Actually, that's one of the reasons Jim thought it would be a good idea if he went with you, Maggie. You have a history of getting involved with murder investigations. Remember what happened at the New York State antiques show? And at the show in New Jersey? Not to speak of—"

"Okay, okay. I get it. You're on his side. It's not my fault I happen to be around when murders are committed. Don't worry. I don't live here, and I have no interest in getting involved in another murder investigation. No interest whatsoever."

"Good to hear that, Maggie. But, even so, I'm going with you," Jim said firmly. "After you finish at the police station I'll drop you at the new store so you and Gussie can plan the rest of your day."

"From there we'll pay a condolence call on Cordelia," Gussie put in. "We won't stay long. Jim, would you pick up a dozen cupcakes at Josie's Bakery that we could take? I don't want to go to Cordelia's empty-handed and I don't have time to make anything."

"No problem. So, Miss Maggie, let's get ourselves over to Ike's place of business. The sooner you take care of that, the sooner the rest of your visit in Winslow can start."

Chief Ike Irons raised his eyebrows slightly when he saw Maggie was accompanied by Jim Dryden. "Good morning, Ms. Summer. Thank you for stopping in."

"Good morning, Ike," Jim interrupted. "*Doctor* Summer is happy to clarify anything she might have said yesterday, but since Dan Jeffrey's death has now been identified as a murder, and Dr. Summer is a guest of Gussie's and mine, I thought I'd accompany her to make sure everything went smoothly."

"Of course you did," said Ike. "But I assure you, Dr. Summer has no need of a lawyer. I just need her to verify the information she gave me under less formal circumstances yesterday afternoon."

"Then we shouldn't take up much of your time," agreed Jim.

Maggie tried to keep a straight face as Jim and the chief squared off in what seemed familiar roles for both of them. She had the distinct feeling they'd share a beer if they met later that day, but right now they were in full male role-play. She could feel the testosterone level in the room rising.

"*Doctor* Summer, I apologize for not recognizing your medical credentials," Chief Irons began.

"I'm not a medical doctor, Chief Irons. I have a doctorate," Maggie interrupted. "Neither of you have to call me Doctor Summer, please."

"Well, then. I had my secretary type up a statement based on our meeting yesterday afternoon." He handed a typed statement across his desk to Maggie. "If you'd read it, make any corrections necessary and initial those, and sign the bottom, that will be all that's necessary."

"Before you make any marks on that paper, I'd like to look at it, Maggie," Jim said quietly. "But go ahead and read it. Any leads in the case so far, Ike?"

"There's hardly been time to do much now, has there? I'll be talking to Bob Silva. He was convinced Dan was the one got his Tony into drugs. And Dan spent time at the Lazy Lobster, so Rocky Costa might have seen or heard something. I have to get one of those interpreters to help me talk with Cordelia. She was mighty upset when I saw her last night, not surprisingly. But she might have information she doesn't know is helpful."

Jim nodded. Maggie handed him the statement so he could read it through. "Any corrections, Maggie?"

"No. It's pretty straightforward."

"Then go ahead and sign it. I'll co-sign as your witness and lawyer." She nodded.

"Maggie here's familiar with ASL. Didn't you say that last night, Maggie?"

"I can get along in it. But I'm not fluent. In a murder investigation the chief will need an interpreter who can understand all the nuances of the language. I couldn't do that."

"I'll keep that in mind, Dr. Summer. I've put in a call to a professional interpreter who'll be here later today." Chief Irons stood. "Thank you for coming in. If you think of anything else from yesterday that might help us, please let us know." He turned toward Jim and bowed slightly. "Or have your lawyer notify us."

"I'll do that," said Maggie.

Gussie's new shop was on Main Street, not far from the police station, within sight of the classic white Congregational Church at the end of the Green that Jim pointed out as the location for the wedding.

"It looks perfect," Maggie agreed. "Just right for a Winslow wedding."

"That's why we chose it," said Jim. "We're not big churchgoers, but Gussie's family have been members there for years. She took her first communion there, and her parents and sister had their weddings there. Plus, it's in the heart of the town, so it's easy to find, and it's classic. It reflects what we wanted for our ceremony. A little old-fashioned, simple, and elegant."

Maggie looked at him. "What does your mother think of it?"

"She's more the high-Episcopalian type, complete with incense and robes, but this is the only church in town, thank goodness, so we said it was this church or no church. I think she's going to add some decorations. She said something about talking with the minister. That'll keep her busy and happy once she gets here. I'm not even going to bother Gussie about it. I'm sure it'll be fine."

Warning lights went off in Maggie's head. The words "decorations" and "not bother Gussie" meant more when they were connected to the woman who'd ordered those dresses she'd seen the night before.

"When's your mother arriving?"

"She's flying in next Thursday night." Jim pulled into a parking space in front of Josie's Bakery. "You stay put. I'll only be a minute. I'm going to get those cupcakes Gussie wanted to take to Cordelia."

The orange and yellow maple trees were brilliant that morning, and their fallen leaves covered the grass on the Green with a patchwork of colors. Few people were out and about this early, and those who were held containers of coffee and bakery bags. She could see a short line inside the bake shop.

Two girls carrying backpacks raced each other across the Green. Were they late to school? Maggie glanced at her watch. Almost 10:00. Maybe they were homeschooled. How old were they? Maybe eleven or twelve. If she remembered correctly, the Winslow Public Library was in that direction.

How soon would she have a daughter? Or two. What would she, or they, look like? African American, with curly black hair? Hispanic? Or maybe they'd have brown hair, like hers. Where was her daughter now? What was she doing?

Jim opened Maggie's door and handed her two pastry boxes. "The bottom one is for Cordelia. The other is for you and Gussie for breakfast." He waved a bag in her direction. "This is for me to take to my office. I couldn't resist the cinnamon rolls. Hope you feel the same way."

"Mmmm." The scent of cinnamon filled the car. "I was hoping you'd get something like that when I saw people coming out with those boxes," Maggie admitted. "Now I'm curious to see the new Aunt Augusta's Attic."

"It's not exactly ready for business," said Jim. "But it's on its way. Gussie's only a couple of weeks from the grand opening."

Chapter 7

Dried Seaweeds, or Sea Mosses. In the nineteenth century sea-weeds were called sea mosses. These delicate dark pink mosses were collected by Miss Marnie Wall of Crescent City, California, pressed in pleasing patterns, dried, placed in an album, and then presented to Charles N. Kendall (perhaps her fiancé?) in 1880. They've been carefully removed from the album, double-matted in dusky pink and moss green to form a shallow shadow box, and then framed. 12 x 15 inch–modern gold frames. Price: $150 each.

"I COME BEARING GIFTS, courtesy of your devoted fiancé," Maggie announced, as she opened the door of Gussie's new store and looked around. "Jim went on to his office. Wow. This is fantastic, Gussie! It's twice the size of your old store." She put the two boxes of pastries on the counter, which looked as though it only needed one more coat of varnish, and started walking around.

Gussie was talking with the carpenter on the other side of a pile of boards in the back of the store. "I'll be with you in a minute!" she called out.

Deep shelves lined the walls on two sides of the large room, and unpainted stands and tables clearly intended for the center of the store were piled in one corner. The rest of the store included the bathroom; a separate office, clearly delineated by the desk, computer, printer, copier, and file cabinets already set up there; and another display room which formed an ell off the front room. That room hadn't been equipped with shelving yet.

Maggie couldn't wait for the cinnamon rolls. "Mmmm. Delicious!" She licked her fingers, as Gussie joined her. "At the rate I'm going, I'll weigh an extra ten pounds by your wedding."

"So. What do you think of the space?" said Gussie, taking a bite of her roll.

"It's perfect. You have so much room, and light. And the large display windows will be terrific showcases for your dolls and toys. Your old store was nothing like this."

Gussie nodded. "I'm especially excited about the windows. The first exhibits will be for Christmas, of course. I'm planning to set up an artificial tree in one window, with Victorian ornaments and Santas and Christmas books and dolls and toys underneath it. The other window will be a fireplace, complete with filled stockings, and of course, more toys. I'm already getting ideas for other holidays later in the year. Valentine's Day, Easter, summer at the beach. One month I could set up a birthday party."

"I can see why window-display designers have full-time jobs."

"True. But at least the first year it should be fun." Gussie dabbed her chin with her napkin. "My one concern for the store is that I'll run out of inventory. In the old shop I never seemed to have enough space. Here, I may have too much. I haven't been doing as many shows recently. Antiques shows aren't as profitable for dealers as they used to be, as you well know, and they're getting harder for me to do physically, so I haven't been buying as much."

"It's hard. The most popular 'antiques' now are twentieth-century design items: architectural elements, furniture, and the kinds of pieces creative sorts can 'repurpose,' the new name for taking something old and finding a use for it that makes it appear modern and unique. That's hard to do with the antiques you and I specialize in: dolls, toys, books, and prints."

"Agreed. Our things are wonderful as 'one of a kind' items, or as small collections, displayed in special ways."

Maggie nodded. "It's interesting, though, to see what used to be considered boring black and white nineteenth-century industrial engravings now framed in black, grouped, and thought very chic and modern. I've sold some that have been featured in decorating magazines. Very far from traditional botanical or bird prints."

"That's why I loved the framed dried seaweed you had at the Provincetown show," agreed Gussie. "And why I sell more individual toys or dolls today. People may not want to collect toys the way customers used to, but they do want one wooden folk art doll to put on a mantel or bookshelf, or one iron bank to give to an executive for his desk. Or perhaps they're looking for an old Tonka truck to remind them of their childhood. They want an antique to make a statement."

"With all this space you could showcase larger things: children's furniture, or rocking horses. Things you couldn't take to shows or put in your old shop," Maggie suggested.

"Maybe in the future. But right now I don't have anything to put in the back room."

"An antique screen could hide the entrance. I have a three-paneled Victorian screen with oil paintings that would be perfect. I wish I'd known. I'd have brought it for you."

"I was thinking of hanging a quilt there. I have a couple I use for wall backgrounds at shows."

"That would work," Maggie agreed.

"But that would be temporary. For the long run I've a better idea for that space."

"Yes?" Maggie turned from looking out the front window.

"There's a fair amount of wall space there, plus room for at least four tables in the center. And easel space, too, depending. How would you like to take that room for some of your prints?"

"What? My prints?" Maggie checked to see if she'd heard Gussie correctly.

"Think about it, before you say no. I have extra space. You don't have a shop for Shadows Antique Prints, and you don't show your prints in any antiques malls. You could use the room however you wanted to. I think your children's prints, and those related to the sea, to Massachusetts, and your shorebirds, ships, sea creatures, fish, that sort of thing, would do well here on the Cape. I'd have an extra draw to bring people to the shop. You'd have a place to show your prints."

"But I use the prints at shows."

"Of course you do, so you'd have to plan around that. And you'd have to come and change them periodically, so you wouldn't always have the same prints here. But you'd always have a place to stay, with

Jim and me, and it's sort of halfway between Will in Maine and your home in New Jersey."

"And when I have a child I might not be able to do as many shows. This might be a way to bring in more income," Maggie mused. "How would you want to do it financially? Would I pay you rent or commission? I'd want to be fair to you."

"Since right now I don't have any inventory to go in the room I wouldn't be making any money from it anyway. What if you supply the tables and table covers and easels—anything you need to set the room up the way you want it to be. And you set the prices. Pay me twenty percent of any sales."

"Twenty-five percent."

"Done," said Gussie, holding out a hand sticky with cinnamon and sugar. "Partner!"

Chapter 8

WHILE GUSSIE UNPACKED cartons in the store office, the only area ready for work so far, Maggie measured off the room she was now excitedly envisioning as a mini–Shadows Antique Prints shop.

Gussie'd been right: she'd have space for several tables, and floor stands for larger shrink-wrapped prints, in addition to the wall space for framed prints. She took careful notes.

The room was larger than her booth at most shows. She had enough table covers, but she'd have to buy two additional tables. The ones she owned she needed for shows. She'd have to invest in more floor stands and easels, too.

She'd also need more permanent, detailed signs than the ones she used for shows. Her prints would have to speak for themselves if she wasn't there to speak for them.

This would take work. But she could already see her large framed Selby Fulmar Petrel, that most people thought was a gull, hanging on the wall where customers would see it as soon as they walked in, and a selection of her Curtis, Sowerby, and Loudon botanicals on one of the center tables. She had enough of those so she could display some here and still have a selection for shows. Morris seabirds. Definitely; she'd bring those. They didn't sell well in New York and New Jersey anyway. And those pages of dried seaweed that Gussie remembered would look stunning on these walls.

Lights. She'd need to bring extra lights.

She'd been thinking of having a new sign made for her booth. She'd have one made for here, too. SHADOWS ANTIQUE PRINTS. She'd named her business that because her prints had always seemed to her like shadows left behind by lives long past. Maybe the concept seemed esoteric. But she loved it.

Bringing Shadows to Cape Cod would take time and money. But it might bring in the extra income she'd need for adoption fees, and for the expenses of having a child. Or children. Being a mother meant more than giving love. There'd be clothes. Toys. Books. Would her daughter want to join the Girl Scouts? Take art lessons? Learn karate?

Doing this would help Gussie, too. The more Maggie thought about it, the better she liked it. Having a branch of Shadows in Winslow, Massachusetts, was a wonderful idea.

"Gussie, you said you're planning to open the shop as soon as you can after your wedding, right?" she asked, as she went into the office where Gussie was transferring files from a carton to a file cabinet.

"Right. The other shop's already closed, and almost everything there is packed. Today's Friday. The guys doing the carpentry and painting here say they'll be finished by late tomorrow. Then it'll be a mad rush to put everything on shelves and decorate the windows. I've already transferred the credit card and computer connections."

"I'll need a couple of weeks," said Maggie. "I'll need to go through my inventory and put together what I'll need. On top of getting caught up with my classes when I get back home, I don't see being able to get the print room set up until Thanksgiving break."

"That's fine," said Gussie. "Whenever you get here. In fact, consider yourself invited for Thanksgiving dinner. You haven't really celebrated Thanksgiving until you've attended the lighting of the Pilgrim Monument on Thanksgiving Eve in Provincetown."

"That sounds like fun. I haven't been to Provincetown in the off-season in years. Put me on your guest list!"

"Will do. In the meantime, I'll hang that quilt we talked about. After you have the print room set up we'll put a special ad in the local paper and have a 'second grand opening.' That way we might catch some of the Christmas traffic. Don't forget to bring your Christmas prints. I'd love to have two or three of your Thomas Nast Santas as backdrops in the windows."

"I'll send those to you as soon as I get home," Maggie agreed. "This is exciting! I'm so glad you thought of it, Gussie. But promise, if the prints don't sell, or if you build up your inventory and want that space for yourself, you'll throw me out."

"Absolutely. I'm just glad you like my plan. I was afraid you'd think it was crazy, or Winslow was too far away for you."

"We'll make it work. And besides seeing you and Jim, I can check out all the antiques stores and galleries on the Cape that I never get a chance to see. In fact, do you know if the Edward Gorey Museum in Yarmouthport will be open Thanksgiving week? I've always wanted to go there."

"Already planning time away from the shop? Maggie Summer, you're coming for Thanksgiving to get Shadows set up here. And I suppose I can check and see if the Gorey Museum is open that week, too." She glanced at her watch. "I want us to get over to Cordelia's house. How did it go at the police station?"

"No problem," said Maggie. "Jim was more protective than he had to be. I signed a statement saying I was walking on the beach and saw the body and dialed 911. No major insights."

"Did you get a hint about who they think might have killed Dan?"

"Ike said someone was angry because he thought Dan had gotten his son involved with drugs. Do you know anything about that?" By that time Gussie and Maggie had left the shop, and were in Gussie's van, headed toward 17 Apple Orchard Lane.

"Not much. Last spring Tony Silva, one of the boys at the high school, died of an OxyContin overdose. People around town talked about where he might have gotten the pills. Some people said he'd gotten them in Boston; others said there was a dealer here in Winslow. Other kids may have known, but no one talked. Dan Jeffrey was relatively new in town and people blamed him. I never knew why. Tony's dad, Bob Silva, made a scene at the Lazy Lobster one night. It made the local paper. Sounded to me as though everyone involved had too much to drink and got all wound up."

"Was there any evidence it was Dan Jeffrey?"

"Not that I know about. But if there were, Ike Irons would know."

Gussie parked in front of a small, weathered-gray home. Gold and orange marigolds bloomed under the windows, and a jack-o'-lantern sat near the doorway. A small yellow VW with Colorado plates was in the driveway.

"Looks like your friend Cordelia already has company," Maggie pointed out.

"It does," said Gussie. "Well, we won't stay long. You bring the cupcakes, while I get my scooter down."

The young woman who opened the door looked like one of Maggie's students on exam day. Her shoulder-length brown hair hung limp. She hadn't attempted makeup, and her jeans and skimpy long-sleeved T-shirt both looked as though they'd been worn a few days. Her swollen eyes suggested a deeper connection to the deceased than that of someone who'd stopped to pay a condolence call. "Yes?" she said. Clearly she also wasn't the Cordelia they were there to see.

"I'm Gussie White, and this is my friend, Maggie Summer. We brought something for Cordelia," said Gussie. Maggie handed the girl the box of cupcakes. "We came to see her; to ask if there were anything we could do to help."

The girl stared at them. "Nobody can do anything. He's dead."

"I know. I was the one who found him on the beach, yesterday," said Maggie, softly. "I'm so sorry."

Behind the girl she saw a woman, perhaps in her mid-forties, looking at them from a room away. Maggie shifted her body slightly so that the woman could see her hands. "We came to say we're sorry for your loss," she signed.

Gussie waved at the woman, who then came forward. She and Gussie looked at each other for a moment. Then Gussie nodded and reached up her arms. Gussie rocked her for a moment as though she was a child, while Maggie and the younger woman watched.

Then the two women broke apart. "Maggie, I'd like you to meet my friend, Cordelia West," Gussie, said, gesturing toward the woman she'd hugged. "Cordelia, this is my dear friend, Maggie Summer, who's visiting."

Cordelia smiled at Maggie and signed, "I'm pleased to meet you. You sign ASL."

"A little," Maggie signed, and smiled. "I'm Maggie. I teach; some of my students use ASL."

Cordelia nodded, gesturing that Gussie and Maggie should come inside.

She indicated a chair in the small living room where Maggie could sit, and then at the box the younger woman was still holding, and the back of the house. The younger woman nodded her head and left, presumably to take the cupcakes to the kitchen.

"We're so sorry about your cousin Dan's death," said Gussie. "Maggie, tell Cordelia."

"Gussie wants me to say we're very sorry about your cousin's death," signed Maggie.

"I thank you both," signed Cordelia. "It's a sad time."

Maggie paused a moment. "I should tell you. I was the person who found your cousin's body on the beach yesterday."

Cordelia winced. "Thank you for calling the police. Chief Irons brought me a note last night to tell me. We'd been very worried. He'd been missing for two, almost three, days."

"We?" Maggie asked.

"Diana." Cordelia indicated the kitchen. "Dan's daughter."

Gussie looked from one of them to the other. "What's she saying, Maggie?"

"She says the young woman who opened the door is Diana, Dan's daughter."

"I didn't know he had a daughter," said Gussie. "Ask Cordelia if she's been here long."

"Only about a week," signed Cordelia. "She's very confused and upset. If you could help her in some way?"

The young lady in question returned, carrying a large tray of cookies, brownies, and the cupcakes Jim had bought at the bakery that morning. Clearly neighbors had started early bringing funeral food. She put the tray on the coffee table. "Would anyone like coffee or tea?"

"No, thank you," said Gussie. "But thank you for asking. Why don't you sit and join us? Let me introduce myself officially. I'm Gussie White. I'm moving into a house a little ways down the beach. And this is Maggie Summer, my friend from New Jersey. Cordelia told us you're Dan's daughter."

"Except he wasn't Dan then!" said Diana. Her tears started to flow. "None of this is right. None of it!"

Gussie and Maggie exchanged looks.

"What do you mean?" Gussie said.

"It's all been so hard! Cordelia's trying to be kind, but she doesn't understand anything I say. I thought Dad was dead, and then I found him again. Alive! And then a few days later he disappears, and now the police say he's dead, again, and someone killed him! And he wasn't even using his real name, and no one will tell me anything!"

"Diana, I don't know what's happening. I'm not even from Winslow. I'm guessing you're from Colorado, right?" Maggie spoke directly to Diana. She felt as though she was back on campus. So many times she'd sat with young people who were close to hysterical about minor issues. Diana's problems were clearly larger ones.

Diana looked confused. "How did you know I was from Colorado?"

"I saw your car outside. The license plates."

"Oh, yeah. That. Not a big secret, I guess. Yeah, I'm from Colorado Springs. Grew up there, and was going to college there, until Dad was killed in a car accident. At least I thought he was killed."

"What made you look for him here?" asked Gussie.

"I wasn't looking for him. I was taking a vacation. I'd decided to sell our house, to help with tuition and all the bills after Dad died. Or after I thought he'd died. So I was cleaning. I found old pictures of Mom and Dad when they were first married. They lived here then. They looked so young! Happy. Dad was so skinny. And his hair was so long!" She smiled a little. "Not the way I remembered him. When he'd died, when I thought he'd died, in Colorado, he was a lot heavier. He had a pot belly, and he'd lost most of his hair. Anyway, I decided to get away. Travel. Dad always said I had no family left, but they'd come from Cape Cod and Martha's Vineyard. I decided to visit where it all started, where my family began. So I came here."

"And?" said Maggie.

"I found Winslow, and I even found the house where we used to live when I was a baby. This house. I got up my courage and decided to ask the current owner if I could look inside. And Dad answered the door." Diana looked from Gussie to Maggie and back. "It freaked me out. For a few minutes I thought it was someone else; someone who looked like him. He'd lost the pot belly, but he'd shaved the hair on his head and grown a beard. He really looked different. Then I thought I was seeing a ghost. Maybe I was going crazy. Or I was in a time warp; I'd gone back in time to when Dad lived here." Diana shook her head. "It's hard to explain. My head was exploding with crazy ideas. I guess he was as surprised to see me as I was to see him."

"Did he explain why he was here? Why he hadn't told you he was still alive?"

"At first he was really upset I was here. Then he told me he wasn't Roger Hopkins anymore. He was Dan Jeffrey. And he introduced me to Cordelia. He told me I could stay a few days, but that was all. Then I had to leave, and forget I'd seen him. I shouldn't tell anyone who I was, or who he was. I needed to go back to Colorado."

"He didn't explain why you couldn't tell anyone, or why he was using another name?"

Diana shook her head. "He said it was complicated, and he didn't want me to get involved. That it would be better if I didn't know. That I should go on living my life the way I had been." The tears started flowing again. Cordelia reached out for a box of Kleenex on a side table and handed Diana some tissues. "I didn't know how I could do that! I was furious. Did he have any idea of what he'd put me through? I kept asking him to trust me! To tell me what was going on! Then Monday he didn't come home. I was so worried. I thought he'd run off; that he'd disappeared again. That he didn't want to see me. I even called the police and told them he was missing. Mrs. Irons, the chief's wife, stopped in. But no one else seemed to care. And now he's dead, so none of that matters, does it? He really isn't coming home again. Ever! This time he really *is* dead!" Diana's tears were flowing.

Gussie and Maggie looked at each other.

"Cordelia doesn't know what to do. She doesn't understand how I feel. She's not used to having me here. I can't talk to her; I just write her notes, and we point. And now the police are going to start asking me questions. I just know they are. That's what happened in Colorado. They've already searched his room." Diana looked up at them. "How can he put me through this again? It just isn't fair! I hate him! You're the first people who've come today who haven't just handed food in at the door and left. We need friends right now, and I don't know what to do!"

"Diana, I don't know what your father was here for, or why he was using another name, but I'm sure you're right. The police are going to want to talk to you again. It might help if you had a lawyer with you. My fiancé is a good lawyer," said Gussie. "He's very easy to talk with. If you'd like, I'll call him right now, and get him to come down here."

Maggie signed that suggestion to Cordelia, who nodded, and signed back, "Yes, please. For Diana."

Diana nodded. "I guess so. I don't know what's important and what's not. I didn't do anything wrong, but I don't know what my dad was doing here."

"Exactly," said Maggie, as Gussie called Jim on her cell phone. "It would be good if you talked with a lawyer. For your own protection."

"Like on television programs, right?" said Diana, brightening a little. "Lawyers aren't only for guilty people; lawyers help protect people who're innocent, too."

"That's right," said Maggie, as Gussie talked quietly on her phone.

"Thank you." Diana sniffled again, and blew her noise noisily on the Kleenex. "I really want to find out why my father ran away from Colorado and came here, and why he was using another name. He let me, and everyone he knew in Colorado, think he was dead. It was awful."

"What about your mother?" asked Maggie.

"She died when I was ten," said Diana. "Breast cancer. I don't have any brothers or sisters. I had to cope with everything. I'd begun to feel I had it under control: the legal mess, the paperwork, the finances: everything. And then this week it all started again." She was trying very hard not to start crying again.

"Jim's on his way over," said Gussie. "He'd be happy to represent you, Diana. And, I'm sorry, what's your last name?"

"Diana Hopkins. My dad was Roger Hopkins," Diana said. "And, thank you."

Maggie looked over at Cordelia, who'd been watching them all closely. "Jim Dryden, Gussie's fiancé, is going to come here to talk with Diana," she signed. "He's a good lawyer. He should be able to help. Would you like to talk with him, too?"

To her surprise, Cordelia stood up and signed, "No thank you." She walked toward the stairs to the second floor. As she reached the lower stairs she turned around. "Your friend can talk with Diana, but not me. Go. Leave. I need to be by myself. I don't need a lawyer."

Chapter 9

"Allow Me To Examine The Young Lady." Winslow Homer wood engraving, an illustration for a story in *Harper's Weekly*, February 18, 1860. A young woman, appearing distressed, is being addressed by a man (perhaps a judge?) standing on a platform. In back of him other men at a desk are checking large books and taking notes. At the time this was published, twenty-four-year-old Winslow Homer was living in New York City and supporting himself by providing illustrations to *Harper's Weekly* and other newspapers. Occasionally he illustrated fiction as well as news stories. Homer did not sell his paintings until the mid-1870s. 4.5 x 4.5 inches. Some foxing. Price: $70.

MAGGIE LOOKED AT Diana and Gussie. "If Cordelia wants some quiet time by herself, that's understandable. Gussie, how long will it take for Jim to get here?"

"He should be here any time," she answered. "Diana, why don't you get your purse, or anything else you need, and meet us outside. We'll wait there for him."

Diana nodded, and ran up the stairs after Cordelia.

"We seem to have found another issue to deal with," Gussie said quietly, as she and Maggie headed out the front door. "She seems very young, and lost somewhere between grief and anger."

"And very alone. It's strange her father lived here for two years, and then was killed a few days after she arrived. He may have told her not to tell anyone who he was, but she told us right away. Who else might she have told? And why was he here in the first place? I can't imagine why he'd leave a daughter her age and let her believe he was dead." How could anyone desert their child? Under any circumstances.

"We don't know anything about their life in Colorado. Maybe she knows something that puts her in danger, too," said Gussie. "That's why Jim should be involved. He'll know how to handle this from a legal perspective."

Diana joined them, a small backpack slung over her right shoulder. A couple of minutes later Jim's car pulled up. Maggie went over to him and gestured to Diana to join her. "Jim, this is Diana Hopkins, Dan Jeffrey's daughter. She'll tell you the details. Could you take her to your office to talk, and then bring her home here?"

"Sure. No problem." He held out his hand, "Nice to meet you, Diana. I'm Jim Dryden. Sorry about your dad. I'll do what I can to help, and make it as easy as I can for you."

"Thanks, Mr. Dryden. I'd appreciate that."

"And I'll see you two ladies for lunch in about an hour and a half, right?" said Jim.

"Right! I'm looking forward to checking out the Winslow Inn in person after that delicious dinner you had them make for us last night," Maggie said.

"And we're looking forward to showing off the reception site to the maid of honor. And, Gussie? Not to worry. I made sure the dresses were FedExed back to Georgia this morning, first thing."

"Maid of honor?" said Diana. She looked from Gussie to Jim. "You're getting married soon?"

"One week from tomorrow, unless there's an earthquake or volcano," said Jim. "Yes, ma'am."

"How wonderful!" said Diana. Her tone of voice showed she'd put aside her grief for a moment and was in full young-woman-in-love-with-weddings mode. "If I can do anything to help, anything at all, please ask me! Doing something for a wedding would keep my mind away from everything else that's happening."

"I'll see if we can think of anything," said Gussie. "There are always last-minute details that need taking care of."

"Please, do. Don't forget." said Diana, as she got into Jim's car. "I really would love to help!"

As the car drove off, Gussie grinned. "Sounds as though the best way to get that young woman to stop crying is to hand her a centerpiece to arrange or a bunch of ribbons to tie. Let's hope Jim decides she's fine, legally. We could use an extra pair of hands for a few days, and I suspect Cordelia would appreciate our keeping her busy."

"You're right. There may not even be a funeral until Chief Irons decides what direction to go with his investigation."

Gussie shook her head. "Even writing her father's obituary will have its challenges, since he had two names. I wonder whether he might even have a third name floating around somewhere."

"In the meantime, where to?" said Maggie, settling herself in Gussie's van.

"Post office. With us between residences, so to speak, they're holding our mail there. Jim's been picking it up, since it takes him less time, but if you don't mind hauling?"

Maggie shook her head. "I'm here to be of service."

"That's what I counted on. I knew Jim would be tied up at his office this week, so I told him we'd do the mail runs. Especially since he agreed to take care of the dresses. He's warned Peggy at the post office you'd be coming in."

"They'll let me pick up your mail?"

"When we've already signed that you can do it. And when you come in with my post office box key to prove it's you," said Gussie, pulling in to the parking lot. "Plus, Peggy's a dear. I wouldn't even bother with the mail except for the wedding RSVPs and the gifts coming in. I don't want us to get too far behind on them." She handed Maggie a key. "My post office box is number 457. Just go in and open the box and get the mail. If there's a yellow package slip inside, give it to Peggy at the window and tell her you're Gussie's friend, come to get her mail, and that I'm in the parking lot."

Maggie saluted. "Got it!" She was back three minutes later with a handful of envelopes and two packages. "Two packages. Peggy says they look like wedding gifts. I could tell she was dying to know what was inside."

"I'll tell her next time I see her. Now," Gussie said, pulling out, "let's stop at the church; I want to check in with Reverend Palmer, and then we'll go straight to the restaurant. It's only two blocks from the church."

"The advantages to being in a small town," said Maggie, as they headed toward the center of town.

The center of Winslow was a lot busier than it had been earlier; almost every parking space on the street was filled, and Maggie noted quietly that it was handy Gussie could use the handicapped van spaces in the church parking lot.

"Reverend Palmer doesn't mind," said Gussie. "Only four of us in town have vans with wheelchair lifts, and all of us attend his church, so he optimistically made sure there were plenty of spaces for us in the church parking lot. The chances we'll all be downtown at the same time, other than for services, is pretty minimal. That leaves the other handicapped spaces in the area for visitors to town."

The church was, as Maggie assumed, handicapped-accessible, with a ramp from the parking lot to the front door so anyone who wished to or needed to could avoid the steps. Maggie pushed a button and the heavy doors opened in front of them.

The sanctuary was classic New England: a center aisle lined by white pews, and high clear glass windows on each side. Small round stained glass windows picturing scenes of the sea set above the tall pillared windows were the only decorations. The pew cushions were dark blue, as was the carpet which led to the simple pine altar raised two steps at the front of the church. A gold cross above the altar was the only other ornament.

"It's beautiful, Gussie. Elegant. I hope your wedding day is sunny, like today." The sun pouring in through the clear glass brightened the whole room.

Gussie smiled at her. "I hope so, too. But the chandeliers," she pointed at classic brass fixtures hanging from the ceiling, "are also lovely. And we'll have candles and a flower arrangement on the altar. Come; I'll show you." She led Maggie down the aisle. "The ceremony will take place here on the floor, in front of the altar. You and Ellen will stand over here," she pointed at her left side, "and Andy and Ben will be with Jim on the other side. All very traditional."

"Music?" Maggie asked.

"The woman who plays the organ for services on Sundays is going to be here. We chose a Mozart piece we like, his Piano Sonata in A, for while people are coming in, and then we'll have the traditional processional." Gussie shrugged, almost in embarrassment. "Ben's been humming 'Here Comes the Bride' since we announced we were getting married, and we didn't want him to be disappointed."

"Makes sense to me," said Maggie.

"Now I need to find Reverend Palmer," said Gussie, heading toward a door on the right side of the front of the church. She was about to knock, when a tall, good-looking man in jeans and an orange WINSLOW BASKETBALL sweatshirt opened it from the other side.

"I thought I heard voices! Gussie, I'm glad to see you. I was going to call you later today."

"Then I'm glad I stopped in. This is my friend, Maggie Summer. She'll be my maid of honor. Maggie, Reverend Palmer."

They nodded at each other.

"I wanted to make sure everything was set. No last minute problems or such. But since you wanted to get in touch with me, I'm assuming something *has* come up."

"Well, actually, yes," said the Reverend. "Shall we sit a moment?"

"Of course." They moved back and Maggie and the Reverend sat in the front pew.

"I'm sorry to have to bother you with this, Gussie, but I thought you'd decided on a simple ceremony, with no decorations in the church except flowers on the altar."

"That's right," said Gussie. "The church is perfect, just the way it is."

"And you haven't changed your mind? You can, you know. But I need to know ahead of time, so we can schedule time to decorate, and there are certain fire regulations that need to be followed."

"Fire regulations?" said Gussie.

"And insurance stipulations."

Gussie sighed. "Let me make a wild guess. Has Jim's mother, Lily Dryden, contacted you?"

"She called yesterday," admitted Reverend Palmer.

"What does she want to do?"

The Reverend looked around, as though he was afraid he'd be

overheard. "I'm in a bit of a pickle here, you understand. She implied you knew what she was doing, but I had a feeling…. I've known you and Jim a long time, Gussie, and it didn't sound like anything you would have wanted."

"Just tell me. What is she planning?"

The Reverend looked like a little boy telling tales out of school. "Big, double, pink-and-white bows tied on the aisle ends of each of the pews. With ribbons that touch the floor. And in the middle of each of the 'bouquet of bows,' she called them, she wants tall candles to be lit right before the ceremony starts."

Gussie's eyes took on a hard, glazed look Maggie'd never seen before.

"And she wants a high trellised arch erected in front of the altar. You and Jim and I would be under it during the ceremony."

Gussie put her hand out, as though to stop the Reverend's words. "And—don't tell me. I'm seeing it all now. This arch would also be covered with giant bows."

The Reverend nodded, slowly. "Flowers, too. And ivy, I think she said. I wasn't listening too closely at that point. I was still trying to figure out how she was going to arrange all this in a little over a week."

"Did she happen to mention *who* was going to do all this?"

"Abigail from Floral Fantasies was conferenced in. I suspect she was taking notes like mad."

Gussie nodded. "Thank you for telling me. I'll talk to Lily. And Abigail. Today."

"You understand. The bows are…"

"Horrible!"

"They may be. But horrible can be done. Has been done. Weddings are…weddings. Some are pretty over-the-top, and bows on the pews are not a catastrophic idea so far as I'm concerned, as long as you take them down before services Sunday. But you can't have candles lit that close to ribbons without a special rider to the church's insurance contract, and it's too late to get one now."

"Did you tell Lily that?"

"I did. But she kept saying I was a darling man and that what the insurance people didn't know wouldn't hurt them." Reverend Palmer shook his head. "I tried to get through to her. I did. But I don't think she heard me."

Gussie patted the Reverend's arm. "Not to worry. *I* get it. No candles. No matter what. As it happens, Maggie and I are having lunch with Jim. I think we just put church decorations on our agenda."

"I'm sorry to complicate your life, Gussie. I know you're in the middle of a move."

"Don't worry. I'd rather hear now than an hour before the ceremony." Gussie turned. "Maggie, let's get going. We're going to have an interesting lunch."

Chapter 10

Crab. Hand-colored lithograph (1843) from *Zoology of New York State*, part of five volumes commissioned by the New York State Legislature to provide a geological and natural history survey of the state; published between 1842 and 1844. American zoologist Dr. James Ellsworth DeKay (1792–1851) was in charge of the project. Born in Portugal, he came to the United States when he was two, attended Yale, and graduated from the medical school at the University of Edinburgh in 1819. More interested in natural history than in patients, he seldom used his medical skills, but made many contributions to the study of zoology. John William Halls provided the illustrations for his books. This crab is beautifully and accurately detailed and colored, and frames well. 7.25 x 10.5 inches. Price: $100.

GUSSIE HAD RESERVED a round table in a corner of the Winslow Inn's restaurant. She maneuvered her scooter so it wouldn't block an aisle and Jim joined them almost as soon as they'd sat down.

"We stopped at the church on our way here. I wanted to show Maggie where the ceremony would be," said Gussie. "We ran into Reverend Palmer." She paused. "Guess who called him yesterday."

"She didn't…" said Jim.

"And what would you ladies like to drink today?" asked the waitress.

"Diet Pepsi," said Maggie. "With lemon, please."

"A cup of green tea for me, also with lemon," said Gussie.

"I think I'd better have a Johnnie Walker Red. Straight up," said Jim.

"She did," Gussie confirmed. She pressed her lips together. Hard.

Jim sat up straighter, as though preparing himself. "What this time?"

"She'd conferenced in Abigail, the florist. She's planning to decorate the pews with large pink-and-white bows. And candles. And add an arch at the front of the church covered with more bows. And flowers."

The waitress brought their drinks. "Would you like to order now?"

"Not yet," said Gussie.

Jim took a deep swallow of scotch.

"Pink-and-white bows, Jim. An arch in front of the altar."

"She did mention something about a surprise."

"You *knew* about this?" Gussie looked across the table as though she couldn't believe her ears. "You *knew* Lily was planning to decorate the church as though it were a birthday cake?"

"She said she was going to add a little to the flowers you'd ordered. I didn't know about everything."

"Well, I can't have it. I cannot have her going behind my back anymore, changing plans we've already made. No more 'surprises.'"

"All she said was, she'd looked at the church on the Internet and it was a little plain."

"Plain! It will be full. Of people. Of joy! Not of pink bows! Or of candles the church's insurance won't allow! If it hadn't been for the insurance issue Reverend Palmer might not even have told me."

"Can't we keep a little something she wanted?" Jim suggested. "What about the bows?" He looked across the table at his bride-to-be. "Maybe white bows? But it's your call. I'll talk to her."

Gussie sighed. "Oh, all right. White bows. Medium-sized white bows. That *don't* drape on the ground so anyone would trip on them or they'd get caught in my wheels. And only on the pews. No arch."

"Maybe you could add a white bow to your bouquet, so everything would match?" Maggie dared suggest.

Gussie glared at her. "I'll think about it."

"Would you all like to order now?" suggested the waitress with a smile. "Crab cakes are our special today, but we also have fried clams, or a New York sirloin."

"I'd like the crab cakes," said Maggie.

"I'll have the steak," said Gussie. "Rare. I want to see the blood."

Chapter 11

Red Astrachan. Hand-colored lithograph of bright red apple of Russian origin from *The Agriculture of New York*, by Dr. Ebenezer Emmons, 1851. Two views; one sliced in half to show seeds and stem. Both apples upside down. At its publication this book included all varieties of apples produced in New York; today most are considered heirlooms. The sweet Red Astrachan, however, is still grown in New York. Lithograph on heavy paper, toned at edges. Unmatted. 9 x 11.5 inches. Price: $40.

THE REST OF LUNCH went more quietly. Nothing more was said about church decorations, and no one mentioned murders, bodies, or the morning's visit to Cordelia on Apple Orchard Lane. Jim told some funny stories about growing up in Georgia which Maggie suspected Gussie had heard dozens of times before, and Gussie asked her if she'd like to have her hair done before the wedding; she and Ellen and Lily all had appointments at Lucky Ladies on Saturday morning, and she'd had them hold an appointment for Maggie, too.

"I don't think so," Maggie said. "My hair's so long I'll just wash it, let it drip dry and pin it up."

When Gussie looked disappointed she added, "But if they do manicures, I could use one of those."

"I'll see if I can get you an appointment," Gussie agreed. "It would be fun to have all of us there primping together."

Maggie had the distinct feeling Gussie was thinking "safety in numbers."

By the end of the meal both the bride and groom were a lot more relaxed. "Sorry you had to see that little scene, Maggie," Gussie admitted. "This getting married has been a true test of love. It's been

64

something new almost every day since Lily found out about the wedding."

"She wants to help. She really does," agreed Jim. "But her system is to push everything one hundred miles further than anyone wants. I'll call her this afternoon and make nice, and tell her she's over the top about the church, but offer her the compromise about the bows. I'm sure she'll retreat. Bows on the pews were probably what she wanted in the first place."

"Dealing with her sounds exhausting!" said Maggie. "How did you manage to grow up sane?"

"I moved to the Cape as soon as I was old enough to get on a bus," Jim grinned. "Or something like that."

"I'm trying hard," Gussie added. "But I may really explode before the wedding if she comes up with any more of her brilliant ideas. You have no idea how glad I am you convinced her to stay in Atlanta until just before the wedding, Jim. If she were here I think I'd be ready to jump off a cliff by now."

"I'll try to keep her busy and under control when she arrives. Not to worry."

"Jim, what happened with Diana this morning?" Maggie asked. "Is she going to be all right? Do you think she needs a lawyer?"

"I'm not sure. But she did need someone to talk with. I'm now on record as representing her, and I told her not to answer any questions beyond what the police know already. I don't think that's a problem; she clammed up right after she got in my car. Her father's murder scared her. She wouldn't talk about their life in Colorado."

"Are you going to follow up with her?" asked Gussie.

"Not unless she asks me to do something specific, or I hear from Ike that she's part of his investigation. At the moment I think he's focusing on what Dan Jeffrey was doing here in Winslow, not on what he did when he was Roger Hopkins in Colorado. I'm not sure Ike even knows about that part of the man's life yet. We have so much to do with the house and the wedding, Gussie, I don't have time to take on a young woman who needs a surrogate family right now."

Maggie was silent for a moment. "I'm worried about her. Maybe it's because I spend so much time with students her age. If you can spare me—" she looked over at Gussie, who clearly wasn't thrilled with what she was saying—"I know, I just got here, but I'd like to check up on her, and maybe get her out of that house a few times while the police are investigating. She said she'd like to help with the wedding. Maybe she could help us with the move, too. Could we offer to pay her a little?"

"Maggie, why is it you're always getting involved with young people in trouble of some sort?" Gussie sighed. "But we could use some young muscles at the house. And I have a feeling Cordelia wouldn't mind if we borrowed Diana. Jim, would that be a problem for any legal reason?"

He shrugged. "None I can think of. If she can help you out, and it keeps her busy, sure, why not? We can pay her a few dollars. That'll make it look as though we aren't looking for free labor."

"We're going to pack at your place this afternoon, right?" said Maggie.

Gussie nodded.

"I'll take my car and go back to Cordelia's and see if Diana's interested. If she is, I'll bring her back with me. I won't be gone long."

Within twenty minutes she'd pulled her van up to the house at Apple Orchard Lane. Diana's Volkswagen was still outside.

After several minutes' wait, Cordelia answered the door. "Good afternoon, Cordelia. Could I speak with Diana for a few moments?"

Cordelia looked surprised, but went to a small table near the staircase where there were several books, a lamp, and a cowbell, and rang the bell. A minute later Diana came down the stairs.

"Oh, it's you, Maggie. I wondered what Cordelia wanted."

"Sorry to disturb you. But you mentioned helping with Gussie's wedding. This isn't directly wedding-related, but Gussie and Jim are trying to consolidate their households and move into their new home and get Gussie's shop set up before their wedding. I know you have a lot on your mind, but if you'd like to earn a few extra dollars, we could use some help packing this afternoon."

Diana looked from Cordelia to Maggie. "Was this Cordelia's idea?"

"No; but if you'd like to come, I'll ask her if it's all right."

"I make my own decisions. I'll get a jacket." Diana ran back up the stairs.

Maggie signed, "Diana's going to help Gussie and me pack some of Gussie's things; she's hoping to finish moving to the new house before her wedding."

Cordelia nodded. "Good. The girl's restless. She has nothing to do. Thank Gussie for me."

Maggie nodded. They'd wanted to help Diana. If Cordelia thought they were helping her, so much the better.

"Let's go," said Diana, heading out the door. Maggie waved at Cordelia, and followed her.

"I'll take my car and follow you," said Diana. "That way I can leave when we're finished."

"Fine." Maggie headed back to Gussie's, the VW following close behind.

Was this a good decision? There was plenty to pack; that wasn't the issue. But with Diana there it meant she and Gussie wouldn't have as much time alone together as they'd hoped.

She hoped Ike Irons was making headway in figuring out who'd killed Diana's father. She'd had a few experiences with murder investigations, and usually the "why" came first. That led to the "who."

The chief certainly should be looking at why Dan Jeffrey disappeared such a short time after his daughter had found him. Could that just be a coincidence? Maggie shook her head. She'd lived long enough not to believe in coincidences.

If Ike Irons wasn't interested in Dan Jeffrey's history pre-Winslow, then he wouldn't worry about Dan's daughter. The more Maggie thought about it, the more she worried about Diana.

What happened in Colorado that made Diana's father leave his daughter? A daughter who'd already lost her mother? Starting a new life somewhere else, with a new name, was something people did only when they were desperate, and either they didn't care about those they left behind, or they needed to protect them.

Diana certainly acted as though she felt her father cared about her.

That only left one other possibility.

By the time Maggie pulled her van into a space in back of Gussie's shop she was determined to find out whatever she could. And make sure no other bodies were found on the beach, or anywhere else, in Winslow.

Chapter 12

EXTRA! PRES. ROOSEVELT DIES! One page, one side, broadside, issued by the *SCIO Tribune*, Linn County, Oregon, Thursday, April 12, 1945, to announce President Franklin Roosevelt's death. Paper tanned, but in perfect condition. "The United States and the World was shocked suddenly this afternoon when the news was flashed over the wires—"President Roosevelt dies suddenly!" Death came at 4:35 P.M. Eastern War Time (2:35 Pacific War Time), at Warm Springs, Georgia, where he had gone two weeks ago to rest before going to the United Nations' Conference called for the 25th of this month at San Francisco." 13 x 20 inches. Price: $350.

"WELCOME!" SAID GUSSIE, as Maggie walked in the back door of her old shop.

Diana followed, looking curiously around her. "I thought we were going to your house."

"You're here. I live on the second floor, above the shop," Gussie explained.

Diana walked around the back room, looking at the inventory items Gussie hadn't packed yet: boxes of antique doll arms, legs, wigs, and bodies. Dolls' clothes, one box of hats, one of shoes. Two shelves of china heads, arms, and legs. One box of eyes. She shuddered. "Those are creepy! But not as creepy as the dolls at Cordelia's house. Now I know why you two are friends. You have weird dolls, too."

Maggie and Gussie looked at each other.

"I use those parts to repair old dolls. I didn't know Cordelia had dolls," said Gussie. "But lots of people collect them. What kind does she have?"

"She doesn't exactly collect them," said Diana. "That would be normal for a kid, I guess, but for an older woman—I mean, she must be over forty! It would be strange." She ignored the half smile Maggie and Gussie exchanged. "She cooks them."

"What?" Maggie blurted. "Cooks them? Are you sure?"

Diana nodded dramatically. "The first night I was there Dad said he'd get Chinese food for us because we couldn't use the stove. I thought it was broken, so when he was out I looked at it. The oven was on, and there were two baby dolls inside. In a roasting pan! Now I know she does that all the time. She has parts of dolls upstairs in her bedroom, too, like you have in those boxes. Eyes, and hair, and arms and legs. Clothes, too."

"Have you seen her working on them?" asked Gussie.

"She keeps the door to her room closed. But I've peeked when she was out walking," Diana admitted. "She has a workbench in there, with half-finished naked dolls all over it."

Gussie laughed.

"Gussie, I'm with Diana. That's strange. Roasting dolls? If she has doll parts maybe she's making or repairing dolls. Okay. But cooking them in the oven? What's that? Voodoo?" Maggie shivered. "I don't see what's funny."

"No, no, no. I've always wondered how Cordelia makes a living, since she stays in that house by herself all the time. Now I think I know. I'll bet she's making OOAK reborns. The best get pretty high prices nowadays."

Diana and Maggie looked bewildered.

"English, please? OOAK? Reborns?" Maggie shook her head. "Whatever that means, it sounds awful. Educate us who clearly have no clue."

"It's not awful." Gussie smiled. "They're dolls, like Diana said. OOAK means One of a Kind. Reborns are dolls that look like newborns or preemies. People make them by hand. Someone, like maybe Cordelia, takes expensive manufactured baby dolls apart, removes the factory paint, cleans them, and then repaints them, adding real hair, eyes, eyelashes, and fillers to make the doll feel like a real baby. Then they dress the doll, often in real preemie or baby clothes. Every OOAK is different. They can be made to look like any race. At several steps along the way the doll has to be baked to set the paint or glue. Making them isn't simple. It takes patience and time, and only someone who's really talented artistically can do it successfully."

"It sounds horrible," said Maggie.

"Not to a lot of people. A reborn isn't the kind of doll most children would play with. It's a baby doll that can sometimes be mistaken for a real infant. People collect them. Some women with emotional issues, especially those who've lost an infant, find taking care of them is relaxing. I've heard of women who can't have children who 'adopt' an OOAK as a substitute." Gussie shot a sideways glance at Maggie, who pointedly ignored her.

"Taking care of them?" Diana looked askance. "You mean people act like they're real babies? Weird!"

"I've seen women with reborns in strollers at doll shows. The best are very realistic. One of the artists, as their makers are called, told me she had a customer arrested for child abuse for leaving hers in a car seat in a parked car. Of course, all charges were dropped when the policeman saw her 'baby' was really a doll."

"Talk about embarrassing moments!" said Maggie. "I'll bet the other cops teased him about that for months."

"How much do the dolls sell for?" asked Diana.

"At the doll shows they can go over a couple of thousand dollars. If you want a custom-made one, perhaps with the facial features of a specific child, maybe even higher. The last time I looked on eBay they were up to sixteen hundred. It depends. Different styles and races are popular at different times."

"You don't have any, do you?" asked Diana, glancing around as though one might pop out of one of Gussie's cartons.

"No," said Gussie. "They're not my sort of doll. I specialize in toys made before 1950, and most of my inventory is nineteenth-century. Reborns are brand new, or made within the last ten years. The collectible doll industry is a diverse one. It's like teddy bears. Thousands of different teddy bears are made each year, and lots of people collect them. The only teddies I have in my shop are from the early twentieth century, when a stuffed bear was a cute way of remembering that Teddy Roosevelt spared the life of a baby black bear when he was hunting. A couple in Brooklyn created a stuffed bear in his honor in 1903. Then the Steiff Toy Company in Germany introduced a stuffed bear the same year, and most of them sold to the United States. In 1904 President Roosevelt used the teddy bear as one of his campaign mascots."

"Wasn't there a *Titanic* connection with teddy bears?" Maggie asked.

"There was. After the *Titanic* sank in 1912 the Steiff company made five hundred black teddy bears and advertised them as presents to give to those in mourning."

Diana made a face. "Gross. And depressing."

"There were happier teddies. Like the one A.A. Milne gave to his son Christopher on his first birthday. That teddy was the model for *Winnie-the-Pooh*, published in 1926."

"I never thought about toys having history," said Diana.

"Don't get her started; she hasn't even mentioned Smokey the Bear," Maggie pointed out.

"And don't forget Paddington!" said Gussie. "That's why I love children's books and toys. They're a part of our lives."

"By the way, Gussie, if you ever want to do an exhibit of special Roosevelt items, like teddy bears, and maybe Theodore Roosevelt games or cards, we could also include prints and political cartoons related to him. And perhaps Franklin Roosevelt, too. Did you know FDR was a major collector of American prints? He started collecting when he was governor of New York State, looking for views of the Hudson River between Hyde Park, where he lived, and Albany. Then when he was Secretary of the Navy he collected American navy prints to decorate his New York City home. Both his collections went with him when he moved to the White House. Today they're all in his library at Hyde Park."

"Interesting, Maggie. But right now I'm not focused on history. I'm focused on getting into my new house before my wedding. If we're going to get everything packed up, we need to start," said Gussie.

"Got it. Sorry," said Maggie. "I get carried away when I'm thinking about history and prints. Where do you want us to begin?"

"Most of my stock is down here in the shop area. It's already in boxes. I only need to add bubble wrap, find tops for the boxes, and label them," said Gussie. "I can do that myself because everything's at a level I can reach. You ladies go on upstairs and start on the closets. Just pack everything." She sighed. "I'll go through things when I un-pack. Cartons and packing materials are in the living room. Maggie, you can show Diana."

"Will do, boss," said Maggie, saluting Gussie. "Come on, Diana. Let's see how fast we can get this done."

They started on the two hall closets. "It's amazing how much can be crammed into closets, isn't it?" said Maggie. "These seem to be full of Christmas decorations and china. Why don't you stand on the ladder and hand the china and boxes down to me? I'll sort, and then we'll both wrap and box so we don't mix up the Santas with Gussie's demitasse set."

Within minutes they'd finished the top shelves of both closets. "I wish Gussie hadn't emptied her kitchen first," Maggie commented, failing miserably to separate tangled Christmas tree lights. "If we had plastic kitchen bags I'd try to put the strings of lights in separate bags."

"Those are so tangled we'd be here all afternoon trying to separate them," Diana commented. "I did those sorts of things at my house in Colorado when I had to clean it out."

"Did the house sell?" Maggie asked.

"Not yet. I left a few boxes in the garage, and some furniture in the rooms. The real estate lady said it would be easier to sell if it looked like a home. It didn't feel like my home anymore, though. If it sells while I'm away she's going to have a few things, like the Christmas ornaments I want to keep, put in storage for me. The rest will go to Goodwill if the new owners don't want it."

"It must have been hard, going through everything alone."

"It was hellish. Everything there reminded me of my mother, or my father, or of what my life would have been like if they hadn't died."

"What did your dad do in Colorado?"

"I don't exactly know. He had an ordinary, boring job. He worked for a bank. He didn't talk much about it, and I didn't ask."

"And then one day he just disappeared?"

"Oh, no! Nothing like that! He died, or at least everyone thought he'd died, in an awful accident. It was a snowy night. He was on his way home from a business meeting on a slippery road in the mountains. His car went off the road and burst into flames."

"And there was no doubt?"

"That he died? No! It was his car, and people at the meeting saw him get into it. The car completely burned up. There was nothing left. A policeman knocked on my dorm room door at college and told me." Diana's eyes filled up. "There was a death certificate. Someone at the bank helped me plan the funeral. No one ever questioned that he was dead."

"When did all that happen?"

Diana blew her nose, and then wrapped the last of a group of fragile Christmas ornaments. "A little over two years ago. Somehow I finished the semester and then I took a leave of absence. I had too much to do, and I wasn't ready to go back to a dorm and focus on books."

"And you haven't been back to school since."

"No." Diana looked guilty. "Mr. Dryden said you're a professor, right?"

"I teach at a community college in New Jersey."

"You probably think I was stupid to drop out."

Got that right, Maggie thought. "People go back to college at all ages. It's up to you. You have to decide what you want to do. But college can help you do that," she said. "Have you thought about your future?"

"Not really. That's one of the reasons I left Colorado. I decided to just drive. See America. So far I haven't seen much. I decided to start in Winslow, so I drove straight through. I thought maybe since my family had come from the Cape, I'd feel at home here."

"But?"

"I found Dad. But he wasn't happy to see me. He was angry, and I was angry, and then he disappeared, and now he really *is* dead. I guess I should have stayed in Colorado. I feel worse now than I did there. And instead of answering questions, now I have more of them.

My dad and I had a second chance to get to know each other, and we blew it. Big time. The little time we had together we argued. I wanted to know what happened? Why he made me go through all that? Why he was here in Winslow using another name?"

Maggie finished folding a stack of holiday napkins and handed them to Diana to fill the carton where she'd stacked boxes of Christmas balls. "What did he say?"

"He never answered anything. He kept saying what he'd done was best for everyone. And that I shouldn't have come to Winslow."

"Did Cordelia say anything?"

"She doesn't talk! Freaked me out when I first met her, but now I'm getting used to it."

"I mean, how did she react when you arrived?"

"Okay, I guess. I was curious about her, but Dad didn't tell me much about her. He'd never told me I had a cousin to begin with. He always said we didn't have any family; it was just us. I thought I was the only one in the family alive. He could sign to her, like you can, though, so I figured he'd known her a long time. It's all so new, and so strange. He was a different person here. He even looked different. But he was still my dad."

Diana paused.

"It's all happened so fast. I drove across the country, feeling free and independent, maybe for the first time in my life. Then suddenly to see Dad again and know he was still alive, but somehow had turned into someone else, someone I didn't know, and I had a relative, but I couldn't ask her all the questions I had, and now, *zap*! Dad's gone again. And here I am, cleaning out the closet of someone I don't even know, and talking to you about it all." She looked at Maggie. "I feel as though I'm in a movie or something. As though maybe the last week never happened, and I just arrived from Colorado. Maybe Dad was never here. Maybe I imagined it all."

"That would make it a lot easier to understand, for sure," Maggie agreed.

"I don't know what I should do, now," said Diana. "Dad didn't want me to tell anyone I was his daughter, but when he disappeared I figured it wouldn't make any difference. Now I'm wondering. Do you think maybe it does? People here knew him as Dan Jeffrey. Maybe that's who he should be."

"I don't know, Diana."

"I want to know why he left me. Why didn't he think he could trust me enough to tell me about it? And what was he doing here? The first time, I accepted that he'd died in an accident in Colorado. But people don't kill other people by accident. He must have been in trouble here."

"That's the job of the police. Chief Irons and his detectives will find out what happened."

"I hope so. But Cordelia doesn't think they'll be able to find out who did it."

"Why do you say that?"

"She doesn't talk, but she writes notes to me. After Chief Irons was at the house the first time, to tell us Dad was dead, Cordelia looked sad. But she wasn't surprised. She wrote, 'Dangerous friends' on a piece of paper, and shook her head. So when the chief came back and said Dad had been murdered, it wasn't really a shock. I think we were both expecting it."

"But why don't you think the police will find the killer?"

"Because I said what you did. I wrote that Chief Irons would find whoever killed Dad. And Cordelia wrote, 'The Cape has many harbors.' And she's right. Dad was on the beach. He'd been in the water. Who could tell where he went in the water? There are lots of towns and harbors on the Cape. How can one little police department know what's happening everywhere?"

"I'm sure Chief Irons has contacts in other departments, and with the state police," said Maggie. "Although you're right that your dad could have been on a boat out in Cape Cod Bay, and his body washed ashore. He wasn't necessarily killed here in Winslow."

"Maggie? Diana? How're you ladies doing up there?" Gussie called from downstairs.

"We've almost finished two closets." Maggie answered. "Do you need help downstairs?"

"I was thinking it might be time for a tea or cola break. Sound good to you?"

"Fine with me," said Maggie.

Diana glanced at her watch. "Oops! I didn't realize it was this late! I planned to stop and get a bottle of port for Cordelia on my way home. She likes a glass after dinner. We have tons of what she calls 'funeral food' at home, but no port. I should get back to be with her."

"Thank you for helping, Diana. And I know Gussie's planning to pay you a little for your time."

"That would be great. But it was fun. Thank you for listening…" Diana hesitated.

"Why don't we exchange telephone numbers," said Maggie. "I'm sure we could use your help with other things during the next week, and if you want to get in touch with me for any reason, don't hesitate to call. Even just to talk."

The two exchanged cell phones, and entered their numbers.

"We're officially on each other's speed dials now," said Diana. "Thank you, so much. I'll say good-bye to Gussie downstairs."

"Tell her to come on upstairs and we'll have that tea and soda," said Maggie. "I'm ready for a sit-down, too."

Chapter 13

Tower Rock, Garden of the Gods. Wood Engraving by Thomas Moran for Volume 2 of *Picturesque America*, two volumes describing and picturing the scenery of the United States. Published monthly and then in bound volumes in 1872 and 1874, they were the first attempt to picture all of America. The two volumes, edited by poet William Cullen Bryant, contained over nine hundred wood engravings and fifty steel engravings. Their publication increased tourism, encouraged population growth in the West, and contributed to the call for preservation of state and national park lands. The Garden of the Gods, which *Picturesque America* says is five miles northwest of Colorado Springs, was later given to that city by the children of General William Jackson Perkins. Black and white; L-shaped. 6.25 x 8.50 inches if it were a complete rectangle. Price: $45.

"SORRY TO BE A party pooper," said Gussie. "But I need to lie down a while."

Maggie was immediately on alert. "Is your Post-Polio Syndrome getting worse? What can I do to help?"

"You're helping by being here," said Gussie. "And of course it's getting worse. That's what it does. Besides: what rational person moves their home *and* their business *and* gets married within a two-week period? Anyone would be tired! You must be tired, too; you drove up from Jersey yesterday, and we've been on the go since then. I just need a short nap; I'll be fine."

"Do you still have Wi-Fi here?" asked Maggie. "If so, I think I'll have that cola you mentioned and check my email and do some research on-line."

"My personal computer's still here so I haven't discontinued the service yet. Make yourself at home. If I'm not up by six o'clock, wake me," said Gussie, as she headed for her bedroom.

Maggie took a Diet Pepsi from the supply in the refrigerator and opened her laptop.

Diana either wasn't telling the whole story about what had happened in Colorado Springs, or she didn't know it. It didn't make sense that a loving father would disappear for no reason and not tell his daughter. Or that a man would be declared dead if there were no body, even if there was an accident.

Maggie searched for "Roger Hopkins Colorado" and immediately there were hits.

Everything Diana had said checked out. Roger Hopkins was a loan officer for the Rocky Mountain Savings and Loan in Colorado Springs. Two years ago he was on his way home from visiting homeowners who were behind in their mortgage payments. (Read: telling them they'd be foreclosed on if they didn't pay up. Nasty job.) His car swerved coming down a steep, icy road and plunged into a ravine, where the gas tank caught fire. Flames could be seen for miles. Fire and police departments were on the scene as soon as they could, but nothing could be done.

Roger Hopkins, widower, had left one daughter, Diana Emily, a sophomore at the University of Colorado.

But that wasn't all.

Eighteen months before the accident Roger Hopkins had made the *Colorado Springs Gazette* for another reason. His name was mentioned in a small story with the dateline Cripple Creek.

Cripple Creek. That was the old mining town in the Rockies where there was now gambling, Maggie remembered. Her brother, Joe, whom she hadn't heard from in years, had once sent her a postcard from there. She'd looked it up because she'd been fascinated by the name.

For some reason Roger Hopkins was in Cripple Creek, in a bar, in the middle of the day. Had he been visiting another homeowner to be foreclosed on? Was he there to gamble?

According to the article, he was by himself. While he was there a group of three young men started arguing loudly. When the bartender

told them to take their problem outside, one of the men pulled a gun
and shot the other two, the bartender, and the only other person in
the bar: Roger Hopkins. Hopkins was seriously wounded. The others
died.

Maggie looked up from her screen.

Clearly, he'd survived. But he'd been the only witness to three
homicides.

She looked through the other references.

Nothing else that added to information about "Roger Hopkins."

What if she looked under "Cripple Creek homicides"?

Sure enough. Good work, Colorado State Police. Six weeks after
the shooting, a young man "with ties to organized crime" was arrested and charged with the shooting deaths of three men in Cripple
Creek and the attempted homicide of a fourth. No mention of Roger
Hopkins by name. But he must have been involved in identifying
the man. He was the only person who could have helped lead them
to the killer.

Maggie searched under that man's name. His trial was eighteen
months ago. The verdict was "not guilty on all charges."

She closed her laptop.

Roger Hopkins should have testified in that trial. He was the only
witness. But he'd "died" six months before then.

Had they bought him off? Had he been threatened and afraid to
testify? In either case, Roger Hopkins hadn't been in the courtroom
and a mob-related killer had gone free in Colorado.

And now Roger Hopkins, aka Dan Jeffrey, was dead. Again.

Chapter 14

Anatomy: Myology. (The study of muscles.) Two plates, both from 1808 medical book. Black and white detailed line drawings, one showing the back muscles of a male figure, the other the front muscles, with details of muscles of hands, feet, arms, and legs. 8.25 x 11 inches. $60 each.

MAGGIE HAD TROUBLE sleeping again that night.

Gussie'd napped until six o'clock, and then they'd raced to meet Jim for a fast dinner, since they all admitted to being weary. Maggie decided not to mention anything she'd found on-line. After all, anyone could find what she had.

The newest wedding-related question was whether a distant cousin of Gussie's, Sheila from Boston's North End, was going to host a bachelorette party for Gussie the night before the wedding. She'd volunteered a month before, it seemed, and Gussie had said that would be fine.

But today Lily had received her invitation to the party and promptly called Sheila and told her that the night before the wedding was an inappropriate time for a bachelorette party. The night before the wedding was reserved for the rehearsal dinner. Sheila had, of course, sent emails to Gussie and Jim asking their help straightening out the schedule.

This time Maggie tended to agree with Lily. She wasn't even sure why there needed to be a bachelorette party for a bride in her late forties. (Or why Lily was invited.) But she kept her mouth closed.

Clearly getting in the middle of a Lily issue was not a wise idea. So she quietly savored her fried clams as Gussie and Jim planned how to explain to Lily that they weren't planning a rehearsal since the wedding was so small, and that the parties, one for the men and one for the women, were set, and basically, that she should not get involved with scheduling.

Right now, getting Jim and Gussie into their new house seemed a lot more important than what would happen next Friday night. Especially since she knew how tired Gussie was. Maggie kept wishing dinner would be over so she could get Gussie home to rest.

When she'd met Gussie twelve years ago her friend walked with braces and crutches, and Maggie hadn't known anything about Post-Polio Syndrome, the relentless result of having had polio, as Gussie had, as a child. Gussie'd explained that after years of physical therapy she'd walked without braces or crutches as a young woman, but then had needed to use them again later.

Now doctors knew that forcing muscles weakened by polio would only work temporarily. People unlucky enough to get polio today, as many still did who lived where not everyone had access to vaccine, were told they would have to wear braces for life, and use wheelchairs when they could. They needed to save their muscles, to make them last as long as possible. Gussie had just moved to her electric scooter two years ago. But every time Maggie saw her, it seemed Gussie tired more easily.

Thank goodness she'd now have Jim to help her on a regular basis. Someone who loved her, and knew her strengths and weaknesses. Gussie was a determined and stubborn woman. But her muscles weren't always going to keep up with her mind.

The more Maggie thought about putting her prints in the back room of Gussie's store, the better she liked it. That would take pressure off Gussie to get out and buy more merchandise, and would help both of them (she hoped) financially. And although it was a long drive from New Jersey to the Cape (or from Maine to the Cape, she added to herself), it would push her to visit Gussie more often.

Maggie pleaded exhaustion after they finished dinner to make sure Gussie went to bed early. "We were up so late last night, and today was a full day. I want to be sure I can finish the rest of the packing tomorrow so we can get everything out of your old shop and into the new one."

"You're not just trying to get *me* to rest?" Gussie looked at her askance. "You're sounding like Jim when he wants me to slow down."

"Me? No! I'm getting old myself," said Maggie, guilelessly.

"Hah! You're ten years younger than I am. What Will's Aunt Nettie would no doubt call a spring chicken. But I'll take you up on it anyway. I have some thank-you notes to write, and I can take my stationery box to bed with me. After I'm married I'll have better things to do in bed!"

The conversation might have taken a slightly different turn, but then Maggie's phone rang.

"It's Will," she said.

"You go," said Gussie. "Give him my love and tell him I'm looking forward to seeing him in a few days."

"Will do!" said Maggie, turning to her phone. "Hi, friend!"

"So, have you got everyone on the Cape organized and ready to march down whatever aisle is nearby in rank order?" said Will's familiar deep voice.

"Not quite. But I'm working on it. I think Gussie and Jim need more help with moving to their new house and setting up Gussie's new store then they do with the wedding. One day at a time."

"I wish I could get away a little earlier, if you need help moving boxes and furniture. But my cousin Tom has agreed to stay with Aunt Nettie for the three days I'll be down on the Cape, and he can't stay longer than that."

"Don't worry. We have it well in hand. Most of it is packing right now. No one's asked me to move furniture. I think Jim will find someone else to do that. I hope, anyway."

"So do I. I've had enough of that, moving the few pieces I wanted to keep from Buffalo to Maine."

Maggie wondered, not for the first time, what it must really feel like for Will. He always talked of the changes he'd made in his life in terms of logistics, not emotions. And the changes he'd made were huge. In the past two months he'd returned to his home in Buffalo, put it up for sale, and given away most of the physical connections to his last twenty years. The few pieces of furniture he wanted to keep, and all the antiques in his fireplace and kitchenware business, he'd trucked to Maine. His books, furniture, and papers were now in a storage unit outside Waymouth; his business inventory was in Aunt Nettie's attic and barn, which he'd cleaned out. She hadn't been thrilled at throwing out her "special things" (like canning jars she hadn't used in twenty years), to make space for his belongings, and neither of them were looking forward to a Maine winter when the barn was too full of cartons for either her car or his RV to fit inside. Will had wanted his inventory nearby so he could continue doing antiques shows easily, and they'd both agreed it would be best if he moved in, "at least for a few months, to see how it works out," after her troubles in August.

So Will had his hands full. Aunt Nettie was a dear. But she was a ninety-one-year-old dear. Will was already finding he couldn't take off for a weekend and head for New Jersey, as he used to, or meet Maggie at a show halfway between them. He'd skipped the Rensselaer County show on Columbus Day weekend two weeks ago. Missing shows meant missing income, too.

"So Gussie's keeping you busy and out of trouble, then?" Will was saying.

Maggie almost told him about finding Dan Jeffrey's body. And then hearing that Jeffrey had been murdered. And then finding out he wasn't really Dan Jeffrey. And about Diana. But why bother Will? He'd tell her to let the police handle the situation, that she should focus on Gussie and Jim.

Not a bad idea.

But not what she wanted to do.

And after all, Will wasn't in Winslow. Yet. What he didn't know…

"How's Aunt Nettie?"

"Doing well. She made a terrific apple–cranberry pie today, but then was too tired to get the rest of the dinner, so she talked me into taking her out to dinner at the Waymouth Inn. We had her pie for dessert."

"I'll bet you'll have it for breakfast too. Aunt Nettie's pies are special. You be careful, though! I don't want you putting on too much weight! Every time we talk you tell me about her great cooking."

"I think cooking for me gives her a reason to keep going. She hasn't wanted to go to her genealogy group or her book group at the library, or invite any of her friends over. And she hasn't been going out for walks, the way she did last summer, remember?"

Aunt Nettie'd walked everywhere in town. She'd scolded if Maggie or Will said they were driving to the post office. "You have perfectly good feet. You young folks should be hoofing it."

"She says she's too tired to walk too far. And once winter sets in it'll be harder for her to get out, because of the ice. So if cooking keeps her busy, then I encourage it. I make the sacrifice of having to eat it all."

Maggie grinned. For over ten years now Will'd been a widower who didn't cook for himself. She suspected he was enjoying being the object of Aunt Nettie's home-cooking demonstrations.

"You give Aunt Nettie a big hug for me. Tell her I miss her."

"She doesn't understand why you don't come up and visit more often. She likes you, Maggie."

"I assume you've told her I have a job, and an antiques business. I can't exactly race back and forth to Maine all the time."

"I've mentioned those other activities of yours. Of course, she seems to think Maine holds certain attractions which should pull you away from everything else in your life."

"You tell her Maggie has bills to pay," said Maggie. "I'll send her some postcards from the Cape. And I'll see you soon."

"Looking forward. Very forward," Will whispered softly.

"Hmmm. I won't mind that," said Maggie. "Miss you."

"Love you."

"Love you, too."

Maggie lay awake, wishing Will were there. But if he were, she'd have to tell him about the murder. He was very patient, but she had a feeling he wouldn't be enthused about her getting involved. Not to speak of the adoption issue, which she was trying to repress this week.

She touched her R-E-G-A-R-D ring, rolled over, and punched her pillow. Hard.

Chapter 15

Homard et Langouste. (Two species of lobsters.) Signed aquatint by Swiss artist Fifo Stricker (1952–) First strike of eight. Two orange-red lobsters, tail to tail, behind jade architectural window-like frame; Art Deco sun above them. Matted in gray; narrow black frame. 25 x 28 inches. Price: $895.

SINCE ALL THAT was left in Gussie's kitchen was teabags, cans of diet cola, and two of the bottles of champagne Maggie had brought, Jim's arrival the next morning bearing hot breakfast sandwiches from the Salty Dog Diner was a happy surprise. "My kitchen's pretty much empty," he admitted. "I had a feeling yours was, too."

"Have you heard anything about the investigation of Dan Jeffrey's murder?" Maggie asked, she hoped casually.

"Talk around town is it was a drug deal gone bad," said Jim. "Bob Silva's saying he was always sure Jeffrey was responsible for his kid's death last spring. He's just sorry he wasn't the one to kill him. Frankly, no one seems too interested. I'm surprised a murder in town hasn't stirred up more feeling."

"Dan had only been around a couple of years. If he was involved with drugs and someone from Boston or somewhere else far from Winslow killed him, then no one here's in danger, so no one needs to worry," said Gussie. "Makes sense. This is a closely knit community."

"Bob Silva. He's the one you were telling me about, right, Gussie?" asked Maggie, taking the last bite of her sandwich. If anyone believed Jeffrey was responsible for his child's death, wouldn't that be a good motive? In addition to a mysterious drug dealer from Boston, whom she wasn't ruling out. Or someone connected to the victim's previous life in Colorado.

"Silva's the one. When his son died of an overdose, pretty much the whole town went to the funeral."

Jim nodded. "At first his dad, Bob, blamed everyone. His teachers, for not teaching drug education. The police, for allowing drugs in the community. Chief Irons had a hard time with him. Then Bob decided someone in the community must have given Tony the drugs, and got the idea it was Dan." Jim shrugged. "No one ever proved where the boy got the drugs. They were prescription meds, so they could have come from anywhere. But Dan was the newest face in town, and he didn't have a history here. Bob followed him around and harassed him. I think he threw a rock through the window at Cordelia's once."

"That's more than just bad-mouthing someone," Maggie pointed out.

"True. Ike talked to him about it more than once, I know. Bob has a tendency to drink when he's angry, and he gets angrier when he drinks. After his son's death…well, the whole town was making allowances for him. I guess Ike was, too. Or else he couldn't do anything about it. Anyway, everyone pretty much ignored the situation."

"It sounds awful for Dan."

"Must have been," agreed Jim. "As I think about it, that's probably why I hadn't seen him around town much the past couple of months. He was probably staying out of Bob's way."

"He's the one Ike Irons said he'd be checking out when you asked if he had any leads in the case. He certainly sounds as though he had a motive."

Jim shrugged again. "I guess. But I suspect Ike thinks he's what they call in Texas, 'all hat and no cattle.' Bob yelled a lot, but I've known him all the years I've been here and the only time I've seen him throw a punch was once last spring when he and Dan got into it at the Lazy Lobster." He looked at Maggie. "But, you're right. He had motive. I'm sure Ike'll be checking him out."

Maggie wasn't convinced. Besides, Dan Jeffrey, as he was called here in Winslow, was shot. You didn't need to get up close and personal with someone to shoot them. "If I were making a list of suspects, Bob Silva would be on it. Just sayin'."

"You've been spending too much time with your students," said Gussie. "Or maybe with Diana."

"Diana?" asked Jim.

"Remember? You said it would be all right if she helped us with the move and the wedding. She was here yesterday to help us pack," said Maggie. "She's had a rough time of it."

"True," Jim agreed. "Just don't get too involved."

"Does he sound like me?" asked Gussie.

"I mean, you'll be heading back to Jersey after the wedding," said Jim. "I don't know how long Diana will be staying here, or what she'll want to do next. She has no roots now. I suspect she'll want to stick around here until she gets some answers about her father's death."

"Do many people in Winslow know Dan Jeffrey was her father?" Maggie asked.

Jim shook his head. "She's only been here a few days. Dan didn't tell anyone he had a daughter so far as I know."

"You don't think she's in any danger, then."

"Diana? I wouldn't think so." Jim looked at her. "Let me guess. You looked up her father on the Internet. Right?"

Maggie nodded.

"You didn't think I'd take her on as a client without a bit of background checking, did you? Sure, I've got some reservations about her father and why he left Colorado so suddenly. But that guy he saw doing the shooting was freed."

"What's this all about? What guy? What shooting?" asked Gussie, looking from one of them to the other.

"I'll fill you in after Jim's gone," said Maggie. "Promise."

"In any case, there's no double jeopardy. He couldn't be tried again. There'd be no reason for anyone connected with that situation to follow Diana or her father to Cape Cod and kill him here. Unless there's something we don't know, that problem was solved. Over. Finito. Somehow I think the now–Mr. Jeffrey got himself into another mess here on Cape Cod. And this one he really did have to die to get out of."

Maggie put up her hand. "One minute." Her phone was ringing. She glanced down. "Diana's texting. She wants to know if we'd like her to help again today. Chief Irons's wife brought over flowers and she's allergic."

"Sounds to me like an excuse to get out of the house," said Gussie. "But, sure. Tell her to come over. The more the merrier."

Jim got up and brushed the crumbs off his lap. "Sounds like my cue to go to the office. I emailed Lily our list of people who hadn't RSVP'd by now. She's going to call them today. I figured she couldn't mess that up. Okay with you?"

Gussie nodded. "Sounds harmless. Although with Lily you never know. I'm hoping we have the rest of the shop packed by noon. After we do I'll call Ellen and get Ben to come and pack both our vans and we'll get them over to the shop. Maybe later this afternoon we could all get together and open the wedding gifts. That'll be fun, and then I could write the thank-you notes in my spare time."

"Right! I've noticed all that spare time you have," Jim agreed drily. "But opening gifts does sound like fun. And then tonight I can tell Mother about them. She's been dying to know what people have sent us. I'm sure she thinks we'll get silver tea sets and punch bowls, like she did back in the dim dark ages."

"I have no idea what we'll get. But we'll need to thank everyone for everything," said Gussie. "And I have my maid of honor here to play secretary."

"'Bye, ladies!" said Jim, backing out the door. "Try to stay out of trouble. See you late this afternoon!"

"What?" said Maggie, who'd been focusing on murder suspects, not wedding gifts.

"That's one of the jobs of the maid of honor, Maggie! Didn't you look all this up while you were researching topics on the Internet last night? The maid of honor is supposed to keep track of who gives gifts and what they are. So prepare to have your pen and paper at the ready."

"Aye, aye, my captain," said Maggie. "Opening gifts does not sound like hardship duty. It sounds like fun."

"And good practice, for when you and Will get married."

"Oops! Missed target," said Maggie. "I thought we'd settled that. Don't you remember in the old, old days when you were single, and not engaged? You do not talk to single women about future marital plans or possibilities at or before the wedding of their close friends. It's a long-standing rule."

"You're right. Forgot!" Gussie grinned. Then she leaned over. "Can I whisper, then?"

"No wedding hints. Or engagement hints. Not allowed! Period."

"Okay, okay. Boring, but you win," said Gussie.

"So we have a deadline. It's almost nine-thirty, and you want to finish packing the store by noon. How close are you?"

"Almost there. I finished the doll and toy parts I was working on yesterday afternoon. You could box up the books still in the book-cases in the front room. While you're doing that I'll check all the drawers in the cabinets to make sure I haven't forgotten anything."

Diana arrived fifteen minutes later, and, with her help, they'd finished the shop by eleven, an hour ahead of schedule. Diana and Maggie decided to pack two more closets upstairs ("I never realized how many closets you had in this place!") while Gussie telephoned her sister.

"Ellen? We're ready for reinforcements. Are you and Ben free to come over? We need someone to help with heavy lifting." She called upstairs, "Diana, do you mind taking a couple of cartons in your car over to the new store?"

"No problem," Diana called back.

"Then, with your car, we have two vans and two cars," said Gussie to Ellen. "I wish I could help but…I know, I know. I'll supervise. Some of the cartons are light. Ben can help with the others. I have the dolly he and I use at shows. I think we can get it all loaded in about half an hour. Then we need to drive everything over to the new shop and unload. Great. See you then."

"Ellen and Ben'll be here in about twenty minutes," she told Maggie and Diana.

"Who're Ellen and Ben?" Diana asked, as they came downstairs and started sorting the packed cartons.

"Ellen's Gussie's sister. She's a realtor here in town," said Maggie. "Ben's her son. He's about your age. Twenty-one?"

Diana nodded.

"Can't believe it, but, yes. Ben's birthday was last month," Gussie confirmed.

"Is he in college?" Diana asked.

"No," Gussie answered. "Although he wishes he were. He misses his friends from town who're away at school now. Ben has Down Syndrome. He lives with his mom and helps at the real estate office, making copies and running errands, and helps at my shop when I need him."

"He goes on the road with Gussie when she does antiques shows out of town, too," said Maggie. "He does the lifting for her."

"That's right," said Gussie. "He and I share one thing in common: people with Down's and people who've had polio both have weak muscles. I had physical therapy for years, and still go for sessions when I can. Ben tries to make up for it by lifting weights and running. He's in Special Olympics, too. He can climb ladders and reach things I can't, and pack and unpack the van. I tell him he's my legs and arms now." The back door of the shop slammed. "And here he is!"

"Hi, Aunt Gussie! Hi, Maggie!" Ben gave them both hugs. "Who are you?" He stared curiously at Diana.

"This is Diana Hopkins. She's visiting from Colorado and she's helping us today," said Gussie. "Thanks so much, Ellen, for bringing Ben over."

"Glad to be a help. Hi, Maggie! Good to see you. And, Diana? I'm Ellen, Gussie's sister," Ellen said. "We were about to take a lunch break anyway."

"Whoops! I forgot lunch," said Gussie.

"I didn't forget lunch, Aunt Gussie," said Ben. "I never forget lunch."

"That's true. You don't," agreed Gussie. "Why don't we load the vans and cars and then stop for pizza on the way to the new shop? Can you wait that long?"

Ben walked around the two rooms of the shop very seriously. "Are we all going to work?"

"I think so," said his mother. "You'll do the heavy work, and the rest of us will carry the other cartons and plan where everything will go. Aunt Gussie's in charge."

"Then, yes. I can wait. We can do this pretty fast," Ben declared. "But let's get started. I like pizza." He stopped for a moment. "Can it have pepperoni?"

"Of course, Ben," said Gussie. "I wouldn't get you pizza without pepperoni."

"Which carton do you want lifted first?" he asked.

Diana just looked at him and laughed. "You're very funny, Ben."

Ben laughed, too. "Yes, I am. And I'm very nice. You look nice, too, Diana. Are you nice?"

The smile Diana returned was the biggest Maggie'd seen her give anyone in the past two days. "I hope so, Ben. I certainly hope so."

Chapter 16

Great Black-Backed Gull. Hand-colored steel engraving from 1865 edition of *A History of British Birds,* written and illustrated by the Reverend Francis Orpen Morris (1810–1893), naturalist and Vicar of Nafferton. Morris, an early advocate of conservation, was also one of the founders of the Royal Society for the Protection of Birds. Illustrations for his seven-volume history were engraved by Alexander Francis Lydon, hand-colored by a team of women colorists, printed and bound in the North Country village of Driffield, and shipped in tea chests to London. It went through various editions from 1851 until 1903. Print shows gull standing on beach, rocks and sailboat in distance. 6.75 x 10 inches. Price: $150.

WITH FOUR OF THEM working together and chatting, and pizza as a motivator, the emptying of the former location of Aunt Augusta's Attic and then the deposit of all the cartons at its new location went even more smoothly and quickly than Gussie'd hoped.

Ben and Ellen were able to wave their good-byes and return to the real estate office by two-thirty. Diana stayed a little longer to help Gussie and Maggie sort the cartons, but it was clear Gussie was beginning to tire when Diana received a text from Cordelia.

"Chief Irons stopped in at the house. He wants me to come to the station. What's that about?" she wondered out loud, picking up her backpack.

"Remember not to answer any questions without Jim being there," Gussie cautioned her.

"I haven't done anything wrong," Diana assured her. "I'm sure it's nothing. He probably wants to know something about my dad. I'll go now, and then go back to Cordelia's. See you tomorrow?"

"Call me in the morning and I'll let you know," said Maggie.

"Tomorrow I'd like to focus on unpacking and arranging merchandise here at the shop," Gussie put in.

"Talk with you tomorrow, then," said Diana as she headed off.

"Why don't you go home and rest," Maggie said to Gussie. "I'll pick up whatever's at the post office, put the cartons Diana and I packed yesterday in my van, and take everything over to the new house when we meet Jim there later to open the wedding gifts."

"Would you do that? I'd appreciate an hour or two of downtime," said Gussie. "I've been keeping quite a pace the past couple of weeks."

"And it isn't going to slow down until you're safely in your new house, you have that gold band on your hand, and your shop is organized and open, the future Mrs. Dryden," said Maggie.

"Not Mrs. Dryden, you old-fashioned woman," said Gussie as they headed to their vans and she handed Maggie her post office box key. "I'll still be Gussie White. I'm not changing my name. But Jim and I will be wearing matching bands. That's a tradition I do believe in."

Peggy the postmistress recognized Maggie immediately. "How's Gussie doing? Is she very excited? Is everything organized for the wedding? Has she managed to move out of her old house and shop yet?" She handed Maggie a stack of cards Maggie recognized as wedding RSVPs. A little late. Those people had probably already gotten calls from Lily Dryden.

"Gussie's tired, but she's going strong. She's almost out of the old house and shop. I think we'll start getting the new shop organized tomorrow."

"I hear Cordelia West's young cousin's been helping her."

The postmistress did know everything happening in Winslow.

"That's right. She's been very helpful."

"Such a shame, that other cousin of Cordelia's, Dan Jeffrey, going and getting himself killed. Cordelia's such a sweet woman. Can't hear or say a word, of course, but she's always baking cookies for people, or bringing me wildflowers to decorate the office. A sweet little woman."

"Then you know her well?"

"Well, she's lived in Winslow for twenty years or so. Gets her mail here most days. And we do a pickup at her place over on Apple Orchard Lane on Fridays."

"Pickup?"

"Packages. The post office does that, you know. Got to compete with those other delivery services. She sends out all her packages on Fridays, regular as clockwork."

"I understand she makes dolls. But I've never seen any. Have you?"

"I've seen a couple of her baby dolls. She makes those newborns. Gets supplies delivered all the time," said the postmistress. "From all over the country, and Canada. Even Europe, sometimes. She ships dolls in the bigger boxes. Maybe one or two a week. Used to ship more. But the past couple of years she's been sending smaller packages. Ten of those every Friday. Those go to post office boxes in different places. Boston, northern Maine, Washington, D.C. She has customers all over."

"What does she sell besides the dolls?" asked Maggie.

"I've wondered that myself," said the postmistress. "But I can't talk with my hands, like she can, so I haven't asked. She puts the value at fifty dollars for each box, so whatever it is can't be too valuable. The big boxes, that hold the baby dolls, those she values at a thousand dollars. Sometimes more. I figure maybe now she's making smaller dolls, and selling on eBay. Lots of people do that today, you know. How're the wedding plans coming?"

"Fine. Did Gussie get any packages today? She and Jim have been saving their gifts. They're going to open a pile of them tonight."

"Let me check." She went into the back of the crowded room. "I'm pretty sure I saw a pile of boxes for those two in here somewhere. Yes, here they are." She reappeared carrying a stack of four boxes. "All different sizes this time. I'll admit I've been curious about these gifts. Most times when people get married we get boxes from the big department stores, or from Sears, or when they're summer folks, even from a place like Tiffany's. But all the boxes Gussie and Jim have gotten have been wrapped by hand. Not a store name in sight." The postmistress handed them over one by one, after recording their arrivals.

"I can see that," said Maggie.

" 'Course, them being an older couple, I suspect they didn't put their names on a bridal registry saying they were looking for a set of white towels or a toaster oven, when it comes to it," she added. "Between the two of them they probably have towels and toaster ovens to spare."

Maggie laughed. "I guess they'll find out once they get everything unpacked," she said. "Thank you!"

She sat in her van for a few minutes and checked her watch. Two hours until the official gift opening.

Why had Ike Irons wanted to see Diana again? Maggie hoped the girl was smart enough to know if she needed to call Jim, or just say the magic word, "Lawyer." Nowadays you'd think anyone who watched TV would know that. You'd hope. But despite all she'd been through, Diana seemed awfully naïve. Or maybe being young was, by definition, naïve.

When I was twenty-one, was I that innocent? Maggie thought back. Senior in college in New Jersey on scholarship. Working two jobs, so not much time for socializing. Not really innocent. But she hadn't guessed the family situation her roommate, Amy, was coping with. She'd thought anyone who lived in a big house in Short Hills must be happy.

Yup. Twenty-one could be very naïve.

That's why she often felt protective of her students at the college. And now she felt protective about Diana. The world took advantage of the young too often.

The sooner Chief Ike Irons and his detectives found out who'd murdered Diana's father, the sooner she could be on her way. Whatever she decided to do with her life, she needed to put the past behind her and get on with her future. It probably wasn't by chance that her father'd been shot and dumped in Cape Cod Bay. But whatever trouble he was in wasn't Diana's trouble. It shouldn't have to make a difference to her future.

Would her daughter or daughters be able to deal with whatever their early lives had dealt them? She'd have to help them begin again. Clean slate. Memories, yes. It would take time. But another chance.

Maggie's mind was whirling with possibilities as she drove through the quiet streets of Winslow. Then, on her left, she saw the Lazy Lobster, the tavern Jim'd mentioned where Dan Jeffrey had hung out. At four o'clock on a brisk October Monday afternoon three well-used pickups were parked outside, and one salt-rusted Ford sedan. She hesitated, and then turned her New Jersey van in to join those with Massachusetts SPIRIT OF AMERICA or CAPE COD AND ISLANDS license plates.

All five men at the bar inside turned to look at her.

Clearly this was an establishment for locals. Fishermen, by their garb and the décor. The nets on the wall weren't the colorful sort hung in places looking to attract tourists. These nets were used and grungy, smelling faintly of long-dead fish and the sea, and now the repository of old pinups, photos of fishermen with their catches, newspaper articles, and assorted empty beer cans and beer bottle labels. Sort of a grease-encrusted work in progress, an ode to those who worked the sea, drank beer and whiskey, and ate the burgers and chowder listed in smudged black marker on the mirror in back of the bar. It was a limited menu, but Maggie suspected the cook didn't get many complaints.

Five teenage boys came in after Maggie. One of them wore a T-shirt that read TOO MEAN TO MARRY. And clearly too young to sit at the bar, at least legally. They sat in a corner booth.

"Can I help you?" asked the tall, bald man behind the bar. He wore a shirt embroidered *Rocky* and had a dragon tattoo on his neck that led down to places Maggie was grateful were left unseen.

"Beer," Maggie said, sliding onto one of the bar stools. She glanced over at the taps. "Sam Adams, please." She almost asked for Oktoberfest, but sensed that wouldn't be on the menu here.

"You got it," said Rocky, drawing her a tall draft. "Visiting Winslow?"

"I'm here from New Jersey for Gussie White's and Jim Dryden's wedding."

"So why aren't you partying it up with them?"

"I heard this was where Dan Jeffrey used to drink."

There was sudden silence. Maggie had the attention of every man in the place. Maybe she'd been too out-front. Why hadn't she been more subtle? Oh, well. Too late now.

"You a friend of Dan's?"

"I know his daughter."

Two of the men looked at each other and one shrugged slightly. The other one spoke up. "Dan never said he had no daughter."

"No?"

"He never said much, did he, Earl, when you think about it."

"Nope. Never did. Never even said where he come from."

"Told me he come from out West," said the bartender.

"Hey, Rocky, but Cordelia West, that deaf-and-dumb broad he was staying with, he said she was his cousin, right? And she's from the Vineyard."

"That's what he said," agreed Rocky, quietly.

"You'd know that, I figured," Earl put in.

The heavier guy added, "I always wondered about that cousin part. But she didn't seem his type, you know. So maybe if they were relatives, that would explain his staying there so long."

"What was his type?" Maggie asked.

The man shifted uneasily. "I didn't mean nothing by that. I meant, you know, he was a real man, with appetites and such, and Cordelia West, why, she's a quiet little woman. Real nice lady, I suppose. Wouldn't you say that, Rocky?"

"So did he have a lady friend?" Maggie sipped her beer.

No one said anything. Then Rocky answered. "Jeffrey didn't talk much. He was in town a couple of years, and I don't think you'll hear from anyone he was exactly a model of piety. He had his women. But he never talked about 'em. Give him that, wouldn't we, boys? He never named names."

"That's the truth," seconded the old codger at the corner of the bar. "And it wasn't for us not asking, that's fer sure, too!"

Guffaws from two of the four gents at the bar and a laugh from the booth in the corner.

"So would you say you were his closest friends while he was here?" Maggie asked.

The bigger guy shrugged.

"Friends? He came in pretty regular. He drank. We drank.

Sometimes we talked. We watched the games. He was a Sox fan. What would you say, Rocky?"

Maggie could almost see an invisible curtain sliding down between the men and her end of the bar. If they knew any of Dan's secrets, they weren't telling. Men didn't tell on each other.

Or maybe they didn't know anything. Somehow she'd believe that, too. She might as well go for the gold. "Who do you think killed him?" Maggie asked. "His daughter wants to know."

"That Dan, he wasn't the most popular gent in town," said the old guy. "Maybe some of the ladies liked him. And some of the kids at the high school did." He glanced over at the boys in the corner, who were now ordering hamburgers and sodas from Rocky, who'd left the bar. "But people like Bob Silva blamed him when Tony died."

"Nobody had proof he had anything to do with those drugs," cautioned the man wearing the faded Pats cap. "No proof. And you know it."

"I know it. And I don't know it. Someone was bringin' those drugs into town. The kids were buying 'em. And that Silva boy was stupid enough to swallow too many." He shook his head. "I don't know if it was Dan selling 'em. Could have been someone else. But I haven't seen anyone else arrested. Have you?"

"I think you've talked enough for today, old man. Had enough beer, too."

"Dan could've gone overboard anywhere in Cape Cod Bay, and washed ashore, you know. Pure chance he washed ashore here," said one of the other men.

"Pure chance, with a bullet hole in his head?" Maggie pointed out quietly.

"Could have been a stray shot, you know? Hunting season and all. You never know where a stray shot might end up."

Maggie drained the rest of her Sam Adams. "No. You never do. Anyone could mistake a man for, say, a quail or ruffed grouse. But if any of you think of something that might explain what happened to Dan Jeffrey, I'd appreciate—and his daughter would appreciate—if you'd let me know. Or tell Ike Irons. It's not healthy to have accidents happening in a nice town like Winslow."

She put her money on the bar. "You can leave a message for me at the new Aunt Augusta's Attic on Main Street. Just say the message is for Maggie. I'll get it."

Herring and great black-backed gulls were crying and circling the sky over the tavern. Maggie watched them for a minute, remembering an old mariner's saying, that gulls were the souls of departed sailors.

But Dan Jeffrey hadn't been a sailor.

Chapter 17

Boston Lighthouse. Steel engraving, 1843, of lighthouse on rocky island, surrounded by vessels of various sorts, from skiffs to schooners to a steamboat to a small lobster boat with one sail. "Drawn After Nature" by an unidentified artist, and published by Hermann J. Meyer, New York. Paper size: 7.5 x 11 inches. Engraving size: 4.24 x 6.25 inches. Price: $60.

MAGGIE ADDED THE packages she'd picked up at the post office to the ones already piled in a corner of Gussie's and Jim's new living room and walked over to look out the wide windows. "Your view is breathtaking. In the summer the Bay will be filled with sailboats and fishing boats, and you'll be able to sit in your own living room and watch them. There can't be many more perfect places than this one."

"That view is the reason we bought this place," said Gussie. "We hesitated because of the price, but then we kept thinking that we'd have that view to look at for the rest of our lives. Two old people looking out at the world together."

"Sounds wonderful."

"So, when does the unwrapping begin?" Jim asked as he came in the room. "I'll admit I feel like a kid on his birthday. I've been looking forward to this all day."

"Now that you're here, we can start any time," Gussie answered.

"I have no idea what our friends will have come up with. Mother keeps telling me about the three silver tea sets she and Dad got for wedding gifts. I keep telling her that when you get married slightly, shall we say, later in life, your needs and interests are a bit different than they are for a couple starting out the way they did, in their early twenties."

"Not that we live the sort of life that calls for even one silver tea set," Gussie added.

"I'm waiting, notebook and pen at hand, to record the salient facts. Jim, why don't you get a knife to help open the cartons, and then you and Gussie open the inside boxes together, assuming there is an inside box."

"Maggie's organizing us! She's stepping up to the maid-of-honor role very well, don't you think?" said Gussie. "Go ahead, Jim, start with that long heavy box in the corner. I wish Ellen could have been here tonight, but she had to show a client two houses. A client with money gets priority in this housing market."

"Maybe Ellen could talk her client into a charming Victorian," said Jim, thinking of his own house. He picked up the first carton and looked at the return address. "This one is postmarked Maine. Your Maine man, I believe, Ms. Summer. It's from a Mr. Will Brewer."

Maggie smiled. "I suggested going together for your gift, but he had his own idea. I don't know what it is, but I can guess why it's heavy."

Gussie leaned over toward Jim. "You remember, Will's a dealer in fireplace and kitchen antiques. Of course, that may have nothing to do with his gift."

Jim finished lifting the inside box away from the heavy outside carton. "All set to open the inside box, my love. But it's heavy, too. Why don't you read the card while I open?"

She read, "'A totally unnecessary gift that will last another two hundred years, although nothing will outlast your love. Will.' Very sweet. Maggie, have I mentioned he's a keeper?"

Maggie raised her eyebrows in mock admonishment, and made a entry in her notebook as Jim lifted out a beautifully burnished, hand-crafted, brass bedwarmer engraved with hearts.

"Oh, I love it! Very apropos. Bedwarmers—no comments, please, Jim, I mean the non-human kind!—are hard to find nowadays. It'll look beautiful next to the fireplace in our bedroom." Gussie reached over and touched it. "Masterful work. Oh, I can't wait to thank Will in person!"

"It's very special," agreed Jim, taking it over and leaning it against the wall next to their living room fireplace.

"This is fun! Next, please!"

Will's gift had set the tone. Knowing Gussie and Jim loved antiques, most of their friends had found gifts for them that reflected love or marriage.

A sailor's valentine, a hanging nineteenth-century shadowbox containing a delicate mosaic design made from small shells in Barbados. A "Home Sweet Home" sampler from 1847 in which the motto was surrounded by small hearts. A small wedding quilt from the 1840s. ("Wherever did she find it?" Gussie, marveled. "What wonderful condition!") Several people had given them nineteenth-century brass or iron trivets decorated with hearts. ("We can hang them all on one of the walls near the kitchen.") And one of Gussie's roommates from Wellesley had sent them a Bride's Basket.

"How perfect!" Maggie said. "I wish I'd thought of that."

"It's a beautiful one, too," said Gussie, admiringly. "So many you see today don't have both the hand-blown basket and the silver-plated holder. I love the deep pink in the inside with the lighter pink on the outside and the ruffle."

Jim didn't look as thrilled at that gift. "That's for your dressing table," he said. "It doesn't exactly go with our stone fireplace."

"Perhaps not. But brides in the 1890s collected them," Gussie said. "And I'm happy Rachel thought to find one for me. Our friends have come up with wonderful gifts. I love the antiques theme."

Not every gift was an antique. An expensive ("Wow! Look at this!" from Jim) bottle of aged cognac was from Police Chief Ike Irons and his wife, Annie, and a hand-woven king-sized blanket came from Jim's law partner, Andy, and his wife.

"And what on earth is this?" exclaimed Jim.

He was unwrapping a delicate blue and red–swirled blown-glass ball, perhaps ten inches in diameter, with a loop at the top.

"How wonderful!" Gussie said, as Jim read the note.

"'This is not an antique, but it does come from Salem. May it keep the bad spirits away from your new home and always keep you safe from things that go bump in the night!'" Jim started to laugh. "From your cousin Sheila. Of course."

"Of course. It would be!" said Gussie. "And exactly what we need for our new home!"

"But what *is* it?" said Jim, again.

"It's a witch ball," Gussie explained. "A modern one. An old one, even if she could have found one, would have been way over Sheila's budget. You hang it in a window or doorway of your house. Some people fill it with herbs—Sheila always told me dill was best—and it keeps bad spirits from entering."

"Your cousin Sheila. Isn't she the one hosting your bachelorette party?" Maggie asked.

"That's right," said Gussie. "I haven't seen her in a while. She's a bit of a free spirit, but she's a dear."

"She's the one you said lives in Boston's North End," said Maggie, trying to keep everyone straight.

"That's right. But she used to live in Salem. Actually," Gussie winked at Maggie, "Sheila's a financial adviser now, but that's her second career. She used to be a practicing witch."

Chapter 18

Mazeppa No. 1, Boston, Massachusetts. Built by Hinckley and Drury, the Mazeppa was the first steam fire engine built at the Boston Locomotive Works in 1858. The model was named the New Era; it was designed by J.M. Stone, and featured a tubular thirty-six-inch boiler, and two hundred and forty-one brass smoke tubes. The double-acting pump and the steam cylinder were placed horizontally on a wooden frame designed to be pulled by horses, or in an emergency, by men. It weighed about 10,000 pounds. This engraving is from a book published in 1886 that chronicled the history of fire engines. Why this engine was labeled the Mazeppa No.1 is a mystery. The only town in the United States named Mazeppa is in Minnesota and it didn't have a fire department until 1886. Perhaps Stone just liked the name. 4.5 x 7 inches. Price: $35.

AT FIRST MAGGIE thought the ringing was in her dream. But when it wouldn't stop she reached out, finally connecting with her cell phone where she'd left it, on the carton next to her bed. "Hello?"

"Maggie! This is Diana."

"Diana?"

"I'm sorry. I know it's early."

Maggie looked at the time on the phone. Five-ten. "What's happening?"

"Someone tried to burn our house down."

"Are you all right?" Maggie sat up straight. "What about Cordelia?"

"We're both fine. The house is all right."

"What happened?"

"I was asleep. Luckily, Cordelia doesn't sleep well. She gets up early and works on her dolls. She went downstairs to make coffee and surprised someone. Whoever it was poured some liquid, maybe gasoline, on the back porch, but when Cordelia turned on the overhead light they got scared and ran."

"Did you call the police?"

"She has a TDD machine to call for help. She did that and then woke me up. By the time I got downstairs the police and a fire truck were both here."

"Did she see who the person was?"

"No. They wore dark clothes and a hoodie." Diana paused. "I'm scared, Maggie. Really scared."

"What did the police do?"

"They said they're going to watch the house. But I'm scared anyway. I think Cordelia is, too. We're both just sitting here."

"Did you tell her you were calling me?"

"Yes. She nodded. I don't think she knows what to do. She keeps walking around the house, looking at everything."

"Try to stay calm. I'll talk to Gussie and Jim, and then I'll come over. I promise."

"All right."

"Be brave. If anything else happens, call me again. Okay?"

"Okay. Thank you, Maggie."

Maggie got up and threw on her clothes. This was not exactly the way she and Gussie had planned to start the day, but she couldn't leave two frightened women alone. At least not without making sure everything possible was being done to make sure they were safe.

"Gussie?" she said outside Gussie's door.

"I'm awake," Gussie answered. "Come in. I heard the telephone. What's happening?"

"Someone tried to set fire to Cordelia's house. She scared them away, but she and Diana are still nervous. The police and fire department have been there, and the police say they'll be keeping an eye on the place, but from what Diana said it doesn't sound as though she and Cordelia are handling it well."

"Why would anyone want to hurt one of them?" said Gussie.

"I don't know. But we don't know why anyone wanted to kill Diana's father, either," said Maggie. "And we don't know what the police investigation has found, if anything."

"Let me guess. You told Diana you'd go over there."

"I can talk to Cordelia. And Diana told me a little. Cordelia didn't want to talk to Jim the other day."

"Jim should be involved. He can talk to the police with some authority."

"I agree. You call Jim, and see if he can stop by. But give me an hour or so to see what I can find out first."

"Maggie, are you sure you want to get this involved?"

"I already am this involved," said Maggie. "I want Diana and Cordelia to be safe. Someone dangerous is out there, and I want him stopped. Maybe I can help. Maybe I can't. But at least I can let those two women know someone cares about them. I haven't seen this town doing much so far besides sending over cookies."

"I'll call Jim," said Gussie. "But remember not to let them depend on you too much. That will just make it harder for them when you have to leave."

"I know," said Maggie. "I keep thinking about that."

"Don't forget it. Sometimes it's better not to get involved than to make promises you can't keep," warned Gussie.

Maggie drove by the bakery and was pleased to see it had opened at 5:30. She was in time to pick up a box of assorted Danish, and not knowing what Diana or Cordelia would want, decided to go for comfort food, and ordered three large hot chocolates with whipped cream. Even she would forego a Diet Pepsi for a hot chocolate on a damp and chilly October morning.

The sky was dark, and the dew was heavy. Wet orange and yellow leaves were pasted onto the sidewalk and street in the center of downtown and stuck under Maggie's windshield wipers. Luckily she didn't have far to drive.

Before she got out of her van the door of the house opened. Diana'd been waiting for her.

"Here," said Maggie, thrusting the box of drinks at Diana, "something to warm you up this dank morning. And I brought other goodies." She followed the young woman into the house, where Cordelia sat at the kitchen table. They both looked pale and tense.

"I'm so glad you came," said Diana. "I couldn't stand the silence any longer." She held up the goodies so Cordelia could see them.

"I brought hot chocolate and…sweet things," Maggie signed,

unsure of how to sign "Danish" except by spelling it. Cordelia smiled at her hesitation.

"Thank you," she signed back.

The three women sat at the kitchen table and opened their cups of chocolate capped generously with whipped cream. Some moments called for chocolate and sugar. This morning seemed to qualify.

A few minutes later Maggie wiped off her fingers and signed, "You have no idea who was on the porch earlier this morning?"

Cordelia shook her head. "It was too dark to see. I only saw the beam from a flashlight, and turned on the porch light. Then I saw liquid thrown out of the darkness onto the porch. At first I didn't dare open the door. Then I did, and smelled gasoline, or kerosene, and called the fire department."

Diana asked, "Is she sure she couldn't recognize the person again?"

Maggie checked. Cordelia was adamant. "I don't even know if I saw a man or a woman. Or how tall the person was. It was all so fast, and so dark."

"Maybe the police will find some clues," Maggie said. "Maybe the person left footprints. And whoever it was will certainly smell of gasoline or kerosene."

"Anyone who works on the water or in a garage could smell of gasoline," signed Cordelia. "And a shower could take the smell away."

"But not off all his or her clothes," Maggie pointed out. "Not immediately. We can hope."

"Why would someone want to burn the house?" asked Diana.

"That's what I would like to know," said Maggie. "Cordelia, can you think of any reason someone would want to destroy this house, or anything in it?"

The woman shook her head slowly, looking puzzled. "My things are here. Nothing anyone else would be interested in."

"What about Diana's father? Is there anything he left that anyone would want to destroy?"

Cordelia stopped for a moment, thinking. "His things are in the bedroom he used. I never went in there. There was no reason."

"Diana, have you gone through what your father left in his room?"

Diana looked down. "Yes. When he didn't come home I wanted

to find out why. I tried to find something that would give me a hint of where he'd gone."

"Did you find anything someone might want to destroy?"

Diana shook her head. "Just a few clothes. He must have had his telephone with him. There weren't any papers. No pictures, and no computer. Nothing."

Maggie translated for Cordelia.

Cordelia looked at Diana. "I knew who he really was. But even with a new name, he was afraid of being tracked. He didn't have credit cards. He didn't have a driver's license or a car. He kept saying he would pay someone to get new papers, but I don't think he'd done that. He only worked for cash."

"What kind of work did he do?"

"At first he tried working on fishing boats, like many men here, but he had a weak stomach." Cordelia smiled. "He got seasick easily. No one wanted him on their boat. Sometimes he worked for Rocky Costa down at the Lazy Lobster, tending bar and waiting tables, when Rocky needed extra help. He mowed lawns and trimmed trees for people during the summer."

Maggie summarized for Diana, who seemed to know most of that. "He told me he volunteered with a baseball league for teenagers. I thought that was cool because he'd been a Little League coach in Colorado," she added.

"He worked with boys here?" asked Maggie.

"He didn't coach. He was in charge of equipment or schedules, " said Diana. "He told me that was one of his favorite things to do, but he didn't get paid to do it."

Interesting, Maggie thought. He was suspected of selling drugs to young people in town, but this was the first she'd heard he'd had a reason to be near young people.

"Was Dan helping with the baseball team this summer?" she asked Cordelia.

"No. He did that a year ago," Cordelia answered. "Last spring he started working with the team again, but there were problems." She hesitated. "He was blamed for the death of a boy who took too many pills. Someone even threw rocks and broke two of our windows." She shook her head. "It was bad. Rocky told Dan he couldn't come to practices anymore. People were too upset."

"Rocky told him that?"

"He was Dan's boss at the Lazy Lobster, and he coached the team. That's how Dan got the job helping out."

Rocky Costa. The bartender at the Lazy Lobster. Funny, he hadn't happened to mention that connection when she was there the other day.

"How did Dan feel about being fired from a volunteer job?"

"At first he was angry. Then he was sad. It wasn't easy for him here. Working with the boys was one of the things he enjoyed. But he understood why he couldn't do it anymore."

"It was kind of you to let him live here for the past two years. That's a long time to open your home to a distant relative."

Cordelia looked up at Maggie in surprise.

"This house belonged to him until three years ago. I was the one who was grateful he'd paid the taxes and let me live here all those years. He had a right to be here."

Chapter 19

Raid on a Sand-Swallow Colony, "How Many Eggs?" Winslow Homer wood engraving of four boys climbing up sand dunes and stealing eggs from the nests of the swallows nesting there. Printed in *Harper's Weekly*, June 13, 1874, one of the last of Homer's engravings to be printed in *Harper's*, and one of his finest. It was done at Gloucester, Massachusetts, and is therefore sometimes considered one of his "Gloucester Series," although it doesn't quite match the four other beach scenes he did there because it's a vertical engraving; the other four are horizontal. 13.75 x 9.25 inches. Price: $450.

"THIS HOUSE BELONGED to Diana's father? Not just twenty years ago when he lived here, but until three years ago?" asked Maggie.

"Yes. I thought everyone knew," signed Cordelia. "When he and his wife moved west I needed a place to stay. They told me I could live here for the rest of my life if I wanted to. Roger sent money to pay the taxes and keep the house painted and the roof from leaking. I paid for the utilities and my food, of course. Then three years ago, for some reason, he signed the deed over to me."

"I see," signed Maggie. She glanced over at Diana, who was finishing her second Danish and ignoring their signing. "Does Diana know this?"

"I haven't told her," said Cordelia. "I don't know if her father did."

Maggie suspected he hadn't. He hadn't told Diana much about her family. How had she gotten so involved with these two women? But how could she not care about what happened to them? "Cordelia, why would anyone want to hurt you or Diana?"

"I have no idea."

A very bright light on the wall between the kitchen and living room started blinking.

"Someone's at the door. I'll get it," said Diana.

Of course. In the home of someone who was hearing impaired a light would signal that someone was at the door; a doorbell wouldn't be heard. Maggie had read about signals connected to TDD machines and doorbells, but this was the first time she'd seen one operating.

Chief Ike Irons came back with Diana. "Good morning, ladies. Maggie Summer. I didn't expect to see you here."

"I came to keep Diana and Cordelia company. They've had a difficult morning."

"And you speak the hand talk, don't you? I remember your saying that. Well, then it's good you're here. You can translate for Ms. West. I wanted them both to know we looked in their yard, and down to the beach from their porch, this morning, but we didn't find any footprints. Of course, the wind has blown considerable, and wet leaves are over everything. But we couldn't find a trace of whoever was here."

"Did you check on the beach? Down by the tide line? Maybe whoever was here was picked up by a boat," Maggie interrupted.

"Doubt it. If there were someone there he probably walked through the water so the tide washed away any footprints."

"Well, he wouldn't walk in that frigid water forever! Wouldn't you see where he walked out?"

"Theoretically, yes, Dr. Summer. But we didn't find anything. For whatever reason. The beach isn't even, and the tide comes up pretty high about now. Maybe whoever it was hopped on a unicorn. In any case, we didn't find anything. But we haven't given up. We're checking marinas and gas stations to see if anyone remembers seeing someone pump gasoline into a container in the past day or so. But that's not unusual around here, you know. And we're going to keep an eye on this house, both from the road and the water, for the next few days."

Chief Irons nodded to Diana and to Cordelia. "Miss Hopkins and Ms West can be assured they're under the personal protection of the Winslow Police Department."

While Maggie translated the message for Cordelia, Diana asked, "Have you figured out who killed my father yet, Chief Irons?"

"That investigation is underway."

"What does that mean?" she asked. "Who are you investigating?"

"We don't have any specific suspects yet," Chief Irons replied, "but we're working on developing a timeline: trying to find out where your father was during the last few days of his life, and who he saw then. Once we know that, we'll be in a better position to start interviewing persons of interest."

"What do you know so far?" asked Diana.

"We know he was here on Tuesday morning with you for breakfast, and he was seen in town later that morning."

"Yes?"

"Well, so far, that's it."

"Where was he in town? With whom?"

Maggie listened as Chief Irons tried to avoid admitting he didn't have too many answers. "He was walking down Main Street, near the statue of the whaling master. He was alone, heading toward the library."

"That's it? That's all you know?"

"We've only had a couple of days to work on the investigation, you know. These things take time. This isn't 'CSI' or 'Law and Order.' This is the real world, young lady."

"And in the meantime someone just walks up to our house and tries to burn it down, with Cordelia and me inside!"

"We're investigating that, too, I assure you. These sorts of things do not normally happen here in Winslow."

"Well, they're happening now! And they're happening to my family! And I want them to stop!" Diana burst into tears, and turned to Cordelia, who reached out to hold her.

"These women are very upset, Chief. Isn't there anything more that can be done for them?" Maggie asked.

"They could go and stay somewhere else, I suppose, but then whoever wanted to burn down their house could do that more easily."

"If they went to stay at one of the B and Bs in town for a few days, very quietly, could someone on your staff stay here to protect their property?"

"Dr. Summer, do you have any idea how much that sort of protection would cost? I have one detective and three regular cops on my force. You think I could spare someone to hang out in an empty house on the chance some stupid kid came back to try to burn it? I'm sending over someone to clean off the gasoline that's there now. I think between Miss West and our guys we scared off whoever was there this morning. I don't think anyone's coming back. Winslow's a small town, Dr. Summer. If you don't like it, you can go back to New Jersey."

With that Chief Irons stomped off, heading for the front door. For once Maggie was glad Cordelia was hearing impaired. She couldn't hear the door slam.

Or the light knock a few minutes later. But Maggie did. Diana was still sobbing, so she went to the door. It was probably too much to hope that Chief Irons had come back to apologize.

Yes, it was.

"Morning, Maggie. Gussie said Diana and Cordelia had a scare here this morning."

"Exactly. Did you pass your friend Ike on your way here?"

Jim nodded. "His car went by mine."

"Probably over the speed limit. He couldn't wait to get out of here. He says he's providing protection for them and for the house, but I don't see it. They're really upset, Jim. And, truthfully, so am I. Attempting to burn a house down is a pretty nasty game."

"You're right. Do either of them have any idea who would have done this?"

"No clues. Cordelia didn't see anything helpful, and Diana was upstairs asleep. Neither of them can think of anything in the house someone might want to destroy, or a reason anyone might want to hurt them."

Jim shook his head. "I don't have a magic solution, Maggie. I'll be moving out of my house in a couple of days, and I could have them both come and stay there, but that would leave this house unprotected. I don't think they'd want that, either."

"I suggested something like that to Ike. He didn't seem impressed."

Diana and Cordelia looked up as Maggie and Jim walked into the kitchen. From the look that passed between them, Maggie wondered what they'd been doing—or communicating. Did they look guilty?

Chapter 20

Harvard College. Cover of *Appleton's Journal of Literature, Science and Art* for Saturday, March 5, 1870, and following seven pages, which are devoted to a history and current view of Harvard, including wood engravings of Harvard Square (which shows men driving cows away from the area), Harvard Church, the Library Building, Appleton Chapel, the Divinity School, Law School, Lawrence Scientific School, The Observatory, and the Class Tree. Special treasure for any Harvard graduate. Page size 7.5 x 11 inches. $75.

MAGGIE LEFT JIM with Diana and Cordelia, hoping perhaps his advice and male calm could provide a different sort of comfort than her hot chocolate and Danish had.

Although the hot chocolate had certainly not been refused.

She headed toward the new Aunt Augusta's Attic. If the schedule was on target, Gussie should be there, and the painters and carpenters should be finished. This morning they'd planned to unpack before, if she remembered correctly, a last-minute wedding cake check at the bakery.

Gussie's van was the only vehicle in back of the new shop; there were no painting or construction trucks there. That seemed a positive sign. Maybe the work was complete.

Maggie walked up the ramp to the back door, knocked, and went in.

"There you are!" Gussie called from the front room. "How are Diana and Cordelia?"

"Physically, fine. But scared and confused. They have no idea who would try to set their house on fire."

"I can't imagine too many things more frightening than fire," said

Gussie. "Jim and I've put ramps at three entrances to our house, and fire alarms everywhere we could think of."

Getting out of a burning house would be so much more complicated for Gussie than for someone who wasn't disabled, Maggie realized. She hadn't ever thought of that. And now that she had, the pictures in her mind were horrific.

"If Cordelia hadn't happened to be downstairs in the kitchen so early in the morning, who knows what might have happened," Maggie said. "She wouldn't have heard anything. But thank goodness she saw a light. Whoever it was had a flashlight."

"She probably has visual fire alarms connected to her heat and smoke detectors, but depending on how well she sleeps, she might not have noticed them." Gussie shuddered. "I'm just glad they're both safe."

"Jim's at the house with them now," Maggie added.

"Good," said Gussie. "And, before I forget or die of curiosity—as that movie said, 'You've Got Mail!'"

"What?" said Maggie.

"When I got here there was an envelope on the floor near the front door. It must have been pushed through the mail slot. At first I thought the carpenter had dropped off a bill, but it's for you. Over on the counter."

Maggie picked up the envelope. It was addressed in penciled block letters to MAGGIE FROM NEW JERSEY.

"Who'd be sending you mash notes here?" Gussie asked, only half in jest.

Maggie started opening the envelope. "Yesterday, while you were resting, I stopped and had a beer at the tavern where Jim'd said Dan Jeffrey drank. The Lazy Lobster. I thought someone there would have an idea of what happened to him."

"Maggie! That's not exactly a social high spot in Winslow. If you felt you had to go, why didn't you ask Jim to take you?"

"Because he wouldn't have. And, besides, no one would have said anything if he'd been with me. I wanted to go on my own." She ripped open the envelope. "I told the men there that if anyone had something to tell me about Dan they could leave a note here. I figured the shop would be a neutral place." She read what was on the sheet of paper inside.

"So? What does it say?"

"'Stay away from bars and balls. Let sand cover sin.'" Maggie shivered. "That's hideously poetic."

"Not poetic to me. Scary, and downright weird!" said Gussie. "Sounds like you made a real fan in that bar. Which someone is definitely telling you to stay away from." She reached inside a carton and pulled out the ringmaster for a Schoenhut Humpty Dumpty Circus, a popular set of toys made in the early twentieth century.

"'Bars and balls. And sand,'" mused Maggie as she paced the front of the shop. "Did you know Dan Jeffrey was involved with a baseball team here in town?"

"Where did you hear that?" Gussie arranged a wooden clown and a glass-eyed lion next to the mustached ringmaster on the shelf.

"From Diana. He'd told her. Cordelia confirmed it. He didn't coach. He kept track of equipment. But his working with the team might connect him to the boy who died last spring."

"Tony Silva. Bob Silva's son. Bob's a widower. He thought the world of that boy. Went to pieces after he died," said Gussie. "Horrible situation. Jim said everyone knew there were drugs in the school. Ike'd been looking for the dealer for months. Thought someone was picking drugs up in Boston and selling them locally. But none of the kids would talk. You know kids. And after Tony died, they closed down even more. Bob accused anyone who had contact with the kids."

"I heard he'd blamed Dan Jeffrey."

"Could be. I didn't hear that, but then, I don't have a child in the school, so I don't have a pipeline into those circles. But it makes sense. Dan was a 'wash-ashore,' someone relatively new in town, and as far as anyone knew he was a bachelor. Parents these days are nervous about single men being around their children." Gussie paused. "Winslow's an old town, Maggie. Most of us year 'round people have known each other since we were kids. My family's been here a couple of hundred years. There are still divisions. Families that were Portuguese fishermen a couple of generations back may still be fishing, but now they're just as likely to own restaurants, or run tour boats for summer people, or be professionals. A few who summered here as children have found a way, with telecommuting and all, to live here full time today. Times change. But a lot of the same families are still here. Jim's one of the few newcomers. He went to Harvard Law and decided to move to the Cape and practice here instead of going into a big firm, or returning South."

"What about Cordelia West?"

"I'm pretty sure she's from Martha's Vineyard, which is considered 'in the neighborhood.' There used to be a deaf community on the Vineyard, back, oh, a couple of hundred years ago."

Maggie smiled. "I read a study about it once. People there didn't think of deafness as a disability; it was just a characteristic some people were born with, like red hair. Everyone, deaf or not, learned sign language, so not being able to hear wasn't a handicap. Fascinating."

"That's right. But as the world changed, people traveled more, and intermarried, and by the middle of the twentieth century that sign language was gone. If there are any deaf people on the Vineyard today they're not part of that genetic cluster, as they now call it."

"And she's Dan Jeffrey's—or Roger Hopkins's—cousin."

"So everyone says. Hopkins is a good old Cape Cod name, of course. There was a Hopkins on the *Mayflower*. Although I don't know if there's any connection to these Hopkins! Around here, everyone wants to claim a *Mayflower* connection."

"Diana says her parents lived in that house when she was a baby."

A lady Schoenhut acrobat with a bisque head fell over, and Gussie stopped to lean her against the larger of the two elephants in the circus parade she was setting up. "That would have been twenty years or so ago. I don't remember. Maybe Ellen would. Ben would have been a baby then, too. New mothers remember other new mothers."

"This morning Cordelia told me the house wasn't hers until three years ago. It belonged to Roger Hopkins."

"Three years ago? That would have been before he 'died' in Colorado," Gussie said. "Did he give it to her or did she buy it?"

"From the way she put it, I assumed he'd given it to her," Maggie said.

"I never had the feeling Cordelia had much money," said Gussie. "Ellen would know more, but that little house of hers must be worth a small fortune. It has beach front. I'd guess its value is over half a million. Maybe closer to a million. Her property taxes must be incredible. A lot of local families have had to sell their homes because they can't afford the taxes in the current market. I wonder how Cordelia has been paying hers? Those dolls she makes don't sell *that* well."

"She told me that until she owned the house three years ago her cousin sent her money for taxes and maintenance," said Maggie.

"Interesting," said Gussie. "He must have had a very good job at that bank in Colorado. Or she must have another source of income." She looked at her watch. "We have to get going. We're meeting Jim at the bakery. A wedding cake tasting awaits us."

Josie's Bakery, home of the delectable morning pastries, employed a pastry chef who specialized in creating spectacular wedding cakes. Luigi Ferrante greeted Gussie at the door and whisked them away to a private room.

"Ah, it is the bride! I have made samples of three cakes, just as you and your handsome groom requested! Come in, come in!" He moved a small table and several chairs so the table was in front of Gussie, and the chairs were arranged around it. "And where is the groom? We do not want to start without him!"

"Here he is," said Jim, slightly out of breath, as he pushed through the heavy door, and kissed Gussie. "What a morning. But I made it! I see you haven't started yet."

"We would not begin without the groom," said Mr. Ferrante, hovering around the three of them. "Now, let me remind you what cake you have selected."

He opened a loose-leaf notebook filled with photographs of elaborately decorated cakes and flipped to the page he'd marked: a four-layer cake with white trim, topped by white roses made of frosting and a cascade of roses curving down the side.

"Oh, it's lovely!" said Maggie. "Very elegant."

"Now, I need you to make very certain this is the one you want."

Gussie and Jim looked at each other. Gussie nodded. "We're

positive. It's exactly what we want. You know we considered a lot of options. But we liked the flowers best. We almost went with real flowers, Maggie, but we decided the ones Mr. Ferrante made were so lovely we would go with one of his special creations."

"Very good," Mr. Ferrante beamed.

"And we want a four-layer lemon cake with chocolate filling between two layers and raspberry for the other one," Jim added.

"Ah, yes! That will be perfect!" agreed Mr. Ferrante. "The flavors of chocolate and raspberry are certainly very…romantic, wouldn't you say? Almost an aphrodisiac! For a wedding night, very appropriate."

Maggie almost choked.

Jim kept smiling. "Shall we taste those cake samples now, Mr. Ferrante? We're looking forward to deciding which of your delicious lemon cakes we'll choose. "

"Of course, of course!"

And as Maggie tasted the samples, all of which were delicious as far as she was concerned, she couldn't help thinking about the note someone from the Lazy Lobster had left for her.

She needed to talk with someone connected with that baseball team.

Chapter 21

Kirtland Raspberry. Hand-colored steel engraving of a raspberry branch, showing seven ripe red raspberries and five leaves. Published by New York Commissioner of Agriculture, 1866. Now considered an "heirloom raspberry," the Kirtland was a new variety in 1866, developed by Dr. Jared Peter Kirtland (1793–1877), a nineteenth-century naturalist from Lakewood, Ohio, who was one of the founders of both the Cleveland Museum of Natural History and Western Reserve Medical School. 5.5 x 9 inches. Price: $45.

ANY FOOD WOULD have been a letdown after tasting that wedding cake, and when Jim said he'd need to talk to Gussie about the guest list ("Some of the Southern cousins don't seem to be on the list at all, and others are having trouble getting plane reservations into Boston") over lunch, Maggie decided to bow out.

"I'd like to wander around Winslow and sightsee," she said, before either of them could interrupt her. "And I know you'll want to rest after lunch, Gussie. Why don't I meet you back at the store at about three-thirty. We can finish unpacking the books and toys for the back wall then." She waved and kept walking.

She wanted some time by herself.

And she couldn't add anything to discussions about Southern relatives.

Her walk took her to the Winslow Library. People kept referring to the death of Tony Silva last spring. The local newspaper would give more details. Not every small-town paper was on the Internet yet.

The librarian at the front desk was happy to refer her to the reading room, where stacks of local newspapers were piled on a bookcase along with copies of the *Boston Globe*. Of course, Maggie immediately realized, the disadvantage to having the actual newspapers in front of her was, there was no index.

But she hadn't gotten her doctoral degree without being comfortable with research challenges. Tony Silva had died last spring; everyone agreed about that. And it had shaken the town. It had certainly been a front page story locally. She'd start there.

She started looking in February; she found the headline in mid-March. TONY SILVA, 15, WINSLOW FRESHMAN, FOUND DEAD. She started reading. And taking notes. Then, based on what she'd read, she went back to issues earlier in the year. And then to later issues.

By the time she'd finished, Maggie had a much better idea of what had happened in Winslow. It was more complicated than one boy having somehow, possibly mistakenly, taken an overdose of prescription medications.

Small towns, Maggie kept reminding herself. Small towns took care of their own.

Beginning as early as January the "Winslow Police Blotter" had reported teen parties that were rowdy and "out of control," and where there was "no adult supervision present." Some of the parties included young people, usually boys, as young as thirteen.

Some gatherings appeared to have been at closed-up homes belonging to summer people, because trespassing was among the charges mentioned. In most cases charges were dropped and the "juveniles were remanded to their parents."

Right, Maggie thought. Send them home with a lecture.

In mid-February a small article on the front page announced a new lecture series at the high school focused on both the medical and legal problems of drugs and alcohol. The school doctor was to talk about the medical dangers of substance abuse, and Chief Irons would discuss the legal consequences. That would certainly make a difference to teenagers, Maggie thought. Explain to the kids they're rotting their brains; they'll change their evil ways and never have another drink or touch a joint again. Right. That's always worked. And make sure you tell them they're breaking the law, since they never knew that.

Similar talks were scheduled at the middle schools.

Clearly, Winslow thought it had a problem last spring.

Maggie thought of the suburban Somerset County towns near where she taught in New Jersey. A student could probably find alcohol or drugs in any of them if they were looking. And drug and alcohol education was a required part of the curriculum in New Jersey. Wasn't it in most states today?

But the public emphasis on it in Winslow last spring was unusual. Something out of the ordinary had been happening here. Something more than a few kids getting their older brothers to buy them beer.

And then: mid-March, Tony Silva was found dead at his home. Not at a wild party at someone's home where everyone brought a bottle of pills filched from their parents' medicine cabinets and mixed them together in a salad bowl. Not a gathering on the beach where crazy kids had built a fire and were warming up with ever-larger shots of brandy or cans of beer, and one dared another to swallow some pills, too.

Tony Silva, who everyone agreed hadn't been to any of the questionable parties, and was a quiet kid who liked to play baseball and work out on exercise equipment in his own basement, had been home alone in his bedroom when he swallowed at least a dozen Oxy-Contin pills.

His dad was out having dinner with friends, and thought Tony was asleep when he came home. He found his son's body in the morning when the boy didn't come down for breakfast.

And the town of Winslow turned all its frustration with their young people into grief for one boy. Maggie read through his obituary, and the letters to the editor, and the tributes from friends. The school declared days of mourning, and brought in grief counselors. The paper ran two pages of pictures of students crying.

What wasn't in the articles or tributes was any reason for Tony to have taken the pills. Of course, he could have taken them as an experiment, Maggie thought. Kids, unfortunately, do. But this particular kid was, according to the reports in the paper, a fitness freak. If he'd taken steroids, that might have made sense. But that many painkillers? By himself, at home?

Had Tony Silva known what he was doing?

But the possibility of suicide was never mentioned. And even if his overdose had been intentional it left open the question of where he'd gotten the pills.

Bob Silva was clear there'd been no OxyContin pills in his home.

Chief Irons was quoted as "looking for the evil snake who has invaded our fair community and poisoned our children."

In an April issue Maggie read the police note about windows being broken on Apple Orchard Lane: the rocks thrown through Cordelia's windows. In June, police broke up a fight between Daniel Jeffrey and Robert Silva at the Lazy Lobster. No charges filed. So Bob Silva was still angry, and still convinced Dan Jeffrey was the one who'd brought the drugs to Winslow that killed his son.

Maggie kept reading, checking the headlines and the Police Blotter.

But after Tony Silva's death there were no mentions of wild parties. Or drug arrests. It was as though whatever had been happening in Winslow last winter and spring had ended with Tony Silva's death.

Chapter 22

MAGGIE ARRANGED SEVERAL McLoughlin Brothers children's books face out on a high shelf in the front room at Aunt Augusta's Attic. "You have a great selection of illustrated children's books. I think McLoughlin did the best chromolithographs in this country in the late nineteenth and early twentieth centuries. You'd have to go to Edinburgh or Germany to equal them."

"I love McLoughlin books," agreed Gussie. "And the prices aren't too high. Most of the illustrations wouldn't make good stand-alone prints, so you print dealers aren't looking to buy them and take them apart. That helps keeps the prices down."

"Usually there are too many words on the pages, and the illustrations are too specific to the stories for prints." agreed Maggie. "I've had some breakers—books in which the binding was already broken—but even then I haven't been tempted to mat and try to sell the prints separately. They just don't work outside the books."

"When I first started dealing in toys, years ago, I looked for the McLoughlin name. They made the finest paper dolls, blocks, and games. I knew if I was in doubt that buying a McLoughlin item was the right choice. I still love them. Now a lot of McLoughlin toys are being reproduced. I can spot them immediately, but sometimes new collectors get fooled. Several times a month people bring me reproductions and ask me their value. Or try to sell them to me, thinking they're authentic antiques."

Maggie nodded. "I wish all reproductions had dates on them. Or were marked 'Reproduction.' But not all do. Wasn't McLoughlin sold to one of the big toy companies?"

"Milton Bradley, in 1920. Early Milton Bradley games are also collectable, if they have all their pieces, but few do after all these years. And their boards aren't as beautifully printed as McLoughlin ones."

Maggie shelved the last of the picture books and started in on a box of books for older children. "Gussie, how long has Ike Irons been in charge of the police department here in Winslow?"

"Maybe fifteen years? I think he came from Mashpee. He's not a native of Winslow. But not from far away. Mashpee has a much larger police force, so he may have gotten his training there. Why?"

"I was over at the library while you were resting. I wanted to read about what happened last spring, when Tony Silva died."

"That was horrible," said Gussie. "Sad. Poor Bob Silva. His wife died of cancer when his son was still in nursery school. Since then he'd focused his life around the boy. He took it hard. The whole town did, actually. It's the sort of thing people in a small town don't expect to happen to their children."

"And yet no one expects murder in a small town, and no one seems too upset about Dan Jeffrey's murder."

"Tony was fifteen. Dan was a quiet man who hadn't been here long; he didn't have a family, except for Cordelia; and he didn't have many friends. I suspect not many people even know about his death."

"And those who've heard his name connect him with Tony Silva's death last spring, because Bob Silva's been pretty vocal about blaming him. Or so I've heard."

"That's possible. Bob isn't the sort to hold his tongue once he gets something in his head."

"I assume Chief Irons is checking out Bob Silva's alibi for the day Dan Jeffrey disappeared."

"I guess so. He's the one in charge, you know. You're here to help me with the shop and the wedding."

"Right! Like, where do you want these Horatio Alger books?"

"Ah, yes. I keep waiting for someone to write a best-selling novel based on some titan of industry who's patterned his life on one of those books, so they'll skyrocket in value," said Gussie. "Or maybe there'll be an expose on Alger, who was probably a pedophile. For now, put them up on the top shelf. They're not exactly big sellers. Although I do sell them once in a while to people whose name, or whose husband's or son's name, is in the title."

"Like *Phil the Fiddler,* or *Paul the Peddler,* or *Joe's Luck,* or *Mark the Match Boy?*" said Maggie.

Gussie agreed. "Rags to riches. Still a great theme."

"I talk about Alger in my American Intellectual History course," said Maggie. "His works really are classics. You can still buy a paperback of *Ragged Dick.*"

"Well, don't tell my customers. Here they can buy a copy from a hundred years ago, or more," said Gussie. "All the dreams of America between two covers. All you need to succeed is to be born a boy, work hard, be virtuous, and then do a good deed for a rich man who'll appreciate your pluck and give you your first big break."

"And it's straight to the top from there," agreed Maggie. "It also helps if you marry the rich man's daughter." She looked around. "Now, where are your other books? I assume you have all the other childhood classics?"

"Of course. I only take a few to antique shows because they're heavy, but I do want to have a selection in the shop for people to choose from. Isaiah Thomas Books in Cotuit is a wonderful antiquarian bookshop on the Cape, of course, and I don't attempt to compete with them. But my selection isn't bad."

"I'm impressed. I know how hard it is to find copies of books for children in good condition. Well-loved children's books are too often in well-loved condition. Where are the rest of your books?"

"They're in cartons creatively labeled BKS and stacked on the wall in back of the bathroom. There's a dolly there, if they're too heavy."

"I'll take them one carton at a time," called Maggie. She returned with one in a moment. "Do you want them all out?"

"One copy of each title, to begin with. Alphabetically by author." Gussie started arranging an assortment of cast iron banks. "Have you talked with Will recently? Is there any chance he'll be able to drive down early?"

"We talked two nights ago." She should have called Will last night. But she'd gotten so involved with Cordelia and Diana she'd forgotten. And then she was going to call this morning, but there was the almost-fire. "He can't come earlier than he'd planned; there's no one else to stay with Aunt Nettie."

"How is she?"

"She's fine. Cooking up a storm. He doesn't like leaving her alone, in case she were to fall, or something else were to happen."

"He's a good man, Maggie."

"I know. You don't have to keep telling me that!" said Maggie, rearranging a set of Louisa May Alcott's Orchard House series so that they were all on one shelf.

"Have you seen him since you were up there in August?"

"We met in New York State one weekend in late September when he was on his way between Buffalo and Maine. That's the only time."

Gussie shook her head. "I don't know how you two have managed a long-distance relationship this long. It's about eighteen months now, isn't it?"

"About," Maggie agreed. "But we're both busy. We don't sit around between visits. And we keep in touch. Email, telephone."

"It's not the same," Gussie declared.

"Anyway. He'll be here in a few days. And I'm busy here with you."

"Which I'm grateful for. And although I know I've said a few things about your spending time with Cordelia and Diana, I know they're grateful, too. I know you, Maggie. You get involved with people. Especially when you think you can help. Or when you think there's danger or injustice involved."

"You know me too well, Gussie. And I'm afraid about both of those things. There's nothing that makes sense about this situation. Just a lot of dangling threads. Twenty years ago a man moves to Colorado with his wife and child, leaving his cousin in his house here, more or less as a house-sitter, so far as I can tell. Then he fakes his own death, probably because he's been threatened as a key witness in a mob-related court case, leaves his only child, and shows up at the old homestead, under an assumed name. Two years go by. No one recognizes him except the cousin, until his daughter shows up, and three days later he's murdered. A couple of days after that someone pours gasoline on the porch of the house, which looks pretty much like an attempt to burn it down, taking the daughter and cousin with it."

Gussie looked at her. "Good summary."

"So? Who would benefit from Dan Jeffrey's death?"

Gussie was quiet for a moment. "No one directly. He didn't even exist. Roger Hopkins was already legally dead. I suppose keeping him dead would be easier, legally, for Diana. But not easier emotionally. The house is Cordelia's, so she loses a tenant, assuming he was paying rent. And he may not have been doing that. So no reason for murder that's obvious."

"Anyone else?"

"Bob Silva blamed him for Tony's death. If he's still angry, there's that."

"Right."

"I'm assuming there's no double jeopardy, so there'd be no problems left over from the Colorado murder case."

"That's what I figured, too," Maggie agreed.

"But the gasoline on the porch. Putting Cordelia or Diana in danger. That doesn't fit. And I'm not convinced it's Bob Silva. This is the end of October. Tony died in March. He may have blamed Dan last spring, but by now I'd think he'd have calmed a bit. Maybe even had second thoughts."

"The local newspaper didn't mention any drug investigations, or arrests, or even other parties with young people. Could everything to do with drugs suddenly have come to a standstill with Tony Silva's death last spring?"

"I don't know, Maggie. The police probably kept looking for whoever supplied Tony with those drugs. But you're right. I haven't heard anything about that in months."

"I need to talk with Bob Silva." Maggie's look of determination left no room for questioning. "But, don't worry." She smiled. "I'll be nice." She looked around at the beginning-to-look-like-an-antique-toy-store Aunt Augusta's Attic. "So. What do you need from the hardware store?"

Chapter 23

Wild Flowers. Bright and decorative hand-colored engraving (1863) of Wood Hawkweed, Chicory, Melancholy Thistle, Corn Bottle, Mountain Cudweed, Coltsfoot, Sea Feverfew, Ragweed, Daisy, and Corn Marigold; by artist, writer, and naturalist Margaret Mary Plues (1828–1901) from her book *Rambles in Search of Wild Flowers*. Plues was born in Yorkshire, England. Never married, by 1881 she was head of a household in Kennington where she lived with sixteen other women, thirteen of whom were dressmakers. Her occupation was listed as "artist and designer." 4.5 x 7.5 inches. Price: $55.

WINSLOW HARDWARE was designed to provide its local customers with supplies they needed immediately. Its owner understood that if you were building a house, buying a major appliance, or painting your barn you'd probably head over to one of the chain stores near Hyannis.

But if you needed twenty-five pounds of birdseed, washers for your kitchen sink, pellets for your wood stove, a few boards of #2 pine for a bookcase, or shovels, salt, or sand when snow was forecast, Winslow's Hardware was convenient and fast, and free advice came with your purchase. Maggie noted that postcards were part of their inventory, no doubt for summer visitors who stopped in to buy a new mailbox or flyswatter. She picked out several colorful ones to send to Aunt Nettie.

Candles, batteries, and flashlights were piled on one large table. Preparation for winter, Maggie thought. Will was probably stocking up in Maine, too.

"Need any help?" A tall, well-built man wearing a flannel shirt and an orange hunting vest (hunting and fishing supplies filled one corner of the store) asked. "You're welcome to take your time, but if you're looking for anything in particular, let me know."

"I'm helping Gussie White set up her new store," said Maggie. "She could use a can of wood filler, and a few picture hangers."

"How much wood filler?" asked the man. Maggie looked for a nametag, but didn't spot one. "The medium-sized one," she guessed, as he held up two cans. "It hardens fast, doesn't it?"

"It does. Better to come back and get more if you're not going to use it right away," he advised. "Next aisle over there's hardware for hanging pictures. You should find what you're looking for next to the electrical section."

Maggie nodded. "You wouldn't happen to be Bob Silva, would you?"

The man smiled. "At your service. Why do you ask?"

"Gussie said you owned the store, and were very helpful. She said to ask for you if I couldn't find what I was looking for."

Flattery never failed. Bob Silva beamed. "Pleased she said that. I try to meet the needs of the people of Winslow. It's a challenge, you know, to run a small business these days, when you're competing with all those big-box stores. Customer service is what separates us from those places." The man was practically preening. "And you are?"

"Maggie Summer. Here for the wedding."

"This next Saturday, isn't it? Nice Gussie and Jim are finally tying the knot. They're good folks."

Maggie looked past the man toward the front of the store. Hanging from the ceiling were sports uniform shirts printed with WINSLOW HARDWARE and player numbers. She took a chance.

"She also told me you do a lot for the community. You work with young people in town. Your store supports some of the teams?" She pointed at the shirts.

"We do. It's a community thing. I sponsor a Little League team, and a bowling team. And I donate money for uniforms for one of the kids' baseball teams." His smile was fading. "Done it for years. Builds good will."

"I'm sorry. She also told me your son died recently. I've reminded you, haven't I? How stupid of me. He played baseball, didn't he?"

Silva nodded. "He wasn't a great player, but he was getting better. He was working at it. A lot of kids need time to mature, you know."

"It must be hard for you."

"It's been a rotten year," Silva acknowledged. "No one who hasn't lost a kid can know what it's like. Do you have children, Ms. Summer?"

"Not yet."

"They'll tear your heart out," said Silva. "They'll fill your heart and make it feel as big as the moon, then they'll break it into little pieces. But my Tony, he was a good boy. Never got in any trouble. Worked hard. No genius at the books, you understand, but got pretty decent grades. And was getting better at sports. He had asthma so it was harder for him than it was for some of the other boys. He had to train a little more. Boys, they mature at different times."

"You sound as though you know a lot about sports, Mr. Silva."

"I was pretty good myself, when I was younger. Made all-state as a first baseman. Even got the attention of some scouts. Thought I might even make it to the majors. Then I busted my leg in a stupid car crash. My left leg was never the same. None of the teams were interested in me after that."

"You must have been very disappointed."

"Oh, yeah. Still think about what might have been. But that was a long time ago. I'd hoped Tony would've had the chance I never had. But someone gave him a few little pills, and—bang! His life is over. And no one's on the hook for it, neither. Burns me up, I can tell you!"

Bob Silva's face was getting redder.

"They never found out how he got the drugs?"

"The police wimped out, if you ask me. I gave 'em my ideas, and the boys on Tony's team told 'em what they knew. Police never followed up. No one was ever arrested. Ike Irons said he was doin' what he could. He knew Tony; even trusted him to baby-sit his own kids, for Christ's sake! And even with that, no one did one day of time for my boy's death. Not one day."

"Tony baby-sat for Chief Irons?"

"A couple of times. That same spring. He and his wife, Annie, like to go out for a nice dinner. They'd put their kids to bed and Tony'd go over and do his homework at their place, so there'd be someone in the house, you know? In case one of the kids woke up. We only lived a couple of houses away. Ike would never have asked him to sit if he hadn't trusted Tony; if he hadn't thought he was a good kid, would he?"

"I wouldn't think so. So you never had any proof of where Tony got the drugs?"

"Not exactly proof. But I had a feeling. A gut thing, you know? There was this guy in town used to hang around when the kids were playing baseball. No one knew him too well. Everyone else was just regular. The same folks been here for years. It couldn't be any of them. So I figured, it was this new guy. What was he in Winslow for, anyway? He didn't seem to have, you know, a purpose to be here."

"So did you talk to him?"

"Oh, yeah. I talked to him. 'Course, he said he had nothing to do with it. Said he had a kid of his own. He wouldn't hurt any kid." Bob shook his head. "I didn't believe him. I'd had a few drinks. I popped him a couple. I probably shouldn't of. But I've been so damn frustrated about this! Wouldn't you be?" Bob Silva's eyes glazed over with tears. "I heard the guy's dead now, so I'll never know if it was him. What if one day your kid came home and just swallowed a handful of heavy-duty pills. Wouldn't you want to know where they came from?"

Maggie reached out and touched his arm. "Yes. I'd want to know, too. Thank you for telling me. I'll get those picture hangers now." She went to the next aisle, leaving Bob Silva a little privacy, and his memories.

Maggie wasn't convinced. Had Bob Silva killed Dan Jeffrey? Jeffrey's death left Silva with too many unanswered questions.

After dinner that night Gussie smiled and announced, "You'll never guess. I've decided to do something for the wedding that Lily suggested."

Jim actually put down the snifter of brandy he'd been savoring. "Did she call again? I thought we had everything worked out about the guests."

"No, this is something else entirely." Gussie looked at them both. "I've been thinking. I know this is Lily's first wedding as a mother of the groom. I'll admit, she's reminded me of it often enough. But maybe I've been underestimating how important that was. So, I've decided to wear the family veil Lily sent. It *is* beautiful."

"Gussie, are you sure?" Jim asked. "I want you to do what's right for you. Not just something for my mother."

She put up her hand to stop him. "I want to. I'll have to fold it, because I don't want it to get caught in the wheels of the scooter. We sent the dress back, but I kept the veil to give to Lily myself so it wouldn't be damaged. Last night I tried it on. And I think it'll work. I can pin it to the top of my hair so it'll be secure. And the soft cream of the old lace will look lovely with my yellow dress. So the veil will be my 'something old,' from your family, and the dress will be 'something new.'" She turned to Maggie. "Do you have something I could borrow?"

Maggie smiled. "You're ahead of me! I was going to give it to you, but if you need it to be borrowed…" She reached into her canvas tote and pulled out a small crimson silk bag and handed it to Gussie.

Jim leaned over. "What is it? I thought I was in charge of jewelry for the big day."

"It's not jewelry," said Maggie.

Gussie opened the bag and emptied it onto the table. "Oh, I don't believe it! You're wonderful, Maggie. And I do want it to be borrowed. Because then you can have it back to use at your wedding someday, too!"

"Okay, ladies. Explain what's so special about that coin," said Jim.

Gussie handed it to him. "The full saying is 'Something old, something new, something borrowed, something blue, and a sixpence for your shoe.' It's a sixpence, Jim. They aren't minted any longer, so in a lot of ways they're antiques. Brides put them in their shoes during the wedding ceremony for good luck."

He looked over the coin and handed it back to Gussie. "That's a new one to me. Won't it be uncomfortable?"

"Usually the bride takes it out of her shoe after the ceremony," Maggie explained. "I thought it would be fun."

"Absolutely," said Gussie. "I'll ask Ellen to bring a pin for the veil, and that will be borrowed. And I guess I'll just have to wear blue panties."

Maggie burst out laughing. "I don't think you're supposed to tell the groom details like that."

"What details? I didn't hear a thing," Jim said, covering his ears dramatically and grinning.

"What are you wearing, Jim?" Maggie asked.

"An elegant dark gray suit, with a white shirt. And it just so happens I have such garments in my wardrobe."

"And," said Gussie, "here's the latest wedding party bulletin. Jim, your mother has found a flower girl. Little Steffie is five, and as it turns out, is the niece of a distant cousin of mine who lives in Connecticut. Lily's talking to Steffie's mother about her dress. Prepare yourselves for flounces galore in a mini size. And that's fine. Actually, I think it'll be fun."

"Does Lily realize the ceremony's not going to be color-coordinated?" asked Maggie.

"She's figured that out. She's a bit shocked, but she's coping. After all, what can you expect from a Yankee wedding?" grinned Gussie.

"True," agreed Maggie. "The country lost all couth when we won The War."

Jim almost choked.

"What flowers are you going to carry?" asked Maggie innocently, anxious to change the subject.

"I wanted to take a page, literally, from the Victorians," said Gussie. "Years ago I found a mid-nineteenth-century book called *The Language and Poetry of Flowers*. I never wanted to sell it. I always knew that flowers, and many trees and fruits, had special meanings then. But it's such fun to look up all the obscure meanings. Did you know the cypress tree meant death and eternal sorrow, for example? Or that the dandelion was an oracle? Or that if someone sent you a daffodil it meant 'deceitful hope'?"

"Well, I'm glad no one has ever sent me a cypress tree!" said Maggie. "And I still love daffodils, although some years they do deceive us about the coming of spring. But what did you decide on for your bouquet?"

"It wasn't as easy as I thought. 'Love Returned'? That's the 'ambrosia flower.' Ever hear of it? Well, we now call it ragweed. Not exactly something you can order at the florist. Or would want in your bridal bouquet. And 'matrimony' is the American linden tree. Again, not exactly right for a bouquet. 'True love' is the Forget-me-not, but those flowers are so fragile they couldn't really be part of a bouquet either."

"Now you really have me curious. What did you come up with?"

"I found a few possibilities, and then I went to Abigail at Floral Fantasies and explained the situation. She loved the whole idea, and is searching nurseries and florists to see what she can find. She's not even going to tell me ahead of time. She considers my bouquet a creative quest. The flowers or plants I suggested were ferns, for sincerity; rue, for reason; everlasting peas, for lasting pleasure; ivy, for fidelity; pinks, for elegance; and chamomile flowers, which look like daisies, for energy in adversity."

"Oh, what fun! So you don't know exactly what your bouquet will look like—or even what colors it will be!" said Maggie. "And by the way, I think I'll lay in a supply of chamomile. I like that 'energy in adversity' idea. And here I always thought chamomile was supposed to relax you."

"I did, too. But I guess not in Victorian times. And no, I won't know exactly what my bouquet will look like until I see it. Abigail has a friend who does calligraphy; she's going to have her friend write down everything that's in the bouquet so I'll have it as a souvenir. Whatever she finds, I'll have a bouquet of good wishes from the past for the future."

Maggie's phone hummed. "Excuse me a minute." She glanced down. "It's a text, from Will," she said. "He wonders whether the storm has made any difference in your plans. Have either of you heard anything about a storm?"

Chapter 24

Professor John David O'Flynn. "Professor John David O'Flynn / Oft played on his dear violin. / Then the people would say: / 'There's a cyclone to-day!' / And to cellars would promptly go in!" Amusing illustration of a wigged gentleman wildly playing his violin; his stool and his music stand are both falling, and his coat-tails are flying. French artist Edmund Dulac (1882–1953) dropped out of law school and studied at the École des Beaux-Arts. In 1904 he left for London, where he and Arthur Rackham became the most popular illustrators of "gift books" of their time, their paintings of wild and wonderful subjects reproduced in the new color separation process and then "tipped in" to illustrate books. This amusing illustration is dated 1906, just before Dulac got his first major contract. Bordered in black. 6 x 8 inches. Price: $60.

"A COUPLE OF days ago Mother mentioned something about a hurricane off the coast of Florida that she hoped wouldn't interfere with her flight to Boston Friday morning," said Jim. "I didn't think much about it."

None of them had been listening to weather forecasts. "Our cable's disconnected at the old house, and not connected yet at the new one," said Gussie. "But that doesn't sound like anything serious. A hurricane off Florida in late October? This is Cape Cod. Not to worry. Jim, Maggie and I moved everything in the store to the new location, and have even started unpacking and setting up. What do you think, Maggie? Another two *full* days," she looked at Maggie meaningfully, "and we'll have enough arranged, and maybe the windows done, and I'll be able to put up the sign saying I'll be open next week."

"That's great," said Jim. "One mission almost accomplished. What about the rest of your stuff?"

"Most of it's ready to go," said Gussie. "A few last-minute things to pack, and there's the furniture."

"How about moving tomorrow? We only have four days left until the wedding. And there's your bachelorette party Friday night," he reminded her. "Maybe you should have a couple of days in the house before then to get a bit settled."

Gussie hesitated. "Maggie and I would need tomorrow morning to pack."

"We'll ask Diana to come and help," Maggie suggested.

"Fine," Gussie agreed. "And after we've finished packing and you and your friends arrive we'll go over to the new house. We'll be there to make sure you guys put the furniture and boxes in the right rooms."

"Plans made, then," said Jim. "I'll call Andy tonight and check about the trucks."

On her way back to Gussie's house from the restaurant Maggie remembered she'd hoped to stop at the Winslow police station the next day to talk with Chief Irons about what was happening with the investigations related to the murder and to the attempted arson. He might not talk to her, but she could try. She'd also thought of having another beer at the Lazy Lobster. She had a feeling the bartender there knew more than he was saying.

Maybe she'd still have time.

But it sounded as if Gussie had her booked for tomorrow. And with Gussie moving to her new house she'd have to move to one of the B and Bs.

Plus, she really should call Will tonight. Maggie took a deep breath. Gussie was right. This weekend she had to tell Will about her adoption plans.

And with him arriving in a matter of hours, she was getting nervous.

She glanced down at her right hand, and her R-E-G-A-R-D ring sparkled back at her. Will was special.

But so much in both their lives was changing. His move from

Buffalo to Maine was still a work in progress. He'd been a longtime widower who hadn't been responsible to anyone but himself. Now he had to think of a woman in her nineties who might need attention twenty-four hours a day.

He'd had made it crystal clear, many times, that he didn't want the responsibilities of parenthood. But without hesitation he'd volunteered to take care of his elderly aunt.

He hadn't asked Maggie how she felt about that, had he?

Maggie shook her head. She was making excuses. She was fond of Aunt Nettie, too, and it had made sense that Will move to Maine to take care of her.

Maggie was thirty-nine. She only had a few years left in which she could be a parent, and not feel as though it would be more logical for her to be a child's grandparent.

If Will had wanted to be a parent, too, that would have been perfect.

But he hadn't. He'd made his choice. Now she'd made hers. She just had to tell him.

The next step would be up to him.

And she had to be prepared for the possibility that her decision would end what otherwise was the most perfect relationship of her life.

Maggie pulled her van into a space in back of Gussie's old house.

"Hey, Gussie!" she called out to her friend, whose van's wheelchair lift had almost reached the ground. "Why don't we open another bottle of that champagne I brought you? Tonight is your last night in this house. That deserves a few toasts."

Chapter 25

Night Sky: September and October. From *Half Hour with the Stars* by Richard A Proctor, 1887. Lithograph showing round dark blue sky with Milky Way and constellations for certain fall dates in the Northern Hemisphere. For October 22, the time is 8:00 P.M. Stars of different magnitudes are shown with different numbers of points. One of a series showing the night sky throughout the year. 9 x 11 inches. Price: $50.

THE NEXT DAY went by in a whirl of activity.

Diana's presence was a big help with the packing. Maggie'd hoped she'd talk a little more about what was happening on Apple Orchard Lane. But today Diana was quiet.

"We're fine," she said. "The medical examiner hasn't released Dad's body yet, so we can't plan a funeral."

And a little later, "Cordelia's back working on her dolls. She's promised customers some special orders, and she says focusing on work keeps her mind off other things. A nice man from the fire department came and cleaned that stuff off the porch. He said it might be paint remover, not gasoline, but whatever it was, he got most of it off, so we're not worried anymore. It still smells a little, but he says it's safe."

She seemed remarkably relaxed, considering all that had taken place in the past week. She and Gussie chatted about the wedding, and the guests, and she oohed and ahhed over Gussie's dress and veil. They were getting along so well that Gussie asked if she'd like to help with preparations Saturday morning before the wedding. "Not too much, you understand. But a few ribbons and plants, and some flowers that the florist is sending. And maybe answer the phone and the door while I'm getting dressed."

Diana nodded her head excitedly, "Oh, yes. Please. I'd love to. Are you going to decorate your house for the wedding, too?"

"No, we're having the reception at one of the inns in town," said Gussie.

"But you have to hang a big white bow on your door!" Diana said. "Everyone does that when they get married. Especially when you have a new house. People from out of town will want to drive by to see it!"

"I hadn't thought of that," Gussie said. "You're right; not many people know where the house is. I like that idea. Let's call Abigail at Floral Fantasies right now and see if she can do a wonderfully large bow for us!"

And off they went.

Maggie repacked her own suitcase; her possible dresses for the wedding were still hanging in her van. Gussie gave her directions to the B and B she'd reserved for "close friends and family," and Maggie decided to check in after she'd made sure Gussie had all her personal things unpacked and accessible this afternoon. Everything might not be arranged exactly where she'd put them eventually, but at least they'd be in the master bedroom. And then everyone could leave her to have some peace.

She deserved some before the wedding.

Maggie was already planning what she might do after she'd checked into the B and B. A little peace for herself might not be bad.

Jim and Andy and two other friends arrived with two pickup trucks at 11:30.

Maggie looked at them dubiously. "You're going to put everything in those trucks? Furniture and boxes and everything?"

"Not to worry," said Jim. "We're only going a couple of miles. And we plan on making a couple of trips. We'll start with the boxes."

Gussie took a final look around the building that had been her home and business for twenty years, blew it a kiss good-bye, and headed for her van. "Let's get out of here, ladies. I don't want to watch what's going to happen now. We'll deal with the results at the other end."

They parked down the street from her new house so the trucks could get close to the door. "Note well," said Gussie, "the advantages to handicapped-accessible homes. Wide doors and ramps make moving a lot easier."

Gussie'd already called a friend who worked at a Winslow deli and who'd promised, as a special favor, that she'd deliver trays of assorted sandwiches, chips, cookies, sodas, and coffee.

The women had time to arrange lunch on the kitchen counter and each eat at least half a sandwich before the men arrived with the first truck to be unloaded.

After that there was little time for anything but organized chaos. Gussie directed the inside operation, telling anyone carrying a carton or piece of furniture what room it went into, and where exactly in that room it should be placed. Jim was in charge of getting the trucks loaded at the old house, and unloaded at the new one, trying to achieve some sort of order, so the pieces of a bed and its mattress arrived in somewhat the same time-frame.

The system worked remarkably well.

Maggie unpacked Gussie's clothes and hung them in her half of the room-wide walk- (or roll-) in closet and filled her drawers while Diana checked all the arriving cartons and made sure they'd been put in the right rooms.

Cartons holding fine china, silver, and extra kitchen accessories went in the extra bedroom, to be sorted later. Boxes of books and seasonal accessories went to the garage. At one point Gussie zoomed down to where Diana was stacking those cartons and directed, "Lights! Hold out any cartons of Christmas lights! I may use them in the shop when I decorate the windows!"

"Will do," answered Diana calmly. She seemed unflappable.

"She's amazing," said Gussie as she stopped to see how Maggie was doing in the master bedroom. "She fits right in, and seems to anticipate what needs to be done."

"You're right," Maggie answered. "I'm almost finished in here. I did leave a little space in the closet for Jim, too."

Gussie touched her arm. "Love you. I couldn't have gotten through all this without your help. And tomorrow we finish the store!"

"I think I'll take off at about four-thirty today, if that's okay. I'll go check in at the B and B and unpack my things. And you need to rest. The closer we get to the wedding, the crazier this week will get."

"You go ahead. We have lots of food left from lunch, so I have plenty for dinner, and Jim had the same idea. He's going to take a plate of sandwiches and plans to collapse at his place. He wants to finish packing his clothes and a few other things tonight so he can move them here tomorrow."

"He's not going to move in officially until the day of the wedding, though, right?"

"No. And since his house hasn't been sold, he's leaving a lot of his furniture there for now. He has a lot more than I did; he has a bigger house. But most of his things are Victorian, and we'll probably sell them, because they don't fit with this house. We're not worrying about that right now."

By four-thirty everything was in the house. It wasn't in perfect order, but Gussie had moved. And was ready for a long nap. The trucks left; Diana left; Jim left; and then Maggie gave Gussie a big hug.

"Your first night in your new home. Three nights to go! If you need me, call."

"I think I'll collapse, thank you. Everything looks beautiful. I'm sorry Jim isn't staying here tonight. But he'll be here soon enough."

"And forever."

They smiled at each other.

Maggie headed toward the B and B, a couple of miles north of town. As she drove she saw windows boarded up on two homes. Funny, she thought. I hadn't noticed those this morning.

And in the center of town plywood boards covered the windows of a gift shop.

The Six Gables Inn, a brown-painted bed and breakfast, was just outside of town. It had an elegant but weathered look, sheltered by tall pines, and located far enough off the main road to have the illusion of country.

Maggie draped her garment bag over her arm and picked up her suitcase. No other cars were parked outside. She must be the only guest tonight. Fine. Quiet sounded good after a long day of toting and carrying.

And trust Gussie to ensure there was a ramp as an alternative to the staircase leading up to the wide porch. Tonight she didn't feel like hoisting her suitcase up stairs.

The inside of Six Gables was elegantly late-colonial. Maggie realized she was truly exhausted when she didn't even care how authentic some of the décor was. She rang the brass Indian elephant bell on the desk.

Mrs. Decker, the owner, appeared almost at once from the door on the left of the entrance hall. "Good afternoon, and welcome to Six Gables. You must be Ms. Summer."

"Yes, I am."

Mrs. Decker smiled at her, with a glint of amusement in her eyes. What did she find so funny? Maggie reached up to pat her hair. Part of it had come undone, and she knew her sweatshirt was smudged with dust. But considering she'd been packing and moving boxes and unpacking all day, she didn't think she looked that strange. "Would you like me to sign in?"

"You can take care of that later. I believe you are who you say you are. I'm glad to see you. Ms. White specified that you were to have the yellow room; it has a king-sized bed. Number one, the first door on your right, at the head of the stairs. Go right up. Here's your key. It opens both the front door and the door to your room. If you have any questions, my room is number nine on the intercom."

"Thank you, Mrs. Decker."

Maggie took the key and started toward the staircase. "Oh, and Mrs. Decker? What time is breakfast?"

"Seven-thirty, dear, unless you specify another time."

She headed up the flight of stairs to the second floor. That was one disadvantage to bed-and-breakfasts. She'd never yet stayed in one where there was an elevator.

She put her key in the door to number one and threw open the door.

A man was in the room.

Chapter 26

"Sabrina fair, Listen where thou art sitting." Tipped in lithograph (from a painting by Arthur Rackham), an illustration for John Milton's *Comus,* written in 1634; this edition published in 1921. Milton's poem about a water nymph was later quoted in a Broadway comedy by Samuel Taylor (1953,) a Billy Wilder movie (1954), and its remake (1995). Here Sabrina is pictured braiding her hair with lilies, under a wave. Rackham was known for his sinuous young women and his fairies, trolls, hidden images, animated trees, and other fantastic creatures painted in muted watercolors. 5 x 7.25 inches. Price: $65.

MAGGIE DROPPED HER BAGS. A dozen thoughts filled her mind. Had she confused the dates? Mrs. Decker downstairs had known! How bad did her hair really look?

And then she didn't think at all as Will pulled her into his arms and she felt safe and warm and as if they'd never been apart.

After a few minutes, she pulled back, stood on her toes to kiss him on his nose, and reached down to pick up the garment bag crumpled at their feet. "I love you, but I want to look decent for Gussie and Jim on Saturday! My dresses for the wedding are in there. Where's the closet, before we get back to more important issues?"

Will threw back his head and laughed. "That's my girl. Even prioritizing her love life. Closet's over there." He pointed at the corner of the large room. Maggie took approving note of the promised king-sized bed, which even had a canopy, and the fireplace, with stacked wood waiting beside it. "This place is like a picture in one of those 'romantic getaway' travel brochures."

"I was thinking of having the fire started when you arrived, but I wasn't sure when that would be, and I thought we might want to save the wood for later tonight," said Will, nuzzling her ear as she managed to hang her garment bag in the closet. "Perhaps after we have a quiet dinner somewhere. And you have some of your favorite sherry."

"Mmmm," said Maggie, sitting on the bed. "You're tempting me. Successfully. When did you get in? And how did you get here? I didn't see your RV in the driveway."

"I didn't bring the RV. I knew I had a room at a wonderful B and B. I borrowed Aunt Nettie's car. It's in back of the building, in case you might have recognized it, or wondered about a car with Maine license plates. I wanted to surprise you."

"Which you did. Although clearly Mrs. Decker knew," said Maggie.

"And Gussie," said Will, joining her on the bed.

"Gussie, too?"

"I wanted to be sure you'd be here tonight." Will kissed her forehead and unfastened the section of her hair that was still pinned up, so it tumbled down her back. "I got the house and Aunt Nettie set for whatever Hurricane Tasha brings, and Tom was able to come a day early after all, so I couldn't wait any longer. Besides, they're talking about closing bridges Thursday, so I might not have been able to get through tomorrow. Wouldn't want to miss the wedding." He started to ease her down onto the pillows, gently combing his fingers through her tousled hair.

"Wait a minute." Maggie popped up. "Hurricane Tasha? You mean there's really a hurricane that close?"

"You really don't have a clue? It's been all over the TV for days. The storm went east of Florida and is traveling up the coast, aimed directly for Cape Cod, the Islands, and Maine."

"But…what does that old mariner's rhyme say? About when hurricanes hit?"

"'June, too soon; July, stand by; August, if you must; September, remember; October, all over.'"

"Right! And this is the end of October. There are jack-o'-lanterns on porches! This is not hurricane season!"

"Well, if you stopped thinking about bridal dresses and wedding cake, you might have noticed that global warming has changed the climate considerably since mariners wrote that rhyme, and most people in the northeast have taken their pumpkins inside in preparation for the storm. The National Weather Service now says hurricane season is from June until November. And Hurricane Tasha appears to be trying her darnedest to be getting in under the deadline."

"Gussie's TV was disconnected and she hasn't got service in her new home yet. Is there a television in this place?"

"Oh, Maggie. A man drives all the way from Maine to the Cape with a hurricane on the way to see the woman he loves, and the first thing she wants to do—"

"I want to listen to the Weather Channel!"

Will shook his head. "The TV's hidden behind the picture over the fireplace. The remote is in the drawer next to the bed. I checked it out before you got here."

Maggie reached over and opened the drawer.

"The white remote moves the painting; then press the power button on the other remote." Will said patiently, the glint of an amused smile on his face. "And, my romantic love, the Weather Channel is number seventeen."

A serious young man was standing at the map. Below him were the scrolling words STAY TUNED FOR HURRICANE TASHA COVERAGE. "…fierce winds, storm surges, and power outages. Tasha continues barreling up the Eastern seacoast, its high winds and heavy rains anticipated to be affecting the New Jersey shore later tonight. Evacuations are underway on Long Island, where it will hit early Thursday morning. As it crosses Long Island Sound it will most likely pick up speed before continuing up the Connecticut shoreline. Thursday night into Friday morning Tasha should be causing heavy tides and rains in Rhode Island and eastern Massachusetts. Tasha is anticipated to cause heavy damage to islands such as Nantucket and Martha's Vineyard, where visitors have already been asked to leave, and Cape Cod, where harbormasters are requiring boats to be put in dry dock by tomorrow morning. In New England there are already shortages of bottled water, flashlights, batteries, plywood, and in vulnerable shoreline communities, sandbags. Stay tuned for the latest coverage, as the Eastern United States hunkers down and waits to see exactly what path Tasha will take. And what destruction she'll leave in her wake."

Will reached over and took the remote out of Maggie's hand. "So. Now you know I didn't invent Tasha."

"I should call Gussie."

"So she can call off the hurricane? Or the wedding?"

Maggie paused. "She won't do that. And the hurricane will have passed by Saturday."

"Some guests may not be able to get here. And if any plans have to be changed, or locations moved…well, that's one reason I came a little early. I figured maybe Jim and Gussie could use an extra pair of hands."

His hands were moving, slowly, surely, over Maggie's body, as she allowed herself to fall back onto the pillows. "I like your hands. They can't have them right now."

"That's good," Will murmured huskily. "Because right now they're busy. Very busy."

Chapter 27

The Sea Serpent. Tipped-in lithograph (from an oil painting) by American artist N.C. Wyeth (1882–1945) for Kenneth Roberts's *Trending Into Maine*, 1938. Wyeth and Roberts both had homes in Maine and were close friends. Old tales say sea serpents were occasionally seen off the coast of Maine, most notably near the Isles of Shoals in 1820 and near Arundel in 1830. The immense serpent illustrated is rising out of the ocean; its head is as high as the sails on the vessel next to it. 5.5 x 7.75 inches. Price: $50.

GUSSIE SMILED WHEN Will and Maggie both showed up at Aunt Augusta's Attic the next morning.

"How's the bride doing?" asked Will, bending down to give Gussie a hug.

"Glad to see you made it here safely," said Gussie. "You're looking well rested this morning, Maggie."

"Why didn't you tell me?" said Maggie, looking from one of them to the other. "Gussie, you didn't even hint you knew Will was driving down a day early."

"Hey, you're not the only one whose telephone is connected to the world," replied Gussie. "Will and I talk once in a while, too. And it was a surprise! Will, before I forget: Jim and I absolutely love the bedwarmer. Not, of course, that we would need such an item."

"Decorative use only, my dear woman, of course," said Will, with a twinkle. "Although if we lose power Friday night..."

"Gussie! Have you heard about the hurricane?" Maggie said.

"Jim called and told me last night. I can't believe we've been so involved we didn't know." She shook her head. "He's going to try to pick up enough plywood today for the shop windows." They all looked at the wide store-front windows she and Maggie'd admired a few days before. "We'll put off decorating them until after the storm. I can do them with Ben's help after you've gone. Why risk having anything damaged? We'll concentrate on the rest of the store today. Will, can you help, too?"

"That's what I'm here for. Do you need anything done at any of your houses before the storm? I can help Jim with the plywood on the shop windows, too."

"The house I just moved out of is fine. There's nothing to move inside, and no large windows to cover. Jim's moving the few pieces of outdoor furniture at his house into his barn this morning. I'm a little worried about our new place, though. It's near the beach, and since it *is* new, we haven't seen it through any storms yet. We don't know where weaknesses might be in the roof or around the foundation. And there are picture windows overlooking the Bay."

"I assume they're the strongest glass you could buy," said Maggie.

"Double-paned and insulated and all of that," agreed Gussie. "It *is* New England, and we live here year 'round. But in a hurricane all bets are off. I'm thinking we should cover them before the storm."

"I haven't seen your house, but if it's that close to the Bay, that sounds like a good idea. The last I heard Tasha was a Category Three, with winds over a hundred and ten miles per hour," said Will. "Of course, she could weaken before she gets to the Cape. And you're on the northern side of the Cape, not the southern. The damage should be worse there."

"When Hurricane Carol hit the Cape in 1953 the storm surge on the south drove salt water inland as far as Route 6. Hundreds of homes were flooded, and thousands of trees were killed. I remember seeing all the dead, white trees, on the Cape when I was a little girl. My father used to call them ghost trees, and talk about how frightening the storm had been. A lot of old-timers still remember. The spire of the Old North Church in Boston was blown down in Hurricane Carol, too. We don't get many bad hurricanes hitting up this far. It's like Maine. But once in a while we get surprised. And I don't want to take a chance with our new home." She picked up her phone. "I'll make sure Jim gets enough plywood for those windows."

While she was talking with Jim, Maggie and Will moved empty cartons from the front room into the back and folded them.

"Look around, Will. This room is going to be the new Shadows Antique Print Gallery," Maggie said, proudly.

"What?"

"Gussie's offered it to me for my prints," she explained. "I've already measured it. I'm going to hang framed prints on the walls, and put three or four of those folding stands I have for large prints on the floor over here, below the windows." She showed him. "I'll bring four of my show tables up for the center of the room, and put stands on them for smaller groups of prints." She turned to look at him. "What do you think?"

"I think it's great you'll have a place to sell your prints that's closer to Maine," he said. "If it works, maybe it'll mean you won't have to do as many shows. And you'll have to come to the Cape to replenish and change your inventory. This would be a great place for us to meet, too." He smiled and gave her a hug. "I can think of a number of reasons why your having your prints in Winslow is a good idea."

Maggie's phone rang. "Excuse me!" she said, untwining herself from Will's arms. "Yes, Diana? No! No." Maggie's face paled. "Of course. I'll be right there."

"What is it?" Will asked, as Maggie almost ran back to the front room, pulling him with her.

"Gussie, it's awful. You won't believe it. Diana just called." She took a deep breath. "Cordelia's been shot. She's dead."

Gussie stopped arranging toys and stared at her. "When? What happened? Oh, Maggie, I can't believe it! Who would hurt Cordelia?"

"Who's Cordelia?" said Will, looking from one of the women to the other.

"Diana slept in this morning. When she came downstairs she didn't see Cordelia in the house. She thought she'd gone for a walk. When Cordelia still hadn't come home after she'd had breakfast Diana decided to see if she was on the beach. That's where she found her."

"Like Dan."

"I don't think she'd been in the water. She didn't say that. She just said she was on the beach."

"She's called Ike?" Gussie checked.

"He's already there. I told her I'd come, too."

"Go, then. My scooter's no use on the sand, and Jim expects me to be here. You and Will go. She needs someone with her." Gussie shook her head. "I can't believe it. Why? I still can't imagine a possible reason."

Will held up his keys. "I assume we're going somewhere?"

"I'll explain along the way," said Maggie. "I haven't told you everything that's been happening in Winslow."

Will sighed as he followed her out the door. "My dear lady, when do you ever?"

Chapter 28

Medical Plants. One of a series of illustrations of plants grown for medicinal use, from *The Practical Home Physician*, 1883. This page illustrates Dill (to increase breast milk and cure colic), Peppermint (for intestinal gas), Spurge-Laurel (a poison), and Black Bryony (for constipation). 6 x 9 inches. $35.

MAGGIE AND WILL had to park several houses down Apple Orchard Lane. The driveway and street were filled by two police cars, an ambulance, and a van marked CRIME SCENE UNIT.

Not to speak of several neighbors, whose cars (and one bicycle) were driving slowly through the area, and one WBZ–TV Boston van that must have been in the area, since it had reached the scene so quickly.

Maggie and Will tried to avoid them all.

The first barrier they ran into was a patrolman Maggie hadn't seen before. "Sorry, folks. This is a crime scene. No one's admitted. No sightseers. Go home. Or at least stay on the street."

"I'm Maggie Summer. Diana Hopkins called me. I'm a close friend of the family. That poor girl has no one!" Maggie chattered. "Chief Irons knows who I am."

The cop hesitated and pulled out his phone. "Chief, woman name of Maggie Summer is out front. Says Ms Hopkins called her. What do you want me to do with her?" Pause. "Okay." He turned to Maggie. "You stay here. The chief's going to send someone out for you. He says the Hopkins girl's really upset; maybe your being here will calm her down." He looked at Will. "I don't know about you, sir."

"He's with me," said Maggie.

The patrolman shrugged.

A few minutes later another policeman came out of the house and beckoned to Maggie. She took Will's hand, and pulled him with her.

"Who's this?" asked the policeman.

"My friend Will," said Maggie. "I'm sure the chief will say it's all right."

The patrolman didn't look convinced, but let the two of them follow him.

Diana was standing at the side of the house, out of view of the street. Her face was pale, and she was clasping a glass of water as though she would never let it go.

She looked up as Maggie came around the corner. "Maggie!"

With that word the tears she'd been holding back began flowing. Maggie reached out and took the glass from her shaking hands and handed it to Will. "I'm so sorry, Diana."

She put her arm around the girl and let her sob.

Finally Diana stood back. She looked questioningly at Will.

"This is my friend from Maine, Will Brewer."

"Right. Your guy. I remember. I just didn't want him to be a plain-clothes cop or something," Diana said. "Maggie, you've got to help me. The police won't let me into the house. They keep saying it's a crime scene. I called 911 and you, but now they've even taken my cell phone away." She began to sob again.

Maggie dug in her bag and handed the girl some Kleenex.

Diana blew her nose. "It's all horrible. I don't know what to do. I should never have come here. I should have stayed in Colorado."

"This isn't your fault," said Maggie, hoping she was telling the truth. Could Diana's arrival have triggered events that ended with the deaths of two people? But how?

"Even if it had nothing to do with me, I wouldn't have known about it. I was beginning to cope with Dad's death. I'd almost finished getting the estate settled. I thought I'd take a break. Take a vacation. See the country a little. And instead…" Diana started sobbing again.

Will was looking down the slight hill at the scrub pines and grasses that were above the beach where, Maggie assumed, Cordelia's body was. Several uniformed police officers were walking around, looking at the ground. Looking for evidence, Maggie assumed. Of what? Of whom? So far she hadn't seen Ike Irons, but he must be here, too. These must be state police. Ike had said he had a small staff, and the place was full of cops.

"What happened, Diana?" said Maggie. "What did you tell the police?"

"What I said on the phone," she said. "I got up, and went down to get coffee. Cordelia wasn't there. I checked and she wasn't in her room, so I assumed she'd gone for a walk on the beach. She likes to do that in the morning. So I drank my coffee and decided to join her. Have you ever been in back of our house?"

Maggie shook her head.

"There's the yard, just below the porch, where there are a few bushes, but not too many, because the land is pretty sandy." Diana pointed. "Cordelia has a small herb garden there in a sort of deep box. This time of year there's nothing left except some mint and parsley and dill. Beyond that there's a narrow stone path that leads to the beach. I found her near the end of the path, in the beach grass." Diana's tears were still flowing, but she wasn't sobbing. "It was awful. She was just lying there. I knew she was dead, right away."

"Did she have any wounds?"

"There was blood. She was lying on her face. I think she'd been shot in the back of her head. There was a...hole."

"The back!"

"It looked as though she'd been coming back toward the house, from the beach, and someone'd shot her. She fell so one of her feet was on the path and the rest of her was in the grass." Diana was silent. "It was so peaceful down on the beach. I stood there for a moment, right over her. I could see the water, and the beach. The gulls were crying, that mournful way they do, and the waves were coming in. I felt like I was in a movie; as though if I backed up and went back to the house and started the morning again it would all be different."

Maggie put her hand out on Diana's arm. "But it wasn't."

"No. It wasn't. All I want is to be away from this place. Horrible things happen here, Maggie."

Maggie was trying to think of something suitably comforting to say when Jim came striding purposefully down the hill in their direction.

"Diana, I'm so sorry. Gussie called to tell me," he said, nodding at Maggie and Will, but focusing on Diana. "Have you talked to the police?"

"I showed them where I found Cordelia's body. That's all. I can't even get my backpack or clothes or telephone," said Diana, clearly ready to begin sobbing again. "Tell them I *need* my backpack!"

"Remember: I'm your lawyer. I'll take over from here. Don't talk to any of the police from now on. Let me do that," Jim said firmly. "I'll see what I can do about your backpack."

"Good morning, Jim," said Ike Irons, joining them. "We seem to be running into each other a lot this week."

"I heard my client was having a difficult morning and came to join her," said Jim. "I understand you have some personal things she'll need."

"We'll need to keep this whole property clear for our investigation," said the chief. "I was about to ask Ms. Summer and that friend of hers," he gestured toward Will, who was being ushered up the hill toward the road by another policeman, "to leave. I'd like to talk to Miss Hopkins. Since she was the person closest to the deceased, and she found the body, she's a person of interest. I have some questions for her."

"Which she won't be answering right now, when she's in such distress, and won't be answering at all unless I'm with her," answered Jim. "In fact, Ms. Hopkins and I were about to leave. When you need to speak with her, you know how to contact me, and I'll make sure she's available. We realize you need to make the house and grounds a crime scene for now, but that means she can't have access to her personal belongings. Could she take her backpack and telephone with her, Ike? With the storm coming, I'd guess you want to get this crime scene, especially the grounds, wrapped up as soon as possible. I'll guarantee Ms. Hopkins won't be leaving town in the next couple of days."

"I can't let her have any of her belongings, Jim. And those

guarantees better be good." Ike said, turning toward Diana. "We've already searched Ms. Hopkins' backpack. We found her gun."

Both Jim and Maggie turned and looked at Diana.

"That's my property! It was for protection! Cordelia gave it to me after Dad was killed," said Diana. "You have no right to go through my things."

"Ah, but we do, you see. The crime lab will know whether the gun was fired recently, and whether it was the one that killed your cousin. Or your father. And you need a license to carry a handgun in Massachusetts. We could hold you right now, before we get the results of any tests back."

"I didn't do anything!" Diana wailed. "Why would I shoot Cordelia?"

"That's one of the things we have to figure out," said Ike.

"Am I being arrested?" said Diana.

"Shush," said Jim. "Don't say anything more."

"No, you're not being arrested. Not yet," said Ike. "But I want to talk with you later. Jim, I'm holding you responsible for keeping an eye on her in the meantime." He looked back at Diana. "Don't think of leaving. You can't get far in any case. Last I heard the governor had closed the bridges and directed the island ferries to schedule their last runs before the storm. Anyone who's on the Cape now is going to be here when Hurricane Tasha arrives."

Ike walked down toward the beach.

"Why in hell didn't you tell me you had a gun?" said Jim to Diana. "Come with me. You and I have to talk. Fast. Before the chief wants to see you."

Diana glanced back at Maggie, and then followed Jim up the hill to his car.

Chapter 29

"My Little Daughter Must Go To Bed." Victorian lithograph from about 1880. Two little girls in their nightgowns, one sitting in a cane-seated rocker and one standing by a window, both holding their baby dolls also wearing night attire, preparing to put their babies to sleep in a dolls' wooden cradle. Classic sentimental print of period. No illustrator or publisher identified. 7 x 9 inches. Price: $55.

WILL WAS STANDING on the road, waiting for Maggie.

"What's happening?" he asked, after taking one look at her face. "I saw your friend Diana go off with Jim. I have some catching up to do but I think I'm getting the picture. Diana thought her father was dead, but she found him here in Winslow, alive and using another name."

Maggie nodded, and got into the passenger side of the car. "And only a few days after she arrived he was killed. She was staying here with her cousin Cordelia while the police looked for her father's killer. Now someone's murdered Cordelia."

"The poor kid," Will said. "And knowing my Maggie, you've been in the middle of it all since you've arrived."

"I was the one who found her father's body." Maggie admitted.

"What is it about you?" said Will, reaching out and fondly stroking her hair. "You may not believe this, Maggie, but until I met you I'd never known anyone actually involved with a murder. And then the very evening we met…"

"I know. A friend of ours was killed. Just remember: I didn't commit the crime. I solved it."

"My very dear lady. If you'd been the killer, do you think I'd still be hanging around?" Will grinned. "But you do seem to have this…

magnetic quality that draws in people in dire circumstances. It's a bit exhausting for those of us who enjoy your company, you know. Never knowing when you might have to rush off to solve a murder or soothe someone's brow who's been accused of a dastardly crime."

Maggie burst out laughing. "I'm not Nancy Drew, you horrible man! And I seem to remember a number of times we've been together that have had absolutely nothing to do with murders or crimes." She looked at him flirtatiously. "Although there may, indeed, have been a bit of that brow-soothing involved even then, now that I think about it."

"In any case, I assume Jim has taken over the Diana situation for the moment."

"For the moment, yes. But she's in far worse trouble that we thought," Maggie said. "Not only are her father and cousin dead. Murdered. But it seems she had a gun in her backpack. Now she's the number-one suspect."

"She hasn't been arrested," Will pointed out, as he headed the car back toward downtown Winslow. "Or she wouldn't have left with Jim."

"No, thank goodness. They need to check her gun, and I'm assuming it will come back clean," Maggie agreed. "I can't think of a motive she'd have for either killing."

"We can't do anything to help her right now," he pointed out. "But clearly Jim's going to be involved for at least the morning. Diana's his client?"

Maggie nodded.

"So let's take over what he was going to do for Gussie and storm-proof her shop and house."

Will made it all sound so simple and logical. "You're right. That's what we should do," she agreed.

"Give Gussie a call and find out whether Jim had time to pick up the plywood for the windows. If not, we'll stop and do that on our way," Will directed.

Maggie smiled. Will knew kitchen and fireplace supplies and tools. He was most comfortable when he was fixing things. And right now she could use someone who could make life work.

She called. Then she turned to Will. "Gussie says Jim ordered the plywood but didn't have time to pick it up. He went straight to Cordelia's house. She'd appreciate our getting it."

"Do you know where?"

"I do. I was at the hardware store the other day, getting some things for the store. Just keep going straight for another mile here," Maggie directed. And this would give her another opportunity to talk with Bob Silva.

"Good to see you again, Maggie," said Silva, as she explained their errand. "We put Jim's plywood aside for him out back." He handed Will an invoice. "Drive to the back of the parking lot and the guys there will tie the wood on top of your car. I'll put it on Jim's bill."

The table that had been full of flashlights and batteries the other day was now empty, Maggie noted. Only a few candles were left, and some bags of sand.

"Have any bottles of water?" a bearded man yelled in the front door.

"None left!" Silva shouted back. "Try the pharmacy if the grocery's out."

"Jim's sorry he couldn't come himself," said Maggie. "But with another murder, and all, it's a busy time."

"Another murder?" Bob Silva's head shot up immediately. Unless he was a really good actor, that was news he hadn't heard. "In Winslow? What happened?"

"Cordelia West. Her body was found on the beach near her home this morning," Maggie said.

Silva looked shocked. "Why would anyone kill her?"

"I heard she didn't have a lot of friends in town."

"Maybe not close friends. She wasn't like those women who spend their lives gossiping in restaurants and trooping over to the shopping malls in Hyannis. She kept to herself, 'cause most folks couldn't talk to her. And she made those weird dolls of hers. She brought them to the church fair a couple of times. But people liked her all right. She always smiled at folks when she went for walks around town, or on the beach. I never heard a bad thing about her, except folks worried she was alone too much. She used to stand by herself, watching the kids play. When Dan came to live with her, people said maybe she wouldn't be so lonely anymore. He took her out to places, sometimes." Silva shook his head. "Sad. Now that's really sad news. Who would want to kill a nice lady like Cordelia West?"

"I guess that's what Chief Irons will be trying to figure out," said Maggie.

"With this storm coming on, everyone's going a little crazy anyway," said Silva. "This time of year we're usually selling candles for jack-o'-lanterns and salt for the first snow storms. This year it's flashlights and batteries and plywood. And two folks murdered in as many weeks. I ain't saying anything about Dan Jeffrey. Mebbe he deserved it. There are those who think he did, and mebbe I'm one. But there's no one who'd think the same of Cordelia West. Bad times for sure."

"Three's a charm, Bob, if you count your own boy. Maybe this is the end," said a man standing patiently at the end of the counter, holding a box of nails in his hand. "Maybe this is the end."

"It's the end all right," said Silva. "I just don't know what of. And I don't like it. No, sir. It's not good, for sure. Folks around Winslow better start locking their doors. If Cordelia West could be murdered, than none of us are safe."

Chapter 30

WORKING TOGETHER, Will and Maggie had no problem covering the windows at Aunt Augusta's Attic with the plywood. "The shop may look dreary now, but at least it's safe, no matter how high the winds are," said Maggie.

"Thank goodness you're both here to help," agreed Gussie. "Shuttering the store was certainly not what I had in mind when I asked you to come to the Cape early, Maggie. But the woman who owns the children's clothing shop next door has someone coming this afternoon to board up her windows, too."

"The Cape's going to be on lockdown by tomorrow afternoon," said Will. "Sounds a bit paranoid if you ask me. Has the governor called out the National Guard yet?"

"Actually, he has," Gussie said. "Or at least put them on stand-by. He's not taking this storm lightly."

"I guess after Katrina no one laughs at hurricanes," added Maggie.

"But this is the Cape. And it's almost November!" said Gussie. "Can you guess who's most upset?"

Maggie didn't have to think long. "Jim's mother. Lily had reservations to fly in tonight, didn't she?"

"She did, but her flight was cancelled. She's been trying to get an earlier flight, but airports all up and down the coast are a mess. Jim's been in touch with her, on top of everything else he's dealing with."

"If the Cape's closed off, that means some of the guests who were going to drive or fly in won't be able to make it," Maggie said.

Gussie nodded. "While you were outside putting the plywood up I had calls from three people off-Cape in other parts of Massachusetts, and one person in Connecticut. Everyone's worried. But there's not much anyone can do right now."

"The storm's due Friday night, right?" said Will. "Assuming roads are passable, people driving should be able to get here Saturday afternoon. Flying will be the problem. Airports down south have been closing all week. A lot of flights have been delayed or cancelled, and there won't be any flights into Boston Friday afternoon or night for sure. Schedules are going to be crazy."

"If I were planning to fly here from Atlanta on Friday I'd be tempted to cancel now," said Maggie. "I'll bet rental cars will all be spoken for, too. Not to speak of hotel rooms."

"At least anyone who can get to Winslow has rooms booked already," said Gussie. "We can't do anything about the storm except prepare for it and ride it out. And be glad it'll be over by Saturday." She paused. "I keep thinking of poor Cordelia. And Diana. Compared to murder, a storm and a few people missing a wedding, even if it is my wedding, are minor problems. Although I do hope Jim's mother gets here. Despite all my complaints about her, she should be here."

"Gussie, you're a real trooper. I keep wondering what Jim and Diana are talking about, too," said Maggie. "But right now we should get to your house and cover the windows there."

The sun was shining and Hurricane Tasha seemed a far distant event as Will and Maggie managed to stabilize the sheets of plywood over the large picture windows. "This is a lot harder than the shop windows," Maggie said as, her arms aching, she tried to hold the bottom of a board up as Will stood on a ladder and nailed the top of it above the windows.

"Sure is," he admitted. "Remind me never to admire homes set this close to the ocean."

"And this is just the Bay," Maggie added, under her breath. "Think of what's going on with buildings on the southern side of the Cape."

"And in places in Maine like Old Orchard Beach, where storm surges usually go ashore," Will added, hitting another nail forcibly into the plywood. "Let's hope all this preparation isn't necessary. I noticed a lot of trees on the way here with branches all too close to electric wires."

Power outages. Flooding. Maggie suddenly thought of her home in New Jersey.

She lived closer to Pennsylvania than she did to the Atlantic Ocean, but if there were a bad storm, strong winds could take down trees. She hoped none of the tall maples or oaks in her yard would go down on her house. She went through a mental checklist. She hadn't left anything outside that could be blown around dangerously. Her neighbors Jerome and Ian were looking after her cat, and they had her phone number. They'd call if there were any problems.

Maggie was about ready to call a time-out when Jim appeared around the corner of the house.

"You guys are the best! Time for a break, though. I've brought reinforcements."

"Can't say I mind that," Will said, slamming in one more nail, and climbing down the ladder, leaving the piece of plywood they were working on swaying precariously.

Two other men joined Jim. "This is Andy, my legal partner and best man, and his brother, Mel. Meet Will Brewer from Maine, and Maggie Summer, maid of honor. And today, my two other right hands."

"Nice to meet you," said Will, shaking hands.

"We did a little boarding up at the office. Then Andy and Mel allowed me to volunteer them to help finish up here."

"You bribed us," said Andy. "Don't forget, Jim. You owe us!"

"I do, indeed. Beer for all, once we're finished here."

"Where's Diana?" Maggie asked. "And have you heard from your mother?"

"Diana's with Gussie, in the house," said Jim, "and Mother's airborne, on her way to Providence. She found a series of connections that will get her in after midnight tonight, and by some miracle, got a hotel room there. Why don't you and Will go ahead inside? Gussie'll fill you in on the details. C'mon, guys. These two already have the job half-done. Maybe I only owe you half as much beer. Especially if it takes us twice as long to get the job done."

Maggie and Will stretched and walked around the house, glad to be excused the rest of the task. The house was built higher than the dunes, and although the windows were on the first floor, covering them was not an easy job.

Gussie was making tea and Diana was pacing, looking out at the men setting the ladders up, when they got inside.

"Tea, Will? Cola?" Gussie asked.

"Do you have any brandy? Hot tea with brandy would go down really well right now," he said, rubbing his hands together to warm them.

"You've got it," Gussie said, as she moved quickly around her kitchen, clearly proud to be able to find everything exactly where it should be. "In fact, that sounds good to me, too. What about you, Diana? You're twenty-one."

"No, thanks. Plain tea for me, please. Jim said I'd better stay absolutely sober and rested in case Chief Irons decides he wants to ask me more questions." Her eyes were still swollen, and her voice was strained.

"You've been to the police station?" Maggie asked, sitting down on a couch from Gussie's former home that had now found a place near the fireplace.

"Yes. But Jim wouldn't let me answer any questions. It was frustrating. I don't have anything to hide! I had to sit there and keep my mouth closed."

"What did Chief Irons ask you about?"

"Everything. Whether Dad and I had gotten along well, and when I'd found out he was still alive, and about the case my dad was supposed to testify about in Colorado. Why I'd come to Winslow, and how long I'd known Cordelia. Why she'd given me a gun."

"Did Cordelia have a gun herself?"

Diana nodded. "I saw them in her room. She told me every woman living alone should have a gun."

Maggie frowned. "Them? How many guns did she have?"

"I didn't see exactly how many. They were under her bed, where she kept her doll supplies." Diana looked embarrassed. "I shouldn't have been in there. I knew she didn't like her things disturbed. But I was curious. So one day when I knew she was out walking I went in and looked. She caught me. She was really angry."

"And you asked her about the guns."

Diana nodded. "I pointed at them and raised my shoulders, the way you do when you're confused."

"What did she do?"

"She took me by the arm and dragged me out of there and slammed the door. Then, later, she wrote me a note on her computer. She did that when she wanted to be sure I understood something. She said she had lived alone a long time and sometimes she got scared. She had the guns for protection. I told her I understood. Then a couple of days ago she told me she'd thought about it, and I should have a gun for protection, too. She gave me that little gun and told me to keep it with me, in my bedroom, and in my backpack. She showed me how it worked, and had me fire it a couple of times, out into the ocean when no one was around, so I'd know what it felt like. That's all."

Her fingerprints would be on the gun, and it had been fired recently, Maggie thought. But was it the same kind of gun that killed Cordelia?

"Did Cordelia ever say why you should be afraid?"

Diana shook her head. "She said life was unpredictable and unfair, and women had to take care of themselves."

"Did you tell Jim all that?" said Maggie.

"Most of it," said Diana. "But he didn't want me to tell the police.

He said we should wait and see what the forensic test results said first."

"Then that's what you should do," said Maggie. "Can you think of anyone who would be angry with Cordelia?"

Diana shook her head. "She didn't talk with many people. I mean, you know, see many people. She did business on eBay. She was frustrated sometimes that she couldn't make herself understood."

"Did she have any special friends in town that you knew of?"

Diana shook her head slowly. "People came after Dad died, like you and Gussie did. They brought food, or flowers. Before that, Chief Irons's wife came over once. I'd been out on the beach. I came back and found her upstairs in Dad's room. She said she was looking for Cordelia, and came in because she knew Cordelia couldn't hear her knocking. I thought that was weird because everyone who visits knows about the light system. Anyway, she left as soon as I got there. She didn't wait for Cordelia."

"Did you tell Cordelia she'd been there?"

Diana nodded. "Cordelia was really mad. She said we had to remember to lock the doors when we went out so no animals would get in." Diana smiled. "I remember because I thought that was funny. And Rocky Costa, the man who works at the Lazy Lobster, he called Cordelia sometimes. She got text messages a couple of times, but she grabbed her phone fast and gave me one of her looks. Like I shouldn't touch it. But I saw the messages were from him. Once I saw him out on the beach with her. He was signing, like you do. But I don't remember anyone else. People left food or flowers. They didn't stay. I think they felt uncomfortable because Cordelia couldn't hear them."

"You may be right," said Maggie. "Do you think Mrs. Irons was looking for something in your dad's room?"

"There wasn't anything to find. I looked through everything when he didn't come home. I kept thinking I'd find a clue to where he'd gone. Or why he'd left. But there were just clothes. It was as though he used his room like a hotel room." Diana looked up. "I kind of hoped he'd kept a picture of me, or my mother. Something to remember his old life. But there was nothing. So if Mrs. Irons was looking for something, I don't know what it was."

Or, thought Maggie, whatever it was had already disappeared.

"Time for those beers you owe us, Jim!" Andy and the others came in, flexing their muscles. "You're safe from the storm now, Gussie, and this man of yours promised us beer as a reward."

"It's in the refrigerator, right over there." Gussie pointed. "Help yourselves. There are chips on the counter. Sorry we're not equipped to offer you more sustenance right now. Another week or so and we'll be totally organized."

"That's my optimistic bride," said Jim, giving her a kiss. "One week until we have all our cartons unpacked, the kitchen cabinets full, and life totally organized? Nice thought, my love. You hang on to that."

Gussie asked him quietly, "Is Ike going to let Diana go back to her house tonight?"

Jim shook his head. "It's a crime scene, and going to be that way for a while, I suspect, with storm preparation taking up police resources. I think he was tempted to find some reason to arrest her—at minimum, she didn't have a license to carry the gun she had—but I convinced him I'd keep an eye on her."

"Which means?" Gussie arched her eyebrows.

"Is it okay if she stays here tonight? I'd have to stay, too. It wouldn't look good if only she and I stayed at my house, and I don't feel comfortable with a murder suspect, even one we believe is innocent, staying here alone with you. Plus, I promised to keep her close."

Gussie looked at him.

"I know, I know. This isn't what we planned."

Gussie nodded. "But she's alone, and she needs us. Understood. It's all right. She's welcome. But there's nothing set up in the guest bedroom right now. You get the guys to put the bed together. I'll take care of the rest."

Jim reached down and squeezed her shoulder. "Love you. Forty-eight hours to go before we prove it to the world."

"And, Jim. One more thing. I don't care where she is tonight. But promise me she's gone before our wedding night," Gussie said.

"Promise," said Jim. "Don't you worry about that!"

"Diana," said Gussie, calling her over. "Jim says you can't go back to your house tonight. We'd love to have you stay here with us, in our guest room."

"But you've got so much to do for the wedding. And that room isn't set up," said Diana.

"A mere detail," said Jim. "It won't take long to set up a bed."

"You and Maggie packed the sheets and blankets. See if you can dig some out of the cartons; they have to be unpacked some time anyway. That room has its own bathroom, so you'll have some privacy," Gussie pointed out.

"Thank you," said Diana. "I'd much rather stay here than go back to that house by myself anyway. At least tonight."

"Then that's settled," said Jim. "Don't drink too much of that beer, guys. We have one more chore to take care of. Diana here needs a bed put together."

"I'll find you a T-shirt and sweats to sleep in," said Gussie. "Come on, Maggie. Let's get Diana organized before we all collapse after this day. Tomorrow night is the bachelorette party, you know!"

"Is that still on?" Maggie asked.

"Oh, yes." Gussie rolled her eyes. "Did I forget to tell you? This morning Sheila called to say she'd put everything she needed in her car and was heading for the Cape today so she'd be sure to get here before they closed the bridges. She was actually very excited that the party might take place at the same time as the hurricane hit. She said that would 'heighten the atmosphere.'"

"Not sure that's what you want during a hurricane," said Maggie, "but…okay."

"You're having a bachelorette party tomorrow night?" said Diana. "During the storm? What fun!"

"You come too," said Gussie. "Why not? I suspect not everyone who's invited will make it, and you've been a big part of this last week. You should be here for the whole celebration."

"I'd love to be there!" said Diana. "You've all been so wonderful to me! I feel as though you've adopted me in the past week."

Adopted her? Maggie felt her cheeks redden as Gussie glanced at her with raised eyebrows. That was an interesting word for Diana to use. With everything else going on, she'd done a good job of repressing how to broach the whole subject of adoption with Will.

But it was still out there. He might not know it, but Hurricane Tasha wasn't the only storm ahead.

No wonder she was focused on finding a murderer. Murders were simple compared with relationships.

Chapter 31

South Boston Horse Railroad Depot, Summer Street. A wood engraving by Alfred Waud, 1859, showing a church in the background and an elegantly dressed couple waiting as three horse-drawn "railroad cars" meet at the depot. The cars resemble trolleys, their metal wheels fitting on tracks in the road, but each pulled by two horses. This horse railroad and another between Boston and Cambridge opened in 1856, replacing the omnibus (stagecoach) providing transportation before then, "proof of the progressive spirit of the day." South Boston, sometimes referred to as "Southie" by those who've lived there, was for many years the center of Boston's Irish community. 7 x 10 inches. Price: $60.

TWO HOURS LATER Maggie and Gussie were alone. Andy and Mel had gone home, and Will, Jim, and Diana had gone in search of pizza for dinner.

"Not bad," Gussie said, surveying the house. "The plywood covering the windows kills the view, but in the past couple of hours with everyone's help we've gotten another room set up."

"Gussie, before the others get back with the pizza. Do you know Ike Irons's wife well?"

"Annie Irons. Not well. Why? She comes into my store once in a while to buy mechanical banks for her sister's husband. He collects them. She seems nice enough, but I doubt she has twenty cartons of books in her garage like we do, if you know what I mean."

"I remember you said she and Ike weren't from here."

Gussie shook her head. "They're Massachusetts people, but not from Winslow. I think maybe Annie's from South Boston." She looked inquiringly at Maggie. "Why all the questions?"

"Just wondering. She must have been a friend of Cordelia's.

Diana said she'd been there a couple of times. I wondered about the connection."

Gussie shrugged. "Maybe she liked the dolls? I have no idea. I still can't believe Cordelia's dead."

"What possible motive could anyone have?" mused Maggie.

"That's one problem for Diana," Gussie said. "Jim told me something Ike probably doesn't know yet. I don't even know if Diana knows. But if she does, it gives her a motive."

"What?" asked Maggie.

"Right after Dan Jeffrey's body was found Cordelia went to Jim and had him draw up her will. I don't know if she'd had one before. But her new will leaves everything, including of course, her home, to Diana."

"Why would she do that? She'd only known Diana a week or so."

Gussie shook her head. "Maybe she liked her. Maybe Diana was her only relative. I have no idea."

"But you're right. If Diana knew she was Cordelia's heir, that would give her a motive. You told me that house is worth a small fortune."

"So let's hope Ike finds someone with a better motive, and a gun that matches the bullet Cordelia was shot with. Otherwise our young friend could be in a lot more trouble than she imagines."

Maggie sat for a moment. "But even if—and it's a big 'if'—Diana shot Cordelia, what about her father? I can't see that she would have shot him. She'd have no reason to do that."

Gussie sighed. "I was thinking about that the other night. Her father faked his own death. She inherited the money from his life insurance and property. If the insurance company discovered he was still alive her father would be charged with fraud, and have to pay back everything Diana inherited after his 'death.' Plus, he'd probably do prison time."

"I don't know how much insurance there was, but I'm sure she doesn't have much money now. She told me she put their house in Colorado on the market to help pay bills and tuition. Would she be liable for the money she inherited when she thought her father was dead?"

Gussie shook her head. "I don't know. But I'll bet the courts would take back anything she hadn't spent. It would be a mess, no matter what, and there'd be a nasty court case. She'd have lost her dad again, for sure. This time to prison."

"You're saying it would be simpler for Diana if he'd stayed dead," said Maggie.

"It's a horrible thought. But it made me wonder...."

The door opened, and pungent odors of tomato and sausage filled the room.

Maggie watched as Diana laughed and picked the anchovies off her pizza, and they joked about changing the wedding reception menu to include spumoni and tortoni.

Diana couldn't be a killer. Could she?

Chapter 32

C. Brandauer and Co.'s Circular-Pointed Pens. Wonderful wood-engraved full-page advertisement from the September 25, 1886 edition of *The Illustrated London News*. An elegantly dressed woman wearing an engagement ring sits at her desk with her pen and open inkwell, writing a love letter. She's assisted by three winged cherubs; one whispering in her ear, one guiding her pen, and one examining the pen points in a box on her desk. Above her, in the clouds of her dreams, three more cherubs paint a large C. Brandauer & Co. Circular Point. In very small type in the margin below the engraving are the words, "The course of a true love letter runs smoothest when written with one of C. Brandauer and Co.'s Circular-pointed Pens. These pens neither scratch nor spurt, the points being rounded by a new process." Page size, 11 x 16 inches. Price: $60.

"WHAT'S ON THE agenda this morning?" Will asked, bending down to nibble Maggie's ear as she attempted to pin her hair up. "The day before the wedding of the century there must be bridal errands to take care of."

"You mean, aside from the hurricane bearing down on the Cape and the bachelorette party I have to attend tonight?" Maggie asked. "I hear Jim's friends have some sort of fun evening in mind for him, too, and you, as the special out-of-town guest of the maid of honor, are included in that gathering."

"Jim told me, last night. I've been to a couple of those fun events in my jaded lifetime. They usually involve beer, shots, and an occasional stripper. I'd rather spend the evening with you."

Maggie sighed. "I wouldn't count on the stripper. Although you never know. I'm not too thrilled with my evening plans, either.

Especially in the middle of a hurricane. Seems to me storm parties should be spent cozily indoors, behind battened-down hatches, preferably with company of one's choice." She turned and kissed her favorite freckle at the base of Will's neck. "And perhaps a bottle of wine and some pâté or cheese."

"A cheeseburger would be fine by me," Will answered. "Although something that doesn't require cooking would probably be a more intelligent choice, since I suspect we'll lose power somewhere along the line." He switched on the television set.

"Hurricane Tasha is currently passing over the eastern end of Long Island," the announcer was saying. "She's still a Category Three hurricane, with winds of approximately ninety-five miles per hour. Towns along the coasts of Connecticut, Rhode Island, Cape Cod and the Massachusetts Islands are preparing for her to hit there later this afternoon or early this evening, before she heads further north, becoming the first hurricane in more than a decade to make landfall along the coast of Maine."

Will clicked off the television. "No change in the forecast. I hope Aunt Nettie will be all right."

"Tom's with her. And you said you'd already taken the porch furniture in and closed everything up."

"And I have her car, so if it's crushed by a tree it'll be a Massachusetts tree," Will said, pacing the room. "Her home won't flood. It's on that hill, and too high above the river to be touched by tidal surges. Wind or rain would be the problems, or falling trees or branches."

"You'll be home in two days," said Maggie. "And other people in your family are near Waymouth. She's not alone, Will. You deserve a few days off."

"I do. You're right. But I worry just the same."

"Let's get some breakfast downstairs, and then call Gussie and check in. Jim probably left hours ago to pick up his mother in Providence, assuming she made it in last night. If there are wedding-related errands we should do them before the weather starts going downhill. And I wonder if anything will change with Diana's status today."

"I'd guess the police will be focused on the hurricane for the next twenty-four hours," said Will as they headed to the dining room. "They know where Diana is, and they'll have to wait for forensic reports before they do much more. This isn't *CSI*. Results take time. I've heard that hundreds of times from my friend Nick Strait. You drove him crazy about that case last summer, Maggie, but since I moved to Waymouth I've seen him a lot. He keeps calling to ask me to have a beer and tell me his State Trooper stories."

Maggie nodded. "You see? I helped you renew an old friendship. Give Nick my best."

"I'll do that."

"Speaking of talking to people, there are a couple of people I'd like to see before everyone closes up today," she added, sitting down at the table. "Those blueberry pancakes look delicious. And are those pumpkin muffins?"

"They are," said Mrs. Decker. "After all, it *is* the end of October. Even if we are expecting Southern company tonight." She sniffed and headed back to the kitchen.

"Southern...oh, Hurricane Tasha." Maggie slathered butter on her muffin. "Let's stop somewhere and find diet soda."

"My poor lady," said Will, pouring himself a cup of black coffee. "I should have thought of that last night at the pizzeria. No diet soda for breakfast."

"I'll manage." Maggie sipped orange juice. "I can be flexible."

"Oh, I know that," said Will, his eyes twinkling.

"Shush!" she said, elbowing him and blushing in spite of herself. "It's already Friday, and we have to head for our respective homes Sunday. I don't feel comfortable leaving..." she glanced meaning-fully toward the kitchen door "...the *situation* the way it is. I'd like something resolved before we leave. I don't want to drive off and leave Gussie and Jim newly married with...the *situation*...on their hands."

"Maggie, it's not your issue. They're grown-ups. They live here. Jim's a lawyer. It's his job to handle..." Will lowered his voice and whispered dramatically in her ear "...*situations*."

"Oh, shush. You know what I mean."

"Drink your juice and finish your pancakes. Call Gussie and see what she has in mind for us to do. We're here for Gussie and Jim, remember? Their wedding? Tomorrow?"

"I do, Will," said Maggie, wickedly. "I certainly do."

But as it turned out, Gussie had no immediate plans other than to "get a little more rest." Diana was happily engaged in making medium-sized white bows for the church pews, and as Maggie'd guessed, Jim had left early to drive to Providence. Lily's plane had touched down at one o'clock that morning.

"You and Will take some time for yourselves," Gussie said. "Relax. Tonight and tomorrow are totally booked. You haven't seen each other in a while. Enjoy!"

"We're on our own?" said Will after Maggie got off the phone.

"We are," Maggie replied. "But you won't mind if I steal a smidgen of time to drop in on the wife of the chief of police, will you?"

"Do I have a choice?"

"I won't take long. Promise." Maggie dug in her bag. "I looked up the address at Gussie's last night. It isn't far. And she might not even be home."

"I know there'll be no peace if I don't agree. Normally I'd check out the antiques shops in town, but I suspect nothing will be open hours before a major storm is expected to hit."

"I'll make it up to you." Maggie kissed him. "The rest of the day is yours."

"Promise?"

"Until the parties tonight, or until Gussie needs something, anyway," she modified.

"Go ahead. I'll call Maine and see how Aunt Nettie is. And I did bring a book," Will admitted. "The new Paul Doiron mystery. Just in case. I'm discovering Maine's home to some terrific mystery writers."

"Love you!" Maggie blew him a kiss and headed for the door.

The storm might be several hundred miles away, but the sky was already darkening, and there was a freshening to the air. Occasional gusts sent the red, yellow, and orange leaves already on the ground whirling through the streets and up over rooftops, almost in warning of what was to come.

Most businesses in town were already closed; those still open had signs posted in their windows declaring NO BOTTLED WATER or WE HAVE CANNED FOOD. Maggie glanced at her fuel gauge when she saw a NO GASOLINE sign at one station and a long line of cars waiting at another. She had half a tank left. That would get her to Connecticut on Sunday, assuming the roads were open and not bumper-to-bumper. Would there be a shortage there, too? She hoped Will had enough gas to get off the Cape when he headed north.

Chief Irons and his wife lived on a street of medium-sized homes about a mile east of town. She pulled up in front. A grayed wooden jungle gym was in the side yard, the posts sunk safely in concrete. The street and yard were silent.

Mrs. Irons would probably think she was crazy. Maybe she was. But in case she wasn't, she wanted to do this for Diana. And Cordelia.

Would the chief of police have already talked to his wife? On the other hand, not all couples shared everything in their lives.

Maggie had a quick flash of guilt about her decision to adopt that she hadn't yet shared with Will. But that was different. She and Will weren't married.

She rang the doorbell.

Although she hadn't consciously pictured Ike Irons's wife, the woman who answered the door wasn't what she'd expected. Taller and slimmer than Ike, at about five feet ten inches, Annie Irons was a bleached-blond knockout. And knew it. Her skin-tight designer jeans and low-cut top left little to the imagination, and she was wearing more makeup than Maggie had seen on any four women since she'd been on the Cape.

Interesting at-home attire for nine-thirty on a Friday morning.

"Yes? May I help you?"

"Mrs. Irons?"

"Yes."

"I'm Maggie Summer, a friend of Diana Hopkins. And Cordelia West. Could I talk with you for a few minutes?"

Mrs. Irons hesitated. "I guess so. Come in. Do you mind the kitchen? I was about to stuff a turkey."

"That's fine," said Maggie, following her through an immaculate living room beautifully decorated with antiques, including a pine corner cupboard displaying a half dozen pieces of Fairyland Lustre that immediately caught her eye. Was Chief Irons's wife a trust-fund baby?

There were no toys in view, but an infant was sleeping in a pine cradle near the kitchen.

The kitchen was in full operation.

The turkey in question was sitting, naked, in a roasting pan, while the stuffing was being assembled. Enticing smells of onions, sausage, mushrooms, and spices came from various pans.

"Make yourself comfortable; sit down over there," Maggie was directed. "I'm Annie. You said you're Maggie?"

"Yes."

"I hope you'll excuse me if I keep cooking. I need to get this bird in the oven. With the storm coming, we may lose power, so I have to cook as much as I can that'll taste good cold. This fellow's a twenty-six pounder." She filled a large mixing bowl with the cooked ingredients and then added celery, parsley, an assortment of spices, and breadcrumbs.

"I'm impressed," Maggie admitted. "You're very organized." Is this what you did when you were feeding a family? When she'd been married she and her husband had eaten out, or taken turns cooking small meals.

Annie began adding heated chicken broth to the bowl and mixing everything together. "Last night I baked a couple of pies and a cake, and two loaves of bread. I have a bin full of carrots and celery and broccoli and zucchini—you know, veggies we can eat raw—so we should be set for a few days even if there's no power."

Maggie shook her head. "I'm impressed. I've never made bread." Or roasted a bird that size, much less cooked that much food in such a short time.

Annie shrugged, and started stuffing the bread mixture into the turkey. "My husband's job keeps him away from home at odd hours, and I have two kids under five. They're at nursery school this morning, so I need to finish this up before they get home. When the rest of the world is crazy it helps me keep sane if I work." She stuffed the last of the bread mixture into the turkey, skewered the opening, and slid the roasting pan into the oven. "Now. Would you like a cup of coffee? Or tea?"

"No, thanks," said Maggie. "I won't bother you for long. By the way, I love the way you've decorated. I noticed your pumpkin pine corner cupboard in the living room. And a beautiful pine table and mirror, too. You must love antiques."

"I do. But on a policeman's salary I can't afford everything I love." Annie didn't slow down. She started cleaning up while she talked.

Maggie nodded.

"I'm a garage and house sale addict," Annie admitted, "and I taught myself to refinish. I know refinishing old furniture isn't in style right now. Antiques dealers have a fit when I say I do that. But I've found old pieces of furniture covered with six or seven layers of paint. Dealers don't want those, either. They want the original blue or red."

"So you buy pieces with good lines and hope you'll like the wood when you get down to it," said Maggie.

"Exactly. It's like discovering a treasure. Or not. If I don't like what's under all the paint, then I finish the piece off anyway and sell it at one of the school fairs, or to one of my neighbors, or even to one of the antiques dealers in town. I've never had to keep a piece I haven't liked."

"You're amazing! I don't know how you find the time to do all that and take care of three children, too."

"Three? I only have two children; I told you—they're at nursery school in the morning. That's my time to work on my projects."

"But what about the baby?"

Annie frowned. "The baby?" Then she threw back her head and laughed. "Oh! You mean the baby in the cradle?"

Maggie suddenly realized what she must have seen. "Don't tell me. It's one of Cordelia's dolls?"

Annie nodded. "Realistic, isn't it? You're not the first person who assumed it's real. I don't let the kids play with it, but once they took her out in the yard and someone driving past stopped their car

because they thought Nicky was dragging his baby sister by the foot!"
Annie laughed again. Somehow Maggie didn't find it very funny. She
changed the subject.

"Is the cradle one of your refinishing projects?"

"Absolutely." Annie looked down at her hands, which were about
to scrub several pans. "I don't have gorgeous manicured nails, but
I've never met a man who looked at a woman's fingers first, if you
know what I mean!"

"I do, indeed," Maggie said, finding herself liking Annie, despite
the doll in the cradle.

"And I noticed you collect Fairyland Lustre. I don't suppose you
found that at garage sales."

Annie glanced at her. "You know your antiques, Maggie. It's pretty, isn't it? Those pieces are just reproductions. But you came here for
a reason."

"You're right. I came because I'm concerned about Diana
Hopkins."

"She seems like a sweet girl," agreed Annie. "I've only met her a
couple of times. How do you know her?"

"I've only known her a short time, too," Maggie admitted. "I'm a
friend of Gussie White's; I came to Winslow for her wedding."

"Wait." Annie stopped scrubbing for a moment and turned
around, drying her hands on a dish towel. "You're the woman from
New Jersey who found Dan Jeffrey's body, aren't you?"

"Yes."

Annie's smile had vanished. "What do you really want from me?"

"You've heard Cordelia was killed, too."

"My husband's the chief of police. Of course I heard. It's very sad.
But that doesn't explain why you're here."

"Did he also tell you Diana's his major suspect in her death?"

Annie looked back at her. "I'm his wife, not his detective. He
didn't tell me that. No."

"That's why I'm here. I don't believe Diana's guilty of killing
Cordelia. Or of killing her father, which she's also suspected of
doing."

"No. I don't think so either." Annie sat down.

"Diana told me you came to their house a couple of times to pay your respects after her father died."

"Yes," Annie said, softly. "I'm sure others did, too. Cordelia's lived in Winslow many years."

"She has. But most who came left flowers or food, and didn't stay. You did. Diana appreciated that."

Annie hesitated. "I'm glad. I got to know her father quite well when he was here."

Maggie nodded. "That's what I suspected." She paused. "Diana also told me she came home once and interrupted you looking for something in her father's room."

Annie flushed and stood up. "Shit. I hoped she wouldn't remember that."

"When Dan disappeared, you were afraid the police would search his room as part of the investigation, weren't you?"

"You're not going to tell my husband, are you?"

"I'm not. But Diana might. In a strange bit of—luck?—your husband didn't search Dan Jeffrey's room until after his death. You found what you were looking for, didn't you?"

"Maggie, you have to believe I had nothing to do with Dan's death. You can't let Diana say anything to my husband."

"I can't promise she hasn't already talked to him about it. But help me to help you. What were you looking for?"

"Letters. Letters I'd written to Dan." Annie turned back toward the sink, and nosily put one pan inside another. Then she turned back to Maggie. "He didn't have a phone most of the time he was here. And it was romantic. He and I were lovers. Nothing serious, you understand. But if Ike knew it would ruin my marriage. My life. I was afraid he'd find out. So when Dan disappeared I panicked. I went to his house to try to find them."

"Did you?"

Annie shook her head. "They weren't there. I hoped Dan had destroyed them. If he hadn't, then either Cordelia found them, or Diana did."

Maggie hesitated. "I don't think it was Diana. She would have said something. And why would Cordelia have kept them?"

"Maybe to try to blackmail Dan."

"Blackmail Dan?" Maggie looked at Annie. "He didn't have any money, did he?"

"That was the problem. She was tired of him living there and not paying her enough rent. The odd jobs he had around town—mowing lawns, substitute bartending—none of them paid much. I met him through Cordelia, and then he did some landscaping for us, and then, one thing led to another. He told me Cordelia complained he didn't contribute enough toward his room and board. She was trying to force him to get a better-paying job."

"I've wondered how she supported herself just making those dolls," Maggie said, glancing toward the cradle in the living room.

"I don't know," said Annie. "Dan said a lot of people underestimated Cordelia. And then Diana arrived, and everything changed. I don't know why; I only saw Dan once after that."

Maggie looked at her. "Can you think of anyone else who knew Dan well?"

"He bartended at the Lazy Lobster sometimes. Men there knew him." Her eyes filled up. "It's all happened so fast. Diana arriving, and then Dan disappearing, and now Cordelia. I hope Ike's able to figure it out. I miss Dan. But I can't let Ike know what I was doing. Please, Maggie. Don't tell anyone."

"I'll do my best," said Maggie. "Thanks for talking with me." She left Annie scrubbing her kitchen counter, tears smearing the makeup on her cheeks.

On Maggie's way back to Six Gables she kept thinking about the Fairyland Lustre in Annie's corner cupboard. She was no expert on china or pottery, but she'd always coveted that particular Wedgwood, probably because it was designed by Art Nouveau artist Daisy Makeig-Jones. Fairyland Lustre was gloriously colored in vibrant golds, blues, reds, and greens, and depicted magic creatures and the forests and fields in which they lived. Few pieces sold for under $4,000 or $5,000, and she'd read in one of the antiques newspapers recently that a large covered vase in the "Demon Tree of the Ghostly Wood" pattern had brought over $36,000 at auction. Not exactly within her budget.

As far as she knew Fairyland Lustre had never been reproduced.

Even if it had, it wouldn't have the same glow, the same luster, as the original.

Those were original pieces in Annie Irons' living room. Maggie was certain of that. But for some reason—maybe fear of burglary?—Annie hadn't wanted to admit it. Well, she was lucky to have a collection like that.

Will was deep into his novel when Maggie got back to Six Gables. "You were right. That didn't take long," he said.

"How's Aunt Nettie?"

"She sends her love," said Will. "Tom's taking good care of her, and Rachel stopped in to see her and brought them lobster bisque for tonight's dinner and a ham in case there's a power outage. The oil lamps are cleaned, the bathtub is filled. They're set."

"That's right. You have a well, but the water pump is electric."

"When the power goes, so does the water," Will confirmed. "I'm thinking we should invest in a small generator. Enough power to keep the furnace and the pump going, and a few kitchen appliances. At Aunt Nettie's age, if we had an ice storm and lost power for a week, I don't think she'd cope well."

"No power for a week in January in Maine? I'm not sure how well *I'd* cope," Maggie agreed. "Sounds as though you should call for an estimate or two."

"Next week," said Will. "How'd your meeting go?"

"Educational," said Maggie. "But I didn't find out anything absolutely critical. I liked Ike's wife more than I thought I would. Tell you what: why don't we go and have lunch? If it's open, there's a place a lot of the fishermen around here eat. Not exactly gourmet, but it would be a bit of local color."

"Do I sense another mission in the offing?" Will asked.

"Perhaps," said Maggie. "But we do have to eat somewhere. Why not try this place? I've been there once, but just for a beer."

"You don't like beer," said Will, raising his eyebrows.

"I'm flexible, remember?" said Maggie.

"What's the name of this fantastic local establishment?"

"The Lazy Lobster."

"A Mainer does not eat lobster on the Cape," said Will, tapping her lightly on the head in reprimand.

"They have hamburgers, too," said Maggie.

"With blue cheese and bacon?"

"It's possible," she said, as they headed out. The wind had picked up, and there was spitting rain in the air. But Hurricane Tasha was still 250 miles south of Cape Cod.

They had plenty of time.

Chapter 33

Rip Van Winkle at the Village Tavern. Wood engraving from *Harper's Weekly,* September 20, 1873, by Felix Octavious Carr Darley (1822–1888), who usually signed his work F.O.C. Darley. He was the first well-known American illustrator and provided pictures for books by Cooper, Irving, Dickens, Hawthorne, Poe, Stowe, among others, during the first half of the nineteenth century. This engraving is based on one he did earlier for Washington Irving's *Rip Van Winkle.* It shows shiftless Rip, beer mug in hand, being routed out by Dame Van Winkle. Other patrons of the tavern include an obese gentleman smoking an extremely long clay pipe, a boy reading a newspaper, and Rip's dog, Wolf, his tail between his legs, who knows it's time to head for home. 9 x 11.75 inches. $75.

THE LAZY LOBSTER was not only open, it was full. Of course, Maggie remembered. Fishing boats were not out. Harbormasters had required them to be dry-docked yesterday.

The storm was closing in, and most men in the Lazy Lobster had either finished storm-proofing their homes and those of their neighbors, or were taking a quick break before returning to their tasks.

One flat-screen TV above the bar was tuned to the Weather Channel. The other was focused on NECN, New England Cable News. Both stations alternated weather maps and scenes of crashing surf, trees bent over in the wind, and scrolling words warning that Hurricane Tasha was moving steadily northeast, and had diminished very little in power.

"Table today?" said a pert young woman who hadn't been visible during Maggie's previous visit. Her hair was pulled back in a ponytail, and she wore her white LAZY LOBSTER T-shirt proudly, and scooped low enough to hint at barely hidden cleavage.

"We'd prefer the bar, if there's room," said Maggie.

"You don't usually like to sit at the bar," Will said, as they followed their hostess to two stools at the far end.

"I like this one," said Maggie. "We can see the weather reports better from here," she added, guilelessly.

"Right," said Will. "How could I forget your new-found addiction to the Weather Channel?"

"A girl can never hear too much about the weather. Especially when there's a hurricane in the offing." Maggie smiled.

"Nice to see you again, Maggie from New Jersey," said Rocky. "What can I get you today? Another Sam Adams?"

"Sounds good. And the fried Wellfleet oysters," said Maggie, pointing at the menu behind the bar.

Will ordered a Narragansett and a blue cheeseburger, extra rare, with bacon.

"You just ordered a coronary," Maggie pointed out.

"Your fried oysters aren't the healthiest choice in the world," Will retaliated. "Especially since you added fries to your order when you thought I wasn't listening. Now, what are we really here for?"

"I'm not sure," Maggie said, under the noise of the crowd. "But Dan Jeffrey worked here sometimes. And Bob Silva, the guy who owns the hardware store, said the bartender here knows a lot about what happens in town."

The waitress slid their lunch plates in front of them with a quick "Enjoy!"

"Speedy service, anyway," said Will.

"Notice anything unusual about this place?" said Maggie.

"You and the waitress are the only females in here?"

"Right. And everyone's a waterfront sort. No lawyers or bankers, at least by the look of them."

"I'd say you're right. Wide age spread, too. I'd guess from about sixteen—too young to be legally drinking and probably should be in school—up to the old guy in the corner. Maybe in his eighties?"

"Today schools may have closed early. But the afternoon I was here some high school kids came in, too."

Will frowned. "Not a good sign. Even if kids aren't ordering alcoholic drinks, towns usually frown on them hanging out in dives like this. Most proprietors throw them out. They don't want to get in trouble with the parents or police. We had a place like this near the school where I taught in Buffalo. Ended up being closed down."

"Because?" said Maggie, taking another bite of her oysters.

"The kids weren't there to buy the beer and pizza. Or even just the pizza. The owner had another business going on the side."

"The kids were buying drugs with their pizza."

"Bingo."

Maggie looked around. "What do you think about that possibility here?"

Will looked at her. "I have no idea. But if that's even a small possibility you don't talk about it here. You finish your oysters and fries, you smile, you leave a nice tip, and you get out."

"You are such a smart man, Will Brewer," said Maggie. "These are really good oysters, by the way. Nice and fresh. Want a bite?"

"I thought you'd never ask."

Chapter 34

"THE BURGER AND BEER were fine in that place," said Will, as they drove out of the Lazy Lobster's parking lot. "But your oysters were definitely the best choice. I also could have done without everyone's staring at us and wondering why we were there. Especially since I wasn't sure myself. Now, where to? And what's all this sudden interest in drugs?"

"Last spring, a boy here, the teenaged son of the owner of the hardware store where we bought the plywood yesterday, died of an overdose. The town pretty much freaked out. Everyone blamed everyone else."

"Did they find the dealer?"

"No. But the boy's father blamed Diana's father. His rationale was that Dan was new in town and he helped out with one of the kids' baseball teams. It got to the point that there was a fight—in the Lazy

Lobster. The police broke it up, and after that Dan Jeffrey didn't work at the Lobster, or at any of his other local jobs."

"Pretty hard for the guy if he lost his jobs, especially if he wasn't to blame for the drugs."

"Right. And no one was ever arrested, so I'm assuming there wasn't proof to charge him. Or anyone else."

"Are the drugs still around?"

"Not so much. Or they've learned to keep it quieter. But drugs never go away, do they?"

Will grimaced. "They go underground."

"Exactly."

"What does all this have to do with Diana and Cordelia?"

"That's what I want to know." Maggie hesitated. "But I've run out of places to look. I can't exactly go up to someone and ask if they're dealing in drugs."

"Good. Glad you see it that way." Will reached over and patted her knee.

"It would have to be someone who could be with the kids and not arouse any suspicion, right?"

"Right. But I thought you were concerned about Diana, and about the deaths of her father and her cousin. The boy at the high school who died last spring doesn't have anything to do with them."

"I'm not sure, Will. I have a feeling that somehow all three deaths are connected. I just don't know how."

"Maggie, be realistic. It's about," Will glanced at his watch, "one in the afternoon. What time do those parties start tonight?"

"Seven."

"So at seven tonight you and I will be heading out, in the middle of a hurricane, let's not forget, to attend separate parties. Which I certainly hope don't run late, because I'm considerably over the age of eighteen and I don't get a real thrill out of being out in a storm with a bunch of drunk guys I don't know. Or of thinking of you out somewhere else with some crazy cousin of Gussie's who thinks she's a witch. Tomorrow morning there'll be wedding preparations, and early tomorrow afternoon your best friend in all the world—which is how you usually refer to Gussie—is marrying someone who's a pretty nice guy. Plus, Maggie, and I do not say this lightly, the man you love, who you are rarely even in the same state with, is here. Now. With you. A situation which will exist for only another, say, forty hours."

"Are you trying to tell me something?" Maggie asked, trying to look innocent.

"Lady, sometimes you have your priorities really messed up."

"Stop at the hardware store again. Please. I'll be really fast. I promise."

Will sighed. "Let me guess. You want to get some candles in case the electricity goes out tonight."

"I was thinking of flashlights. But candles might have to do if they're sold out of flashlights," she said as he pulled in. She leaned over and kissed him lightly before opening the car door.

Winslow Hardware looked as though the storm had already hit. Most of the supplies she'd seen there earlier were gone. Few customers were in the aisles. She suspected everyone was hunkering down at home before the storm. Any supplies they didn't have now they'd do without.

Bob Silva was behind the counter. "Maggie, we're getting to be old friends. What have you forgotten? I'm afraid we're out of most hurricane supplies."

"Flashlights?"

"The large ones are gone. I still have a few small ones, over there." He pointed at a display of camping gear.

Maggie selected a light so small the entire case fit in the palm of her hand. "Are these any good? I mean, will they light a path in the dark?"

"They're not exactly torches," said Silva, "and I wouldn't try to read with one, but they'll be better than nothing. People put those in glove compartments or pockets so they can see a map or find a keyhole."

"I'll take two," she said, reaching for her wallet. "And I've been thinking about what you said about your son's death. Would you mind if I talked to a couple of the other boys on his baseball team?"

Silva stopped making change. "I don't think it'll do any good,

Maggie. Either those boys don't know anything, or they won't talk. Ike Irons tried several times last spring. And you're not from here. Why would they trust you?"

Maggie shrugged. "They might not. But maybe they'd talk to me *because* I'm not from here. And the situation has changed since last spring. If Dan Jeffrey was involved, they might say something now that he's dead. I'd like to try to talk with them. If you wouldn't mind."

"I'll give you stubbornness, Maggie Summer. I hope this Hurricane Tasha isn't as persistent as you are. I hear it's made a mess of the Connecticut shoreline. Here." Silva reached for a pad and scribbled down two names. "These are the names of two of my boy's best friends. If any of the kids on the team talk, they would. When do you think you might try to see them?"

"Will they be at home this afternoon?"

Silva paused. "Likely. Everyone's home today because of the storm. Schools let out at noon. I'm going to close up here at two o'clock. Tell you what. Those boys probably wouldn't talk with their moms and dads hovering over them. But they're kids. They like to eat. The pizza place in town is staying open until four o'clock. I just sold my last sandbags to the guy who owns it. Let me call their moms and tell them you're here for Gussie's wedding. You're a college professor, right?"

Maggie nodded.

"I'll tell 'em you're doing research on the effects of drugs on kids. You'd like to talk to their boys about how they feel about what happened to Tony, and you'll buy the boys pizza if they meet you at two o'clock. No moms or dads. Just half an hour with you, and the kids get pizza."

"Bob, that's a fantastic idea! I love it!"

"I don't know if it'll work. But I'll try. Sean Jacobs and Josh Sewall. Be at the pizza place at two o'clock and we'll see if they show. Give me your cell number. If both families say 'no way,' I'll let you know."

"Thank you; thank you so much," said Maggie, scribbling down her number.

"No one's asked about Tony in months," said Bob Silva. "You care. I don't know why. But you do. If you can find out anything, I want to help. Let's hope your idea works. If it doesn't?" He shrugged. "Nothing ventured." He turned. "I'll make those calls now."

Will didn't look happy when Maggie got back to the car. "I was about ready to come in after you."

"I got flashlights for us, for tonight," said Maggie, showing him her purchases.

He picked one up. "Not exactly super-strength, are they?"

"They were the only lights left. A couple of hours before a hurricane you don't have a lot of choices."

"Not surprising," said Will. "And now, back to Six Gables?"

"Yes," said Maggie. "But I'm going to have to go out for a short time in about half an hour."

"Where are we going then?" asked Will, his voice very calm. "More sleuthing?"

"Just me this time," said Maggie. "I'm going to meet with one or two of the boys who played baseball with Tony Silva, the boy who overdosed last spring."

"You're *what*?" said Will. "I thought we were going to have a quiet afternoon. Resting. Spending time together. Saving our strength for the craziness of whatever this evening brings."

"We will! I promise. You'll just start your rest a little before I start mine. I won't be long. The boys are only going to be at the pizza parlor for half an hour. That's what we've promised their parents."

"Who's this 'we'?"

"Bob Silva is calling their parents now, trying to convince them to talk with me."

"And, let me guess. You're bribing them with the pizza."

"They're teenagers. Of course I am."

Will didn't answer. He turned the key in the ignition, and headed the car back to the B&B.

The silence in the car would have been even denser if it hadn't been for the winds that were picking up and swirling leaves and small branches on the roads and lawns. A few larger branches had already fallen. Will swerved around one that blocked part of the road.

When he pulled into the parking lot at Six Gables he turned to her. "Maggie, I don't want you to go. The roads are getting worse."

"I told you, Will. I've already made plans. I won't be gone long. This is important."

"More important than listening to me? More important than being with the man you love?"

"I love you, Will. You know that."

"If you love me, why don't you ever listen to me?"

"I do listen to you."

"Then why don't you ever take anything I say seriously? You always do exactly what you want to do, without thinking about how it might affect someone else. About how someone else might worry about you. About how someone else might have a legitimate idea sometime."

"But I—"

"You get involved in one of these missions of yours to help someone, or to solve some crime, and there's no stopping you. Sometimes I love you for it, Maggie. But I need you to make time in your life for me, too. I don't want to spend my life waiting around for you to have an extra minute for me, when no one else needs you."

He got out of the car, closed the door carefully, and went up the stairs into Six Gables, leaving Maggie alone in the front seat of Aunt Nettie's car.

Chapter 35

The **American Base-Ball Players in England—Match Between The Red Stockings and The Athletics, Prince's Ground, Brompton.** Wood engraving (black and white) full-page illustration from *Harper's Weekly*, September 12, 1874. View of field from behind catcher, where bats have been flung. "Boston" is clearly visible on the shirts of both the player at bat and one player waiting his turn. The Cincinnati Red Stockings became the first all-professional baseball club in 1869. In 1871 a pro club was organized in Boston. It hired away half the players from Cincinnati and called itself the Boston Red Stockings. That club eventually became the Boston Braves. Today's Boston Red Sox was established in 1901. Early baseball prints are rare. 10.5 x 15.5 inches. $250.

THIS WAS NOT THE WAY Maggie had intended the weekend to go.

She wanted to follow Will into the B&B and explain. He didn't get it. This was something that had to be done, and no one else was doing it.

Damn. It wasn't as though no one else *could* do it. She wasn't that egotistical. But no one else was. And there was a chance. Maybe a small chance. But still a chance, that she could help figure out who'd killed one, or two, or maybe even three people.

She refused to throw that chance away. Not even for Will.

She stalked over to her own van. After all, the hurricane wasn't here yet. She wouldn't be in any danger. She was only going to talk to a couple of high school kids. And she'd be back in, what? Thirty minutes. Forty-five minutes, tops.

She'd spend the rest of the weekend with Will.

If he couldn't cope with that, then no wonder he didn't want to be a father. He'd never be able to share her attention with a child. It was a good thing she'd found that out now.

She was pulling into the pizza parlor before she'd finished talking to herself. Only a few cars were there. Most people in Winslow were spending their afternoons at home, not ordering pizza.

A tall man came out of the restaurant carrying three pizza boxes, put them in the back seat of his car, and drove off.

Except for those who planned to nosh on pizza while waiting out the storm.

Almost two o'clock. Bob Silva hadn't called. That should mean Sean and Josh were coming. Good for Bob; he must have been convincing. She'd been afraid the boys' parents wouldn't want them to come.

A man and a woman were standing at the restaurant counter, waiting for orders. Only one table was filled: a mother and pre-teen daughter starting on a veggie pizza. The girl was carefully picking the mushrooms and onions off her piece. The mom watched her for a minute, and then took the discarded vegetables and put them on her own slice. Neither of them spoke.

Would she be that way with her daughter? Had those two argued? Or were they so comfortable with each other they didn't need to speak? Were they waiting for someone to join them? That large pizza looked like a lot for only two of them.

The restaurant door behind her opened.

"Are you Dr. Summer?" The young men who came in were both taller than Maggie; the taller of the two had an acne problem he'd tried unsuccessfully to cover with medication. The other had a tattoo of an anchor on his forearm. "The college lady?"

"I am. You're Sean and Josh?"

They nodded. Josh was the taller one.

"What would you like on your pizza?"

They agreed on an extra-large pepperoni, meatball, and sausage pizza and large Cokes. And a large bag of barbecue-flavored Cape Cod potato chips to hold them until the pizza was ready. Maggie ordered two bags of the chips. She'd take one bag back as a peace offering for Will. For privacy, they sat at a table as far from either the cook or the mother and daughter as possible.

"Thanks for coming," said Maggie. "I really appreciate it."

"No problem. We were vegging out at Sean's place anyway, since they canceled school this afternoon," said Josh. "Free pizza's good."

Maggie smiled. Whatever worked. Pizza seemed appropriate under all circumstances in Winslow. "Mr. Silva told me you were friends of his son, Tony."

The boys looked at each other. Sean shrugged.

"I'm not going to tell Mr. Silva anything you tell me. And if I tell anyone what we talk about, I won't say who it was told me. Okay with you guys?"

Sean nodded. "It's just that, Tony was okay and all. And we were on the same team, sure. But we weren't exactly the closest."

"Got it," said Maggie. "Did Tony have any close friends?"

Sean looked at Josh and shrugged. Josh shook his head. "Not really. He wasn't exactly the most with-it kid around."

His dad had played baseball, and said Tony was getting better. "Could he play baseball?"

"He stunk," said Josh bluntly. "Mr. Costa, the coach? He didn't put him in too often. Tony struck out, and he couldn't run fast. Part of it was, he had asthma, and he had to stop to use his inhaler. You can't play baseball when you have to stop to breathe."

"He was supposed to play left field. But most of the time he couldn't catch fly balls, and when he did, he dropped them," added Sean.

"His dad was always at the practices, yelling at him to try harder, and telling Coach to put him in, to give him another chance. But Tony was a disaster."

Their pizza arrived and the boys lost no time digging in.

"He played baseball because his dad wanted him to?"

"For sure. He hated it. Some of the guys made fun of him for even trying."

"Who wouldn't hate being the reason we'd lose games?" added Josh, wiping tomato sauce off his chin. "He was an embarrassment."

"What about the drugs? If you guys wanted to get drugs, where would you go?"

The boys looked at each other.

"I'm not asking if you use, or if any of your friends do. But in most schools, or towns, there's a place or a person where you can go. I'm from Jersey; I don't know Winslow. Where would someone go in this town? If a person were interested."

Sean glanced around, as though someone else were listening. "You said no one would know what we said, right?"

"Right. I'm telling you straight. Did you know Dan Jeffrey?"

"Sure. Friend of Coach Costa. Helped with team equipment last year."

"I heard he got killed a week ago," said Josh.

"He did," said Maggie. "Tony's dad said Dan Jeffrey was the one who gave Tony the pills that killed him."

Sean looked sideways at Josh. "Tony's dad got that wrong. I never heard of anyone getting anything from Mr. Jeffrey. He was just a nice guy who liked baseball. He used to give us tips, sort of like a second coach. He helped me with my fast ball. He wouldn't have done anything to hurt Tony."

Josh shook his head. "Mr. Jeffrey used to talk to Tony about his asthma. Once I heard him tell Tony's dad not to go so hard on him; to let Tony drop off the team and do something he was better at. Mr. Silva got real mad. He told Mr. Jeffrey to mind his own business."

Sean said quietly. "It wasn't Mr. Jeffrey who had pills."

Josh elbowed Sean.

Neither of them said anything more. They both focused on their pizza. They didn't look at Maggie or each other. No one said anything for several long minutes.

Then Maggie asked. "Who was it, then? Who had the pills?"

"We can tell her, Josh. It don't make a difference anymore," said Sean.

"I guess." Josh didn't look as sure. "But you won't tell our parents? 'Cause Sean and me, we didn't do pills. Honest."

The two of them looked so young and so scared Maggie was almost certain they were telling the truth. But they knew something.

"I won't tell your parents. But I won't lie to you. I might have to tell the police."

"Just don't tell our parents you heard it from us. It could have been a lot of people who told. Everybody knew," bargained Sean.

"I promise," said Maggie, hoping no one would else would break her promise.

Sean took a deep breath and looked around. Then he lowered his voice. "Maybe there were other places in town to get stuff, but kids I know got pills from that deaf lady who came to watch the games. Miss West."

Chapter 36

Silver Maple. Chromolithograph published by Stecher Lithographic Company, Rochester, New York. c. 1890. Probably part of a sample book for use by nurseries and tree salesmen. Shows stately home, with tree in yard, elegant carriage beneath, and inset of leaf. "A very rapid growing tree, forming an open spreading head, has abundance of clean, healthy foliage and makes a fine shade tree" printed in small letters at bottom that could easily be matted over. Silver maples are common in the northeast United States; their leaves turn yellow in the fall. They do, however, have the disadvantages of shallow root systems and brittle wood, so are vulnerable in storms. 5.5 x 8.5 inches. $50.

MAGGIE DROVE THE BOYS back to Sean's house through increasingly heavy rain. The wind was stronger, too. In the short time they'd been at the restaurant gusts had turned to gales. Maggie's van rocked as she turned one sharp corner.

Hurricane Tasha might not have reached the Cape yet; forecasts said major winds wouldn't arrive for hours yet. But she was definitely sending warnings that she was on her way.

The boys pointed at branches that had already fallen and excitedly speculated about how high the surf might get and whether anyone they knew had wetsuits and surfboards they could borrow.

Maggie was relieved when they reached Sean's house and the boys ran for cover. Let their parents warn them of hurricane dangers. She'd have to cope with young people's sense of invulnerability soon enough. Listening to them she'd been reminded of how fearless kids could be. And how hungry. In twenty minutes the boys had consumed an entire extra-large pizza, plus chips and large sodas. She was taking this as a personal warning that her food budget might have to change drastically in the near future.

She turned the van carefully, managing to miss a garbage can rolling erratically down the street. Luckily, the Six Gables Inn was only a couple of miles away.

Had Cordelia really been the kids' source for drugs? Or at least one source, she told herself; there might have been another. Thinking about Cordelia as a drug dealer was totally changing the way she looked at Winslow, and the people who lived here.

Who would've suspected that the quiet deaf woman who took long walks along the beach and streets of Winslow, who stopped to watch children play, who smiled at everyone and never spoke was also the source of illegal pharmaceutical medications?

She tried to put it all together.

Those boxes Cordelia received from all over the country. And from other countries, the postmistress had said. She'd specifically mentioned Canada, Maggie was sure. Small quantities of prescription medications could be hidden and shipped, perhaps mixed in with the supplies she received to make her dolls. And those eBay sales she made, and the packages she sent out. Were they dolls, or was she sending drugs, too?

Gussie'd wondered how Cordelia managed to pay the high taxes on her house. Perhaps selling drugs had solved that problem.

A strong gust of wind sent the van shimmying across the road.

Maggie turned her windshield wipers on high and refocused on getting back to Six Gables. Rain was now hitting the van from all directions. The sky had darkened enough so she not only turned her headlights on because it was the law, but because she needed them.

If this was the prequel to the hurricane, what would tonight be like?

Maybe Sheila would come to her senses and cancel the party. It would be crazy to go out in weather like this.

Luckily, not many other people were stupid enough to be on the roads. Leaves that had been on the trees this morning now filled the air like rain. Or were they blowing up from the ground? Wherever they'd come from, they were sticking to the windshield. The wipers couldn't get them all off.

Maggie slowed down even more.

Should she stop and remove the leaves? Or would stopping mean more leaves would get on the van?

She kept going, but even slower.

She crossed the downtown area. Main Street was empty. None of the stores looked open. Although if one were, she couldn't tell and couldn't take the time to look. No cars were parked on the street, which was beginning to flood. Leaves must be plugging storm drains. That happened this time of year in New Jersey. The center of Winslow looked like the set of a science fiction movie after all the humans had been vaporized. Prime for a Martian takeover.

Maggie smirked at her own fantasy. Those Martians had better be wearing heavy-duty L.L. Bean slickers, or they'd be mighty wet when they arrived to take charge. She made her way around the town Green and headed north.

Not far now. She slowed down even more. She didn't want to miss the entrance. Thank goodness there were no other cars on the road.

Finally. There it was. She turned into the driveway with relief.

A police car was parked in front of the entrance to Six Gables.

Chapter 37

Donovan's Humble-bee and Great Humble-bee. Delicate hand-colored steel engraving (1843) from Sir William Jardine's forty-volume *Naturalist Library*, published by W.H. Lizar of Edinburgh. As with other engravings in the volumes, the subjects are carefully and vibrantly hand-colored; backgrounds are uncolored. The humble, or bumble, bee, is black with broad bands of yellow or orange. Humble bees often nest in the ground. Each nest has a queen, drones, and workers. 3.75 x 6 inches. Light foxing. Price: $50.

WHAT BUSINESS DID the Winslow Police Department have at the B&B?

Maggie's thoughts were almost drowned out by the rain pounding on the van roof.

Why hadn't she thought to bring a raincoat to the Cape? The door to Six Gables was only twenty steps away, but she'd be soaked by the time she got inside.

The rain and wind weren't easing up. She hoped Will's mood had. She grabbed the bag of potato chips she'd bought for him, opened the van door, and ran, splashing through puddles already an inch deep that filled her sneakers with frigid water. Sodden leaves made the driveway treacherous. By the time she reached the ramp to the porch her hair was soaked, and she could practically feel her favorite wool sweater shrinking as it clung to the dripping turtleneck beneath it.

Cold, drenched, and focused on thoughts of Will, hair dryers, and towels, she opened the door to the B&B. All four people standing in the lobby turned to look at her.

"Here you are," said Mrs. Decker. "Finally. We were wondering when you'd get back. It's blowing a gale out there."

"It's dreadful. I got here as soon as I could." Maggie stood, drip-ping, on the mat inside the door. Will was in back of two other women, one of whom she didn't recognize. He wasn't smiling. "I'm sorry. I should have called, Will. But I got back as soon as I could." She shook herself a little and carefully stepped across the worn ori-ental carpet to hand him the bag of barbecued potato chips covered with beads of rain. "Here; these are for you." She wanted to add: a peace offering. But she wouldn't say that in front of the others.

"I'm so pleased to meet you dear," said an elegantly coiffed gray-haired woman she hadn't met, putting out her hand. Maggie knew immediately who she must be.

"You must be Jim's mother, Mrs. Dryden," she said, taking the woman's hand in her damp one. "Gussie told me you'd be stay-ing here. I'm so glad to finally meet you. I've heard so much about you."

"You must call me Lily," she said. "Gussie and Jim said you and your friend," she glanced at Will, "were staying here. Jim took me to see their new house, and then brought me here to rest and dress for the party tonight. Although I'm not sure the party's going to happen. There were telephone calls going back and forth when he dropped me off. A number of guests who'd planned to come to Winslow to-night have wisely decided not to travel until tomorrow morning."

So that left the questions no one had answered. Why was Annie Irons here? And why was a police car parked out front?

Maggie turned in her direction. "I didn't think I'd be seeing you again so soon, Annie." Mrs. Irons was wearing a Burberry trench coat. Maggie'd coveted one just like it at the Short Hills Mall in Sep-tember, but its price tag had been higher than her mortgage payment.

"My husband heard the governor is probably going to ask all non-essential drivers to stay home tonight. The roads are getting more treacherous every hour, and Hurricane Tasha's not due to hit here full force until early evening," said Annie.

Yes? So the Winslow Chief of Police sent his wife to deliver a weather bulletin? That seemed unlikely. But no one else was here. She must have come in the police car.

"The car out front is yours, then?"

She nodded. "Ike will kill me when he finds I borrowed one of the station cars, but I enjoyed our talk this morning so much I thought maybe we could get together this afternoon to chat a little more. But your friend Will told me you'd gone out, and now the storm is so much worse. If the party does go on tonight, perhaps I could get Ike to pick you ladies up in the patrol car when he takes me? Police cars are heavy, and wouldn't skid as easily on the leaves."

"Why, that would be lovely, Annie; wouldn't it, Maggie?" said Lily. "Wouldn't it be fun to have a police escort?"

"Will's given me your telephone number, so we can be in touch. We should be hearing from the governor's office very soon now," said Annie. "In the meantime I'd better get the car back to the station. Maybe I'll see you later. For sure, I'll see you all tomorrow at the big event!" She waved, pulled her coat's hood over her head, and left.

Mrs. Decker shook her head. "Maggie, there's a hair dryer in your room. Can I get you a cup of tea, or anything else right now? You need to get out of those wet things."

Maggie shook her head. "Thank you, but no tea. I want to dry off, and maybe take a hot shower."

"You'd better do that soon, dear. If we lose power, we lose hot water, too, and with that Hurricane Tasha getting closer all the time, you never know," advised Mrs. Decker. "I'll be downstairs if any of you need anything. And I'll have sandwiches, and if the power holds, hot soup in the dining room for supper at six o'clock. No extra charge. A hurricane calls for special measures. I'm guessing none of you will be going out for dinner. I just checked. All the restaurants in town have closed."

"You're a wonderful hostess, Mrs. Decker," said Lily. "I'm going to lie down and maybe turn the Weather Channel on in my room. I was up very late last night flying in, and tomorrow is a big day. I wouldn't mind at all if this to-do tonight were cancelled, to tell the truth." She went ahead up the stairs.

Maggie put her hand out for Will's. "Coming?"

Will hesitated.

"We need to talk. Upstairs?"

Will nodded.

Behind their closed door she added, "Give me five minutes to shower and warm up. Then we'll talk," she promised. "And I apologize."

"May I eat the chips in the meantime?" he asked, holding the bag out, "since you're setting the agenda for the next hour or so?"

"Of course," she agreed, stripping off her wet clothes and stretching the wet sweater out as best she could on a towel on the floor. "And I hope you'll forgive me for being such an idiot earlier. And I do have news! That pizza was worth a lot more than its weight in information. But first I desperately need that hot shower!"

By the time Maggie rejoined him, one towel wrapped around her head and one around her body, Will'd finished about a third of the potato chips.

"Cape Cod does wonderfully well by chips," he commented, taking another handful. "But we still need to talk."

"Will, I'm sorry."

"So am I. But I'm serious about not liking what happened. First, though, I know you're dying to tell me your news, so go ahead. Talk. What did you find out that was so important?"

"Bottom line? The boys talked. They told me they'd never bought drugs."

"Of course they hadn't," Will agreed. "That's your news? I could have told you that before you left."

"But, if they'd wanted to, guess who they said they could have gone to?"

"Haven't a clue. The Wizard of Oz. Plus, I only know a handful of people in Winslow, and if you say it's Gussie, I will be genuinely surprised."

"Very funny. No, not Gussie. But almost as strange. They said it was Cordelia."

"The deaf woman who was shot yesterday morning?"

"That's what they said."

Will was silent for a moment. "You're right. That puts an entirely different light on her murder. And on Diana's father's, too."

"Diana told me she'd seen guns in Cordelia's room. Now the reason for the guns makes more sense. But when the police searched the house they must not have found drugs. And if they found the guns, no one mentioned them."

"If the guns were registered, maybe they didn't seem important at the time. Or maybe they were somewhere the police didn't look. When they searched the house the first time they were looking for things related to Dan Jeffrey, weren't they? Not related to Cordelia."

"I'd think they'd have paid attention to several guns. Especially since Dan Jeffrey had been shot. And they'd definitely have noticed if they'd found drugs."

"True. So if the boys were right, and Cordelia was dealing, then either she'd stopped, she had a really good hiding place, or her inventory was temporarily out."

"That would have been almost too convenient," Maggie said. "But even if Cordelia was dealing drugs, it doesn't tell us who killed her. Or who killed Dan Jeffrey."

"No. But it puts her in a position to have had some unsavory colleagues. She might have owed money to her supplier. Or maybe one of her usual customers wanted drugs, and for some reason she couldn't get them for him. Anything to do with drugs can get nasty and violent quickly. It's not a gentlemanly sort of crime. And because of that, now that you've stumbled onto something critical to these murders, you definitely have to tell the police, and step away. Because when you're talking drug violence you're in over your head." Will reached over and drew her next to him. "And much as sometimes you drive me totally crazy, I do love that head of yours, Maggie Summer. I want it to stay intact, and attached to these beautiful shoulders." He gently pulled the towel away from her hair, which fell, damp and wavy, down her back. He took one strand and twisted it around his fingers, and then bent down and kissed her neck. "I love the way you stride in, wanting to conquer the world and make everything right. But, truthfully, an hour ago I was ready to strangle you. There are times it's best to leave law enforcement to the professionals."

"Yes, Will," Maggie said, looking into his eyes, which looked very blue.

"I don't want to spend the rest of my life worried about what trouble you're getting yourself into. If I wanted to marry a policewoman or a detective, I'd ask my friend Nick to introduce me to one of his colleagues. But I want to marry you, Maggie Summer. And I want us to have a wonderful, long life together." Will reached down and picked up Maggie's right hand and kissed the R-E-G-A-R-D ring he'd given her.

Maggie's eyes opened wide and she leaned back slightly. For a moment she didn't say anything. "Are you…"

"I was going to buy you an official engagement ring, but then I decided it would be more fun for us to buy one together. Is that horribly unromantic?"

Maggie stood up, holding the towel around her. "Will Brewer. Did you just propose to me?"

"I hope so. Would you like me to try again? I haven't had a lot of practice."

"No, no. I mean…"

"All you have to do is say 'yes;' it's a one-syllable word. You're usually good with words."

"I know." Maggie moved from the bed.

Will just looked at her. "You're not going to say yes."

"I love you. I want to say 'yes.'"

"Then?"

"I have to tell you something first."

"I know, I know. It's complicated. You live in New Jersey. I live in Maine. There's Aunt Nettie. I know we can't get married right away. But we'll work things out. We'll make it work! We love each other, Maggie!"

"We do. But it's none of those things. It's something else." Maggie sat on the bed, but not next to him. "Will, I was going to tell you this weekend. I still want to be a mother. I've applied to Our World, Our Children to adopt a child. My home study should be finished by Christmas. You remember—the agency we did the benefit for last spring."

It was Will's turn to be silent.

"You liked the people there, Will."

"They were nice people. But a child, Maggie. That's a lifetime responsibility. And you know how I feel about that."

"It's important to me. And if I wait much longer, I'll be too old."

"How could you do that without talking to me? How could you plan the rest of your life without discussing it with the man you say you love?" Will walked over to the window. He stood for a few minutes, looking out at the darkness, his hands clenched. "I'm sorry, Maggie. I can't change that much. I've taken responsibility for Aunt Nettie. I've proposed to you. But I can't take on parenthood. I can't. And you can't expect me to. I've never pretended I could do that."

"In relationships everyone has to give up something; everyone has to change."

He turned and looked at her. "Hell, Maggie. Don't tell me I can't change. In the past year I've changed almost everything in my life! I've given up my house. I've moved to Maine. I've changed the way I do business. I've taken on responsibility for Aunt Nettie. I've just proposed to the second person in my life I've ever loved. Don't tell me I won't change! What are you prepared to give up, Maggie? What are you prepared to change?"

Maggie didn't answer.

"Think about it, then. Because it sounds to me as though you don't want to change much in your life at all. Nothing that has anything to do with me, anyway."

Chapter 38

Camomile: Engergy [sic] Will Surmount Adversity. Hand-colored steel engraving from *American Flora*, 1851. Woman on columned balcony, staring at storm clouds above; man on ladder who has climbed to the balcony reaches up to her. Below the title is the poem, "We must on, —be our pathway o'er flowers or o'er thorns, / Do thunder-clouds gloom it, or sunbeams adorn! / Then sigh not! It never will lighten our woe, / But smile, and e'en pleasure from sorrow may flow." Chamomile flowers surround the picture. Page, 7 x 9.5 inches, toned edges. Picture, 5.5 x 7.5 inches. Price: $50.

THE SOUND OF Maggie's cell phone interrupted them.

"Forget the proposal, Maggie. Forget me. I was wrong to think this was going to work. If it weren't for this damn hurricane I'd leave for Maine tonight. I'm going downstairs. I need time alone." The door slammed behind Will.

Maggie stood, shivering, as though a cold wave had just broken over her.

No. This couldn't have happened. Will couldn't have walked out on her.

But he had.

Her phone. That had probably been Gussie, cancelling the party. She'd check the message and then go and talk with Will. They'd make up. It would be all right.

Wind was hammering at the windows, shaking the panes. Somewhere a shutter had come loose and was hitting the side of the house. The banging felt as though it was inside her head.

Maggie looked for her bag, where her phone was. She found it under the wet clothes she'd hurriedly peeled off. Before the outline of her world changed.

Her phone was in the bottom of the canvas bag she used as a pocketbook. The bag was still damp; she should have emptied it and put it near the radiator. Too late for that now.

The message wasn't from Gussie; it was from Annie. Because of the storm, the party'd been moved to an earlier time. Lily'd decided not to go, because of the storm, but Annie would pick Maggie up at five-thirty at Six Gables.

Five-thirty! She only had fifteen minutes to get ready. And no time to talk with Will; no cozy dinner here at the inn. If she weren't the maid of honor, she'd be tempted to opt out, as Lily had. But she didn't have a choice.

Somehow through her emotional fog she found clean, dry under-wear, a pair of decent slacks, and a dry sweater. The sweater wasn't as nice as the one she'd had on earlier, but that one wouldn't be dry for hours. In this weather she couldn't be expected to be elegant. She looked at the leather shoes she'd planned to wear, and then at her soaked sneakers. Neither was a good choice. She opted for the wet sneakers and a pair of dry socks. Her feet wouldn't stay dry long anyway. Why ruin a good pair of shoes?

She made an attempt at braiding her still-damp hair, which no doubt would get soaked again, and added a minimum of makeup, hoping it wouldn't run. She didn't really care what she looked like anyway.

In case she didn't see him downstairs, in case he cared, she left Will a note. *Time of bachelorette party moved up. Getting ride with Annie. Back as early as possible.* She hesitated before signing it, *Love, Maggie.* She did love him, damn it. She left the note on the bed.

As soon as she got downstairs, Annie pulled up in front of Six Gables, although not in the police car she'd promised earlier. Probably the chief had other plans for the patrol cars tonight, Maggie thought as she climbed into the passenger seat. "How are the roads?" she asked, as they took off.

Tonight was a night to think about Gussie; not about Will.

The rains were still torrential.

"Not good," Annie admitted. "A half dozen streets have already been blocked off because of flooding, and I had to detour around another because a tree had fallen. Luckily, it hadn't hit a house, just another tree and a mailbox. I called the station to let them know so they could put roadblocks up there, too. It's going to be a long night."

"I'm surprised Sheila and Gussie didn't cancel the party," Maggie said. "It's ridiculous to ask anyone to come out in this weather. It must have been a challenge for you to find a baby-sitter tonight."

"Luckily there are a lot of teenagers in the neighborhood," Annie said. "I can usually find someone willing to earn some money." She swerved, barely missing a large branch blocking one lane.

The only lights were from swaying streetlights that gave a ghostly appearance to the wildly blowing tree tops and the garish reflections of the car's headlights on the wet road.

Maggie looked around. "How far is the Snow Squall Inn? I thought Gussie said it was close to town. We passed downtown a while back."

"I told you some streets were blocked," Annie assured her, wiping the inside of the windshield so she could see more clearly. "I'm going around that area."

Maggie nodded. But she had a growing sense that something was wrong. Even with weather this bad, from what Gussie'd said they should have been to the inn by now. But she didn't know the area, and it was dark, and with the storm making it even harder to see than it would have been usually, she couldn't be sure.

Where would Annie be taking her if not to the Snow Squall for the party?

Annie was the wife of the chief of police.

She'd also been Dan Jeffrey's lover. Diana had caught her searching for something in Dan's room. Had she really been looking for love letters?

What if she'd been one of Cordelia's drug customers? Annie was the wife of a busy man. She had two small children, an immaculate house, and still found time to cook almost everything from scratch, and have time-consuming hobbies. Maybe she was one of those housewives who needed a little chemical help to get her through her day.

And Tony Silva, the awkward boy who didn't have close friends, whose dad was pushing him to excel at a sport he was failing at, baby-sat for her.

Maggie's mind raced, as Annie's car skidded around another corner. Annie was driving faster now, focused on the road ahead of her.

They were heading further away from downtown Winslow on roads Maggie was pretty sure she'd never seen. Or maybe it was seeing them through a canopy of wavering tree limbs and drenching rain that gave every twist and turn in the road an eerie feeling, as though whatever was ahead was unknown, and unpredictable.

Maggie tried not to focus on the road, but on what she knew about Annie Irons.

Was it possible Tony Silva hadn't bought the OxyContin pills he'd taken? Could he have found them at Annie's house when he'd been baby-sitting? He'd had serious asthma. His father had said that, and so had Sean and Josh. OxyContin was a depressant. It would have slowed Tony's breathing down faster than it would have in someone without breathing problems. Slowed his breathing down enough to stop it.

And Ike Irons hadn't found the person who'd sold the pills to Tony last spring. Could that be because no one had sold them to Tony? Because Tony'd gotten them from Ike's wife?

How many teenagers died or overdosed from prescription medications in their parents' or grandparents' medicine cabinets, or those in the homes of their friends?

Too many, Maggie knew.

Sean and Josh had told her where kids *could* get drugs. They didn't say they knew for sure where Tony had.

On the campus where she worked students bought and sold their own prescription medications, especially those for anxiety or ADD. Sales like that were almost impossible to control.

Annie's knuckles on the steering wheel had looked white in the glare of the occasional streetlight. But now there were few streetlights, and no lights from houses on Annie's side of the car. Unless this area had lost power, they must be on the beach road. On a clear night you'd be able to see stars, and the moon, and lights from boats on Cape Cod Bay.

But tonight all boats had been brought in to dry dock, and the sky was low and dark. The tide would be high about midnight, Maggie remembered. That's when houses near the Bay would be in most danger from a storm surge.

"Where are we going, Annie?"

"To the party, of course."

"We left town behind a while ago," Maggie said.

"I want to show you something," said Annie.

The car sped through the narrow streets. Annie might know where they were going, but Maggie had no idea. She reached for her telephone.

It wasn't in the outside pocket of her bag, where she always kept it. Damn. She must have left it on the bedside table at Six Gables.

She felt for it again, to be sure. It definitely wasn't there.

But even if she had it, who would she call?

What would she say?

That she didn't know where she was? That she was out for a drive with Annie Irons?

Even if Tony Silva had gotten OxyContin from Annie's home, Maggie had no proof, and there was nothing to be done about it now. And if he'd taken it from her medicine cabinet, he'd stolen it, and she'd been guilty of nothing but trusting a baby-sitter not to invade her privacy or steal from her.

Maggie clutched the sides of her seat. Now Annie was driving through sections of flooded street. How deep was the water? The headlights reflected back rain pounding on water, not pavement.

Annie gunned the car, trying to get out of the flooded area.

If Annie knew about Cordelia's selling drugs, maybe she knew something else.

Something that would help find Cordelia's killer, and clear Diana.

Now the rain was coming sideways as well as vertically. Annie swore under her breath as she squinted at the windshield trying to see through sheets of water. She'd turned off the flooded street onto a narrower street, or alley, or maybe a wide driveway. Bushes and low branches of trees scraped first Maggie's and then Annie's side of the car.

Annie, bent over the steering wheel, stared straight ahead. She never slowed down.

At the end of the narrow passageway she turned abruptly left onto a wider street, swerving as she turned. Suddenly, through the rain, Maggie saw a high brick wall maybe thirty feet in front of them.

Instinctively, she braced herself.

Annie slammed on the brakes, but nothing happened. Then she turned the steering wheel as far as she could to the right.

The car began to skid.

Maggie watched helplessly as the car fishtailed in slow motion and the driver's side crashed into the wall, bounced back into the road, and then the left rear end hit the wall. Hard.

Chapter 39

Panax Coloni. Outstanding copper engraving of plant now called Marsh Woundwort, from Jacob Trew (Berlin) edition of Elisabeth Blackwell's *A Curious Herbarium*, her volume of "useful plants now used in practice of physic," published in 1757. Also called All-Heal, Panay, or Clown's Woundwort, as a tea it was used to stop internal bleeding and as a poultice to stop external bleeding. It was also said to aid dysentery, and as a gargle, sore throats. Artist and engraver Blackwell began working when her husband was imprisoned for starting a printing business without serving the apprenticeship required by English law. Her book was a success, and she was able to obtain his release. He was later executed for treason in Sweden. She was an artist and entrepreneur well beyond the norm for a woman of her time. 9 x 12.5 inches. Price: $250.

THEY'D CRASHED. She was alive. Her neck and shoulders ached, and pain slashed through her left ankle. Blood? None she could feel. Maggie tried to focus in the dark.

The car's engine was running.

She looked over at Annie. "Are you all right?"

Annie didn't answer. Blood was dripping down her forehead, into her right eye, onto her raincoat. She was breathing, but her left arm was at an odd angle. Probably broken. Getting her out of the car wouldn't be easy. Her airbag had probably saved her life, but now she was pinned between the steering wheel and where her side of the car was crushed and pushed in. Jagged points of what had been the door and roof of the car had hit her head. Rain dripped through openings in what a few seconds ago had been the car's two left-hand doors.

Maggie unfastened her seat belt, reached over, and turned off the car engine.

She needed to get Annie to a hospital.

She didn't have a telephone.

Annie would have one.

She pushed aside the now-deflated airbag on her side, found her canvas bag, and foraged for the small flashlight she'd bought that afternoon.

Annie's pocketbook wasn't in what was left of the front seat. It must have been thrown somewhere during the accident. Maggie tried to open her own door. The latch on the handle worked, but the door was jammed. The crash had changed its alignment just enough so it wouldn't open more than an inch or two.

She, too, was imprisoned.

She managed to turn around in her seat enough to flash her light over the back of the car. There. Annie's pocketbook was on the floor, but its contents were strewn all over the backseat. Her phone was in back of the driver's seat, caught beneath a piece of the caved-in back door. Despite the searing pain in her ankle, Maggie managed to crawl halfway over the console between the seats. Annie's seat was bent backward and sideways.

The throbbing in her ankle was worse when she moved it. Maybe it was broken.

A maid of honor with a cast on her ankle. Gussie would love that.

She squirmed around the broken seat and finally was able to reach the phone, and dial 911.

"We've had an accident. We need an ambulance. They'll need to bring equipment to cut us out of the car. No. I don't know where we are. Can you track this phone with GPS?"

The 911 operator pointed out there was a hurricane. Emergency vehicles were busy.

"I know there's a hurricane. No, I don't see any street signs. I told you. I can't get out of the car. Yes, I'll stay on the line. The woman who's badly injured is Annie Irons, Police Chief Irons's wife."

She held on another minute. Then the line went dead.

Was that enough time for the Emergency Center to track the call? She hoped.

Annie's cell phone battery light was blinking. Just what she needed. A dead phone.

She started to dial Will's number. Maybe she could get through before the phone died completely. Then, only inches from her head, someone knocked on the glass of the passenger seat window.

"You folks need help?"

From outside, in the pouring rain, a face peered in at her.

She rolled the window down. Thank goodness Annie had an old-fashioned car. No power windows.

"We've had an accident. We're both trapped in the car. I've only hurt my ankle, but my friend is unconscious. I called 911 but I didn't know where to tell them we were. If you know, could you call and tell them?"

"No problem, Maggie. Let me see if I can get you out of there."

Maggie looked closer. Through the heavy rain it was hard to see, and the man was wearing a dark hoodie. But, yes. It could be. "Rocky Costa?"

"In person."

"Where did you come from?"

"Didn't Annie tell you? I live over that way." He gestured in the general direction of the brick wall. "You were coming to pay a call on me. You're late, so I came to see what was holding you up. And here I've found you had a bit of a problem along the way." Rocky stood and looked over the car, shaking his head. "Women drivers. Annie always did have a heavy foot."

"I'd love to talk with you, but why don't you call 911 first? Let them know where we are. Annie needs to get to a hospital."

"Actually, I'm thinking this is working out just fine the way it is. Two birds in one car crash, as it were."

"Why was Annie bringing me to see you?"

"You were getting a little too nosy, Maggie from New Jersey. I heard from one of the kids on my baseball team this afternoon that he'd talked with you. He wanted me to tell him he'd done the right thing. He figured it would be okay, telling you about the drugs, seeing as Cordelia isn't exactly in the business anymore. He didn't see the big picture. But I figured you, being a smart professor and all, you might put all the pieces together. So I told Annie what the boy'd done, and we decided it would be best if you didn't tell anyone what you'd heard."

"I haven't told anyone," said Maggie. Except Will, she thought. "I talked to the boys this afternoon, and was planning to spend the weekend celebrating a wedding, as you'll remember. I'm going back to New Jersey Sunday."

"Annie and I decided to change your plans a little. To make sure you don't open your mouth and share any information someone here in Winslow might find of interest, you understand," said Rocky. He stood back a little, his clothing and hoodie dripping, rain running off his nose and fingers. The wind had let up a little, but the rain hadn't. Water coursed down the street, creating a new waterway. "But I believe now this little accident opens up new possibilities."

"What do you want from me?" said Maggie.

"Simple. I want you to disappear," said Rocky.

Not good. Would the emergency operator be able to trace her call? She couldn't count on it. Caught in the car she had no defense. Maggie pressed down on the door handle again. "I don't understand enough to be dangerous. Sean and Josh said Cordelia was dealing the drugs. Why should you worry about that? Cordelia's dead." She pushed on the door. It stuck at the same place it had before. Rocky didn't seem to notice.

"For a professor you really aren't that bright," said Rocky. "Sure, Cordelia sold a few drugs to some high school kids. Those dolls of hers were a good cover. She was a nice lady. She and I were together a lot of years. But there's no way Cordelia could have organized the business. She was small-time. All she wanted was money to pay her taxes."

Suddenly Maggie understood.

"Annie. Annie was the one who managed the operation, wasn't she?" Annie, who collected high-end antiques and wore expensive clothes on a small-town police chief's salary.

Annie, who kept busy every hour of the day proving she was a perfect wife and mother. Annie, who had friends and family in South Boston. Suddenly it all fit together.

"But what about Dan Jeffrey? Why was he killed?" Maggie moved closer to the car door and kept pushing it with her shoulder and arm. She had to get out. The metal creaked and moved another fraction of an inch.

"He panicked when his daughter showed up. He thought she'd tell her friends in Colorado he was still alive, and it'd get back to the police or insurance people there, and he'd be arrested. He didn't want that. He was going to take off. Annie said she loved him. I don't know the details. But what Annie wants, Annie gets. Dan hired me to take him to Boston in my old fishing boat. I hardly use it anymore, but he was desperate to get away and not have anyone see him go, so I agreed. Somehow Annie found out. She met us at my dock at dawn the day we were going to leave. They argued, and she shot him. She paid me to take him and the gun and throw them both overboard in the Bay. I guess I didn't go far enough out."

"And Cordelia?" She tried to keep her voice steady, and Rocky talking, while she put as much pressure as she could on the jammed door. Every tenth of an inch counted.

"She wanted out of the business. At first she wanted to scare Diana, get her to leave Winslow. Get her away from the drugs and the craziness. That was the fire."

"Cordelia was going to burn her own house?"

"She was pretending to. Then she told me she'd decided to get out of the business. She'd changed her will, Dan was gone, and she was going to ask Diana to come and live with her. She wanted a family. She was going to tell Annie she wasn't taking any more product. She was going to return what she had, and that was the end."

"And?"

"Next thing I knew Cordelia was dead." Maybe Rocky's eyes were filled with tears. Maybe the rain had just gotten harder.

"And so now you're supposed to kill me," said Maggie. "Because I know too much."

"Idiot. You've made sure she knows more than she did before." Annie's voice was weak, but her eyes were open, and beginning to focus. "You're even more stupid than I thought you were, Rocky."

"Annie, I may be stupid, but I know enough to know I'm through with you. Through with all this. Killing Cordelia put it over the line for me. I loved that woman. You knew that, but it didn't make a difference. You had no reason to kill her."

"If she wasn't in the business, she could have turned on us."

"She didn't know about Dan."

"But I do. And now you've been crazy enough to tell this Maggie person. You're an accessory to Dan Jeffrey's murder, Rocky. There's no way you'll get away with that."

Rocky reached under his hoodie.

Through the rain Maggie saw the end of Rocky's gun. She pushed her shoulder even harder against the car door. The metal was groaning, but pounding rain on the roof of the car and the wind all around them masked the sound.

"You think you can get away with shooting both of us?" Annie managed to shriek. "Two defenseless women, trapped in a car, shot by a madman? My husband will hunt you down!"

Maggie, focused on trying to get her car door open, and on Rocky outside in the rain, heard Annie groan. She glanced back. Annie was looking for her pocketbook. "My gun," she whispered. "In my bag. My gun."

No way was Maggie giving a killer a gun. Especially a killer who'd lured her to wherever this place was and planned to kill her. She hoped the pocketbook was far enough back in the car that Annie, jammed in the front seat with a broken arm, wouldn't be able to reach it. The gun must still be in her purse since she hadn't seen it on the car floor.

Rocky was pointing his gun now, aiming it through the open car window, only inches from Maggie's head.

If she closed the window would the glass deflect the bullet?

Not at such close range.

Besides, it would take too long to close the window.

"I think it would be simpler for me to shoot now," he said, calmly. "At least I won't be shooting either of you in the back of the head, Annie, the way you shot Cordelia. I'm giving you each a chance to think about what's going to happen. Who wants to die first?"

One chance. Luckily the darkness and rain meant Rocky couldn't see inside the car as well as Maggie could see out. She took every bit of strength she had left and pushed on her door.

This time it gave way, with the loud sound of metal scraping metal. The door sprang open, hitting the unsuspecting Rocky's torso, including his gun arm, knocking him into the muddy street, and taking Maggie with it, as she held on to the door handle.

Rocky's gun fired, and Maggie grabbed at the arm holding the gun, and kneed him in the groin.

He screamed and doubled up in pain as she grabbed the gun and managed to pull herself upright on the open door and limp a few feet away from both Rocky and the car.

She stood, gun pointed at Rocky, but with an occasional glance toward the car to make sure Annie hadn't figured out how to reach her purse. And her gun.

Her ankle wasn't just throbbing, she realized. It gave her no support. She couldn't run.

She checked the gun. It was loaded. She'd hated going hunting with her father when she'd been a child, but she had learned a few things from those days.

She aimed, and she could shoot if necessary.

She didn't say anything, and all Rocky did was swear a couple of times.

It seemed they were there, Rocky on the ground, Maggie standing in the rain and wind, forever.

But it was probably only a couple of minutes before they all heard the screams of an ambulance, and then a police car, in the distance. And then coming closer.

Chapter 40

Papaver somniferum. Hand-colored print from A.B. Strong's *The American Flora, or History of Plants and Wild Flowers*, 1846. White Poppy, with yellow center and green stem and leaf. This variety, whose botanical name means "sleep-bringing," is the plant from which opium is derived, which is why L. Frank Baum had Dorothy and her friends fall asleep in a field of them in *The Wizard of Oz*. 6.5 x 9 inches, toned at edges. Price: $50.

AFTER THE AMBULANCE and police arrived, the flurry of activity and explanations was confusing, but adequate.

Rocky ended up at the police station. Annie and Maggie were both taken to Winslow General Hospital, with police escorts.

"Sorry to break up the bachelor party," Maggie'd explained, after she was finally able to borrow a telephone at the emergency room and call Will. "But I hope you and Jim are still sober. There was a car accident, and I know you're mad, but I need you to pick me up at the hospital. Bring Jim, too. I think I might need a lawyer."

"Jim's not with me," Will had said. "Both pre-wedding parties were cancelled. You have no idea how worried I've been about you. Right after you left Gussie called to tell us to stay safe and dry and not go out tonight. I'll call Jim now. You're sure you're all right?"

"Except my ankle. "

"I'll be there as soon as I get directions."

Maggie was propped up on one of the emergency room beds when he arrived. She had an IV in her arm, a bandage on her left hand, and her left foot was raised and covered in ice packs.

He started to reach out to hold her hand, and then pulled back. "How are you?"

"Glad you came. All I could think of when I thought I was going to die was that I'd been a fool. That I loved you."

Will smiled a little, but didn't move closer.

"I'm okay. Bruised all over. Not too many cuts, though, and the X ray of my ankle showed it's a clean break. As soon as the swelling goes down the doctor's going to put a cast on it. What do you think about a blue cast? He's out of pink, and I refused purple. They don't seem to do white casts anymore."

"This is from the car accident?" said Will.

"Most of it. I'll fill you in," said Maggie.

"And what's the good news?" he asked.

"Oh, there's lots of good news," said Maggie. She wanted to say, *The good news is that you came.* "The best news is, I'm getting some good pain meds through this IV, so my ankle doesn't hurt very much anymore, and my bruises and cuts are getting better all the time." She stopped talking for a minute, and closed her eyes. Then she opened them. "And I know who killed Dan and Cordelia. And where Tony Silva got the pills that killed him. That's all very good."

Jim appeared in the doorway. "Maggie! I just talked to Ike Irons outside. He says you not only got into a car accident with his wife, you also got yourself into the middle of his investigation."

"I solved all the crimes," said Maggie. "Did he tell you that?"

"She's on heavy meds," said Will quietly. "I don't know how reliable she is right now."

"Ike told me when he and the ambulance arrived she was standing in the mud waving a gun at Rocky Costa and saying he'd told her he was going to kill her and Annie."

"She was…what?" said Will.

"Absolutely right," said Maggie. "He was. That was Rocky's gun. You can check it out. I got the gun from him. One bullet's been fired, but I didn't fire it. He did. Ask Annie, too."

"Annie won't be answering any questions soon, Maggie. Her arm's shattered, and she has some internal injuries. She's in surgery."

"I think I'd like to talk to my lawyer now. In private."

Will looked at her. "Maggie, why don't you wait until your cast is on, and you're feeling better?"

"I need to talk to Jim now. Please, Will."

Will shook his head and shrugged and left the room.

"Okay, Maggie. I'm here. What is it?" Jim sat down next to her bed.

"Jim, I found out who sold drugs last spring, and who supplied the drugs to Tony Silva. And who killed Dan Jeffrey and Cordelia West. The problem is, I don't have proof. Annie Irons is at the center of it all. If I tell Ike Irons he could just ignore what I say. I think he may already know Annie was connected with Tony's death last spring; that's why he stopped investigating. Tonight Annie and Rocky were going to kill me because of what I'd found out."

"Maggie, those are serious allegations." Jim hesitated. "Are you very sure? Because you're not only accusing two people of murder and drug trafficking, you're suggesting there may have been a police cover-up."

"I don't know for sure about the cover-up. But it seems strange Chief Irons has never questioned the amount of money his wife spends. Jim, she collects very high-end antiques, and her clothes cost a fortune. Unless she has a very rich family or Ike is paid a lot more than most police chiefs in small towns, that money's coming from somewhere. Ike may not know everything she's involved with. But I think he suspects, and closes his eyes. And there's circumstantial evidence to support what I've found out. There's probably more, once someone knows who to investigate. But the investigation has to happen quickly. Chief Irons was right: I was holding a gun on Rocky Costa when the police arrived tonight. Rocky and Annie both know I found out about the drugs and murders."

Jim paused, then said, "Costa's in jail right now, because you said he threatened you. That was enough to hold him. Annie's in the hospital. You're in no danger tonight or tomorrow. And you've been given painkillers tonight."

"What does that have to do with anything? I'm fine!" said Maggie.

Jim pointed to the IV and the ankle. "I'm talking about legalities, Maggie. The fact that you're under the influence of drugs could be used to invalidate anything you say now. Get your cast on. Go back to Six Gables. Get a good night's sleep. I have a couple of ideas. Let me make some calls. I'll talk to you in the morning."

"You're getting married tomorrow," said Maggie.

"There is that," said Jim. "Don't worry. I don't think Gussie will let either of us forget the wedding. We'll talk in the morning. In the meantime, get some rest. Tomorrow you have to be the maid of honor."

Chapter 41

The Bride. Classic lithograph, 1909, by Harrison Fisher (1875–1934). An elegantly attired bride sitting in a full-length satin wedding gown, with train and bouquet of white roses. Fisher, a third-generation artist, was the top magazine cover illustrator of the early twentieth century. His "American Girls" were considered the epitome of feminine beauty. He described his ideal as "well-bred and healthy-minded, delightfully free of pose. Mistress of herself, she looks out upon the world with frankness and assurance." Fisher's girls were on every cover of *Cosmopolitan* from 1913 until his death in 1934, and on eighty *Saturday Evening Post* covers. Trim, athletic, and educated, his "girls" helped define the "new woman." 8.5 x 11 inches. $100.

THE SUN HAD the audacity to shine Saturday morning, displaying to the world the damage Hurricane Tasha had left in her wake.

Downed branches were everywhere. High tides and surf had brought seaweed, driftwood, and parts of collapsed buildings into villages close to the beaches. Beaches themselves had lost quantities of sand. Sections of boardwalk had disappeared.

Shingles, parts of roofs, and street signs were now on lawns and streets and hanging from trees. Trees had fallen on houses, cars, and other trees. Electric lines throughout Cape Cod and the Islands were down, leaving most homes and businesses dark. Many wires had fallen on flooded streets, creating the danger of electrocution. NSTAR Electric trucks seemed to be everywhere, but never in enough places.

The governor was on television and radio telling people to stay off the roads, leaving those that were open for clean-up and emergency vehicles, but most people didn't have electricity so they didn't hear his warnings and pleas to stay home.

Despite posted signs warning people of the continuing dangers of unusually strong high tides and rogue waves, people wandered the dunes and beaches, taking pictures of the dramatic breakers and looking for treasures the storm might have washed ashore.

At Six Gables Mrs. Decker served a breakfast of cold muffins, eggs hard-boiled on Friday, apples, and canned pineapple. No one complained, although Maggie knew Will was longing for hot coffee. She sponged herself off with cold water and was glad she'd showered the afternoon before, although her adventures after that had not left her in wedding picture–perfect condition. She pulled out the heels she'd planned to wear for the wedding, and Will tried not to laugh as she considered wearing one with a cast on the other foot and a crutch. At least the sapphire blue cast didn't clash too much with the navy dress she'd decided to wear.

Maggie settled on one sandal and the reality that she'd be limping down the aisle.

She and Will were on speaking terms. Neither of them had said anything, but they had to stay civil for Gussie's and Jim's sakes, and they were doing that.

At nine o'clock Gussie called. "Maggie? How are you? Jim told me about your adventure last night."

"I'm surviving. Your maid of honor will be using a crutch. That's all," said Maggie. "How's the bride. Nervous?"

"Haven't had time!" said Gussie. "And I need you and Will to help. We have a bit of a challenge."

"Yes?"

"The manager of the Winslow Inn just called. Seems the hurricane flooded their dining rooms last night. There's no way we can have the reception there."

"Oh, no!"

"The good news is, they have a generator, so they can cook. And we have a generator, because I need one to keep my scooter battery charged. So we're moving the reception to our house. They're bringing the food here. The guest list has shrunk anyway; I've been getting calls all morning from people who can't get here. But we'll still have thirty-five or forty guests, and the show must go on."

"Oh, Gussie. I'm thinking of your house. That means—"

"Right! We need the plywood off the windows, and the house decorated, and I still have to get dressed. We'll serve the food buffet-style so that has to be set up. The hotel staff's going to bring tables and dishes and silverware, so all that's good, but we have to make space. Diana's here. She's going to help, and Lily will, too. Jim said he needs to see you right away, so could Will drop you at Jim's office, and then bring Lily here, and stay and help?"

"He will," Maggie said.

"You and Will had better bring your clothes for the wedding here, too. We'll all get dressed and go to the church together. That will save time," Gussie added. "And we have hot water."

"That works," Maggie agreed. "Weren't you going to have your hair done this morning?"

"Lucky Ladies doesn't have power," Gussie said. "Which reminds me I'd better call the bakery and tell them to bring the cake here, not to the restaurant."

"Keep calm. I'll get there as soon as I can!" Maggie put down the phone and turned to Will. "We're on wedding duty. The restaurant where the reception was to be is flooded, so they've moved the reception to their house."

Will caught on immediately. "Those windows!"

"Exactly. And a hundred other details. You're to drop me at Jim's office, and take Lily to their house. Jim will bring me over as soon as I finish whatever he wants me to do."

Will looked at her. "Don't get too far into that legal mess, Maggie. It's Jim's wedding day."

"I am aware. I also know I have to head for New Jersey tomorrow and you'll head for Maine, and I can't forget what happened yesterday. Any of it."

"We have to get through the wedding, Maggie. And then I have to get back to Aunt Nettie."

Maggie nodded, turning away to fix her hair so Will wouldn't see the tears in her eyes. "Thank goodness she made it through the storm fine. Although I know you're not thrilled with those dents she said that tree made in your RV."

Will shrugged. "Dents aren't critical. I'll see how bad they are when I get back to Waymouth."

"And right now we have to get going. Where's your suit?" Maggie asked.

"I'll get it. Tell me what you'll need for this afternoon. You get yourself and your cast down those stairs to the lobby. I'll take everything to the car."

Fifteen minutes later, after a few detours to avoid streets blocked because of downed trees or wires, or both, Maggie was knocking on the door of Jim's office.

Andy Sullivan was there with another man Maggie hadn't met. The three men stood when she came in.

"Maggie, thanks for coming," Jim said. "I'd like you to meet John Tolland. He's a special agent with the Federal Bureau of Investigation in Boston in charge of investigating drug trafficking. John, this is Dr. Margaret Summer, a friend of mine from New Jersey. While she's been visiting my fiancée and me, Maggie's learned some things about drugs sales here in Winslow that we feel the FBI would be interested in."

"Dr. Summer, I appreciate your willingness to share whatever information you've found out. Do you mind if we record you?"

Maggie shook her head.

"Then, let's go ahead."

Maggie spent the next hour telling the three men everything she had learned about Dan Jeffrey, aka Roger Hopkins, and Diana Hopkins, and especially Cordelia West, Annie Irons, and Rocky Costa.

"We'll be getting you a copy of this statement to sign," said John Tolland, taking Maggie's business card and giving her his. "And we may be contacting you to clarify details. For now, however, I think we have everything necessary to proceed."

"What's going to happen?" Maggie asked.

"I can't tell you exactly," said Tolland. "But I suspect your friend Jim will keep you updated when he can."

"He will," Jim agreed. "But right now Jim has to get going. Because in about two hours he's getting married."

Chapter 42

Pleuronectes Passer. Der Lincke Strachlflunder (The Flounder). Rare 1783 hand-colored copperplate engraving by Dr. Marcus Elieser Bloch (1723–1799), a German medical doctor and naturalist, and the most important eighteenth-century ichthyologist. His series of folios (Berlin: *Ökonomische Allgemeine Naturgeschicte der Ausländischen Fische)* illustrating the world's fishes, from which this flounder comes, is often cited as the best work on ichthyology until the twentieth century. The beautiful engravings are on thick, cream-colored paper. Folio-sized, in excellent condition. 10 x 16.5–inch sheet. Price: $295.

DIANA'S BOWS ON the pews looked lovely, and the extra-large bow on the house door did help guests find their way to the new location of the reception after the ceremony.

Steffie, the flower girl, arrived from Connecticut at the last minute, bearing a large basket of rose petals. When she forgot to drop them until she was almost at the altar, and then threw them liberally at guests seated in the front pews, everyone smiled.

Gussie's hairdresser, worried about a bride not having her hair done on her wedding day, arrived at Gussie's home an hour before the wedding and managed to shampoo and pouf her hair into a miracle of elegance, and set her veil perfectly in place. She looked beautiful, as every bride should, and Lily beamed as people admired the heirloom veil.

Gussie's bouquet smelled a little unusual, but was the subject of much conversation, and Diana said someday she wanted one just like it.

Jim kept smiling and accepting congratulations, while Andy and

Ben stood straight and proud. Ben only giggled at the flower girl's antics once.

After the interview with John Tolland Maggie popped one of the pain pills they'd given her at the hospital, hoping he wasn't the sort of drug agent who checked everyone's pocketbooks, and was able to gamely hobble down the aisle in her blue cast while Gussie's sister Ellen followed, sure Maggie would tumble with every step.

To make up for the lack of a reception hall the Winslow Inn chef had turned the dinner into a constant array of hors d'oeuvres. There were platters of miniature crab cakes and lobster puffs, and small pieces of filet mignon with dabs of horseradish sauce en brochette that were, as Will said to Jim with a sly look, "To die for," along with bowls filled with cold shrimp, and platters of both fried and raw clams and oysters, and bowls of steamed mussels in wine and herbs. Small potatoes filled with cheese and chives. Mushrooms stuffed with sausage. And of course, flawlessly arranged platters of raw vegetables and fruits.

Champagne flowed. Maggie's one regret was that because of the pain pill she had to drink club soda, although she did allow herself one glass of champagne for the toast. No extra libation was needed to make the day any better.

Late in the afternoon Jim told her quietly that her new FBI friend had gone directly from their meeting to the jail to talk with Rocky Costa and offered him a deal to testify against Annie Irons. He'd agreed. Annie would be in the hospital for at least a week, and the FBI was requesting a search warrant for the Irons home based on Maggie's information and what Rocky'd said. It looked as though the drug case would be a simple one to close. The murder investigations would be turned over to the state, not to local police because of the potential conflict of interest.

Gussie was glowing. Diana was happily running errands. She was no longer a suspect, and would be spending the night at Six Gables. Gussie whispered that Jim planned to tell Diana on Monday that Cordelia's house would soon be hers. Would she choose to stay in Winslow? Who knew? Diana had her whole life ahead of her.

Maggie sat by the window overlooking the Bay, where the waves were breaking higher and much more dramatically than usual on the beach. New England was a beautiful place. Even in a hurricane.

At five-thirty Diana started announcing, "Attention, everyone! Cake! Cutting the cake!"

One of the caterers walked in carrying a beautiful floral-decorated cake that matched the one they'd seen in the bakery picture book.

He placed it on a table in the middle of the room, to the "oohs" and "ahhs" that usually accompanied the arrival of such a creation. And in this case, Maggie thought, they were deserved. The cake was a work of art.

Gussie and Jim stood together, holding a Victorian silver cake knife his aunt had given them as a wedding gift, ready for the classic pose and cut.

But the young man who'd brought in the cake stopped them. He whispered something. Gussie shook her head. Jim looked puzzled, but then looked over at his mother, shrugged, and grinned.

He put up his hands for silence. "As most of you know, I grew up in Georgia. In the South, it's the custom to have two cakes at a wedding. One is the traditional wedding cake, like this one, which is cut by both the bride and groom to signify the beginning of their life together. The other is the groom's cake. And, it seems that tonight, here in Winslow, we are carrying on that Southern tradition."

The guests looked at each other in surprise. A groom's cake was not a familiar custom in Winslow.

The young caterer raced back to the garage. He returned bearing a large flat cake in the shape of a flounder. It was covered with thick chocolate icing, and then carefully decorated with additional icing that outlined the fish's scales. Hundreds of them.

Jim looked down at the cake. As did everyone else. He tried to keep a straight face as he continued his tutorial. "A groom's cake is usually chocolate, often laced with liquor, and is shaped in a design symbolizing something important to him." He looked at Gussie. "I may be wrong, but, my dear wife, I suspect you were not the one who ordered this cake in my honor."

Gussie shook her head. She'd had a few glasses of champagne, and was trying her best not to burst into giggles.

"Mother?" Jim walked over to Lily, who was trying to back into the crowd. "Mother? Were you the wonderful person who ordered this special groom's cake for me?"

"Oh, Jim!" said Lily, clearly aggravated. "It was supposed to be a surprise!"

"Well, I assure you it was!" said Jim, as more and more people started to laugh quietly. "What, may I ask, inspired you to have the cake made in the shape of a fish?"

Poor Lily looked as though she was going to burst into tears. "That Yankee baker! Our telephone connection was all static-y, and he must not have understood. I told him I wanted a cake in the shape of scales. Of justice! For a lawyer! He made it look like a dead fish."

The guests erupted into laughter.

Jim reached over and hugged Lily. "And no one else in Winslow, Massachusetts, has ever had a cake like it. Thank you, Mother. It's beautiful."

He put his arm around her and brought her back to stand with him and with Gussie. "Gussie and I are going to cut the first slice of our wedding cake. And then I'm going to cut the first slice of my groom's cake. And then, everyone, no excuses: it's time for dessert!"

Will pulled a chair over next to Maggie's as they watched Gussie and Jim perform the traditional cutting of the cake, and then Jim cutting the groom's cake. Jim gave Lily the job of cutting the rest of the slices. She looked happy to do it, and even happier when more people wanted slices of the chocolate "dead fish cake" than of the white wedding cake.

"How does your ankle feel? Are you going to be all right to drive home tomorrow?" Will asked Maggie. They'd managed to smile politely but spend as little time as possible together during the reception.

"Luckily, it's my left ankle. I'll be fine," said Maggie.

"This hasn't exactly been a relaxing ten days for you."

"Not exactly."

"And you're coming back in a couple of weeks to set up your print room at Gussie's shop."

"She and Jim invited me to come for Thanksgiving." Maggie hesitated. "Will, do you think maybe if we had more time to talk, things could be different? Maybe you could come down from Maine then? I could ask them to set an extra place at their table."

"Aunt Nettie's planning on roasting an enormous bird and inviting the whole Brewer clan. She's counting on my being there to help."

"Oh."

"I noticed you're still wearing the R-E-G-A-R-D ring."

"Do you want it back?"

Will hesitated. "No. I gave it to you. It's yours."

"Will, I do love you. Yesterday you caught me off guard."

"You sure as hell surprised me, too."

"You were right when you said I needed to be able to change. To compromise. But I have to think about what that means."

"I love you, too, Maggie. And I'm willing to stretch. But I've always been serious when I said I couldn't be a father. I don't think I can be the man you want me to be."

"You asked me a question yesterday. I messed up the answer. Can I have some more time to think it through?"

"How much more time do you need, Maggie? We've been together for a year and a half."

"Another couple of months?"

Will sighed. "I don't know what to say. I'm not sure that's going to make a difference. But, all right. What about Christmas? You get a couple of weeks off from school. How does a Maine Christmas sound?"

"Christmas in Maine sounds wonderful."

Will looked around at everyone celebrating the wedding, and then at Maggie. "I love you, Maggie. I do. But I can't change the way I am."

"I love you, too. And I don't want to lose you."

He reached for her hand and helped her to her feet. They turned and stood together, looking out at the rough waters on the Bay. "Maine, then. Christmas."

About the Author

Lea Wait. Although Lea Wait did summer on Cape Cod once as a child, and has visited since, her heart belongs to Maine, where she writes full-time and lives with her artist husband. She's the mother of four, grandmother of eight, and has been a fourth-generation antique print dealer since 1977. She also writes novels for young people. *Shadows on a Cape Cod Wedding* is the sixth in Wait's Agatha-finalist Shadows mystery series. She may be visited at www.leawait.com and on Facebook.

MORE MYSTERIES
FROM PERSEVERANCE PRESS
 For the New Golden Age

ALBERT A. BELL, JR.
PLINY THE YOUNGER SERIES
Death in the Ashes *(forthcoming)*
ISBN 978-1-56474-532-3

JON L. BREEN
Eye of God
ISBN 978-1-880284-89-6

TAFFY CANNON
ROXANNE PRESCOTT SERIES
Guns and Roses
*Agatha and Macavity awards
nominee, Best Novel*
ISBN 978-1-880284-34-6

Blood Matters
ISBN 978-1-880284-86-5

Open Season on Lawyers
ISBN 978-1-880284-51-3

Paradise Lost
ISBN 978-1-880284-80-3

LAURA CRUM
GAIL McCARTHY SERIES
Moonblind
ISBN 978-1-880284-90-2

Chasing Cans
ISBN 978-1-880284-94-0

Going, Gone
ISBN 978-1-880284-98-8

Barnstorming
ISBN 978-1-56474-508-8

JEANNE M. DAMS
HILDA JOHANSSON SERIES
Crimson Snow
ISBN 978-1-880284-79-7

Indigo Christmas
ISBN 978-1-880284-95-7

Murder in Burnt Orange
ISBN 978-1-56474-503-3

JANET DAWSON
JERI HOWARD SERIES
Bit Player
Golden Nugget Award nominee
ISBN 978-1-56474-494-4

What You Wish For
ISBN 978-1-56474-518-7

Death Rides the Zephyr
(forthcoming)
ISBN 978-1-56474-530-9

KATHY LYNN EMERSON
LADY APPLETON SERIES
**Face Down Below
the Banqueting House**
ISBN 978-1-880284-71-1

**Face Down Beside
St. Anne's Well**
ISBN 978-1-880284-82-7

Face Down O'er the Border
ISBN 978-1-880284-91-9

ELAINE FLINN
MOLLY DOYLE SERIES
Deadly Vintage
ISBN 978-1-880284-87-2

SARA HOSKINSON FROMMER
JOAN SPENCER SERIES
Her Brother's Keeper
ISBN 978-1-56474-525-5

HAL GLATZER
KATY GREEN SERIES
Too Dead To Swing
ISBN 978-1-880284-53-7

A Fugue in Hell's Kitchen
ISBN 978-1-880284-70-4

The Last Full Measure
ISBN 978-1-880284-84-1

MARGARET GRACE
MINIATURE SERIES
Mix-up in Miniature
ISBN 978-1-56474-510-1

WENDY HORNSBY
MAGGIE MACGOWEN SERIES
In the Guise of Mercy
ISBN 978-1-56474-482-1

The Paramour's Daughter
ISBN 978-1-56474-496-8

The Hanging
ISBN 978-1-56474-526-2

DIANA KILLIAN
POETIC DEATH SERIES
Docketful of Poesy
ISBN 978-1-880284-97-1

JANET LAPIERRE
Port Silva Series
Baby Mine
ISBN 978-1-880284-32-2

Keepers
Shamus Award nominee, Best Paperback Original
ISBN 978-1-880284-44-5

Death Duties
ISBN 978-1-880284-74-2

Family Business
ISBN 978-1-880284-85-8

Run a Crooked Mile
ISBN 978-1-880284-88-9

HAILEY LIND
Art Lover's Series
Arsenic and Old Paint
ISBN 978-1-56474-490-6

LEV RAPHAEL
Nick Hoffman Series
Tropic of Murder
ISBN 978-1-880284-68-1

Hot Rocks
ISBN 978-1-880284-83-4

LORA ROBERTS
Bridget Montrose Series
Another Fine Mess
ISBN 978-1-880284-54-4

Sherlock Holmes Series
The Affair of the Incognito Tenant
ISBN 978-1-880284-67-4

REBECCA ROTHENBERG
Botanical Series
The Tumbleweed Murders
(completed by Taffy Cannon)
ISBN 978-1-880284-43-8

SHEILA SIMONSON
Latouche County Series
Buffalo Bill's Defunct
WILLA Award, Best Original Softcover Fiction
ISBN 978-1-880284-96-4

An Old Chaos
ISBN 978-1-880284-99-5

Beyond Confusion
ISBN 978-1-56474-519-4

LEA WAIT
Shadows Antiques Series
Shadows of a Down East Summer
ISBN 978-1-56474-497-5

Shadows on a Cape Cod Wedding
ISBN 978-1-56474-531-6

ERIC WRIGHT
Joe Barley Series
The Kidnapping of Rosie Dawn
Barry Award, Best Paperback Original. Edgar, Ellis, and Anthony awards nominee
ISBN 978-1-880284-40-7

NANCY MEANS WRIGHT
Mary Wollstonecraft Series
Midnight Fires
ISBN 978-1-56474-488-3

The Nightmare
ISBN 978-1-56474-509-5

REFERENCE/ MYSTERY WRITING

KATHY LYNN EMERSON
How To Write Killer Historical Mysteries: The Art and Adventure of Sleuthing Through the Past
Agatha Award, Best Nonfiction. Anthony and Macavity awards nominee.
ISBN 978-1-880284-92-6

CAROLYN WHEAT
How To Write Killer Fiction: The Funhouse of Mystery & the Roller Coaster of Suspense
ISBN 978-1-880284-62-9

Available from your local bookstore or from Perseverance Press/John Daniel & Co. at (800) 662-8351 or www.danielpublishing.com/perseverance.